Zombie Takeover

Michele Israel Harper

Love2ReadLove2Write Publishing, LLC
Indianapolis, Indiana

Published by Love2ReadLove2Write Publishing, LLC
Indianapolis, Indiana
www.love2readlove2writepublishing.com

Library of Congress Cataloging-in-Publication Data is on file at the Library of Congress, Washington, DC.

ISBN: 1-943788-08-1
ISBN-13: 978-1-943788-08-8
Library of Congress Control Number: 2016906878

This is a work of fiction. Names, characters, incidents, and dialogues are products of the author's imagination and are not to be construed as real. Any resemblance to actual events or persons, living or dead, is entirely coincidental.

Cover Design by Sara Helwe (www.sara-helwe.com)
Model and Photography by Jessica "Faestock" Truscott

For my brother

So many of these phrases are you.
I miss you.
Thank you for being the best brother in the whole wide world!

And my dad

This book wouldn't have happened without you.
I love you.
Thank you for all of the book title brainstorming sessions!

Chapter 1 ☣

My fingernails dug into the armrests as strains of eerie music floated across the cinema, infusing my spine with ice and trailing chills down my arms.

What had I been thinking?

I jumped as a thunderous crash rattled our reclined seats. Slamming my eyes shut, I slumped in my seat, wishing the next couple of hours were already over.

Better yet, what had Peter been thinking?

The movie roared to life, skipping any previews. Come on! Seriously? They couldn't let me avoid the movie a few minutes longer? Of course, the previews were probably as gruesome as the stupid movie we were about to watch.

My boyfriend poked me.

I opened one eye and followed his pointing finger to the domed screen above our heads. Peter leaned close and whispered hoarsely, his hot breath blasting my ear.

Two lesser-known actors he enjoyed—probably because they were in every slasher flick known to man—filled the screen. They were yammering something about a virus killing everyone. Now they—the dead people—were somehow alive, chasing more people and trying to kill them as well. It was tragic, horrible, blah, blah, blah—I didn't care. It was scary. And I don't do scary. Anyway, it was just another lame excuse for a plot so one more blood-curdling movie could be made.

I couldn't hear Peter over the ear-shattering volume of the film, so I nodded and retreated behind my eyelids once more.

Listening to it was only slightly less horrible than watching it. Maybe.

I braced myself for the carnage about to begin. I don't know how he'd done it, but Peter had talked me into seeing the latest horror zombie flick. You don't understand. I do *not* watch horror movies. Especially about zombies. It means weeks of no sleep and jumping at every little noise. And sleeping with a nightlight on. Seriously. But here I was, in the nicest state-of-the-art cinema New Mexico had to offer, preparing to spend the next two and a half hours cowering, eyes squeezed shut, hands clamped over my ears.

He was so going to pay for this.

I peeked at my boyfriend. He was staring at the screen in sheer excitement, eyes sparkling. I don't understand it. Why couldn't he look at me with the same enthusiasm, huh? I don't even know. But get this. He had somehow gotten pre-screening tickets as a *surprise* for me. For *me*. I wanted to stuff those pre-screening tickets down his…

I gasped and jumped as the blasting volume of the film was ripped away, leaving a void of silence. You know, that horrid, awful silence right before something jumps out at you? Yeah. That one.

I cringed away from the screen, knowing I was going to scream no matter how prepared I was for it.

The lights grew bright, and our seats returned to their upright positions. My eyes flew open. The screen was blank. Not a horror movie in sight. Yet, I could still hear the actors. What? Their voices were hollow, distant, but there. Hope began to blossom in my chest as a slow grin spread across my face.

The screen remained void of life. Yes! The movie had crashed! I stifled my victory dance and glanced at my boyfriend, smoothing my face until all evidence of celebration melted away. I could act disappointed. I could. Now to console him as I tugged him away from the theater as fast as humanly possible before they repaired anything.

And, well, if he didn't move fast enough, maybe I could run for it while I wasn't terrified of moving through a dark theater all by myself.

Okay, I wasn't that bad. Most of the time. Who am I kidding? I'm that big of a chicken.

"Peter, I'm so sorry. Next time, huh? Why don't we just—uh, Peter? Hello?"

Tears weren't streaming down his cheeks, his face wasn't a mottled red, nor were there any other obvious signs of distress. In fact, he wasn't even paying attention to me. The stoic, always bored-looking guy practically bounced in his seat—something I had *never* seen him do before, by the way—and his face held adoration. I followed his stare, my heart plummeting to my toes.

Something that made him that excited couldn't be good.

What in the—? What were *they* doing here?

There, on a raised stage, the same actors who'd been on the screen moments before continued their scene. Tattered clothing and all. Yep. Called it. I knew there had to be something more to our little date for Peter to act so crazy about it.

My surprise for *my* birthday was really a chance for *him* to meet his favorite actors.

I kinda wanted to kill him.

My curiosity got the better of me and halted all devious plots—for the moment, anyway. But what were the actors *doing* here? Were they going to act out the whole movie on that minuscule stage? The thing was ridiculously small. They were all clustered together, still reading their lines. Yep. Reading them. "We're all gonna die" can't be that hard to memorize. I cringed and shook my head. They were B-list actors for a reason. Good. Night. Bad doesn't even begin to describe their performance.

On film, they had been stellar—well, not as terrible—but now their acting was stilted. Dry. Boring. Come to think of it, not much had changed from the film. Now they just didn't have ear-shattering music to cover their dreadful acting. I frowned. What on earth were they doing? They weren't focused on their scene but were sending glances to the front of the room, excited about something. I mean, extremely excited. Excited enough to butcher their scene and not care. I grimaced at my choice of words.

The scene came to a close. They lowered their scripts—thank the Maker—stopped speaking, and stared at the front of the room. Excitement rippled through them. I could tell. What were they so blasted excited about? Was the movie going to start again?

I craned my neck and rose off my seat an inch or two to try to see over the ridiculously high seats in front of me, half-wondering if I should be closing my eyes instead. A dry, monotonous male voice echoed around the chamber, and my gaze sought the speaker.

Oh, goodie. Another bottom-of-the-line actor. Gracing my fair town. The light grew brighter. Actually, I didn't recognize him—not that that's saying much. Was he an actor, too?

At the front of the room, an older, distinguished gentleman in a meticulous suit sat at a short conference table. The table was wedged between the wall and a row of seats, and the guy was shuffling papers and commenting on the scene we'd just watched.

I studied him. Nope. Still didn't recognize him. I started to sink back down in my seat until I glanced at the person sitting next to him. I squealed and jumped forward, clinging to the seat in front of me, my nose plastered on the grimy surface. I peeked between the two chairs instead of over them so *he* couldn't see me.

Right there, in my theater, in my small town, sat Gavin Bailey, my *favorite* actor. I peeked further over the seat, oogling him as I'd never had the chance to do before in my life.

Our eyes met.

He smiled at me.

I gasped and dove for my seat, disappearing from his view. I held my racing heart, reliving those few seconds over and over. He was here. In the same theater as I was. And he'd smiled at me! His eyes even crinkled at the corners in that maddening way. Eek! I could now die a happy woman. Not that I wanted to die anytime soon. At least, not until one more peek...

I inched forward and glanced down my row. Everyone in it was leaning forward, staring at me.

I flushed and sank down in my seat. I *so* did not like being the center of attention.

Peter nudged me. "What is it? You're acting a little...strange."

I clutched his arm like a lifeline, my dopey grin making me question my own sanity.

"Gavin Bailey is sitting up there!" I shriek-whispered in sheer panic and total excitement. Yep, definitely was making a fool of myself.

"Oh?" Peter stretched to see after tossing me an annoyed look. He shook off my grasp. "So...what do you think of him in real life?"

A knowing grin erased his annoyance, but jealousy tinted his tone.

I smiled, then frowned, halting the word vomit that was about to gush forth about how amazing Gavin Bailey was. The last time he'd been jealous, he'd gotten up and left in the middle of a date, dragging me with him. He'd said the waiter was flirting with me, and he wasn't going to stay and watch it. It was obnoxious. And it totally wasn't true. The guy had only wanted a bigger tip, and he definitely wasn't flirting. Guys just didn't flirt with me.

I weighed my response carefully. I didn't want to watch a horror movie, but I didn't want to leave yet either. *Gavin Bailey* was up there! Besides, what did he have to be jealous over? Gavin Bailey wouldn't look twice at me, unless it were out of pity. A thought brought a glimmer of hope. Did Peter know Gavin Bailey was going to be here? Maybe he'd actually been thinking of me. How sweet!

I stole another glimpse, but Mr. Bailey wasn't looking at me this time. He was talking with the dude next to him, laughing and looking down at the table, his hands folded on top of it. My eyes traced his every movement. I loved that laugh. I loved everything about him. The confidence, the easy poise—he was a gentleman on and off the screen. Or so I'd heard. I soaked in the sight of him. The thirty-something actor may have had premature gray frosting the temples of his close-cut, dark hair, but it did not take away from his charm one bit. If anything, it enhanced it. I thought it best not to mention that particular fact to my boyfriend.

My mind scrambled after every fact I knew about him, searching for one that wouldn't set Peter off.

Eight years older than my own age of twenty-four, Gavin Bailey was my dream. True, I didn't know him, and true, movies are vastly different from real life, but that made him even more perfect. He was what every guy should be. Heaven knew—six years of college, floating from major to major, then moving to this nearly ghost town even though I didn't want to—my dreams rarely came true. So I was going to enjoy every second of this—experience—to its fullest, and Peter was not going to ruin it for me.

"He looks older than I expected," I managed, still awe-struck and trying to think of a way to diffuse the situation.

This apparently relieved Peter, because he lost interest and began talking to me about something. Only heaven knows what, because my heart was still racing at the thought of my secret crush sitting a few rows away from me. And my boyfriend had asked me to wear my favorite jeans and sturdy hiking boots. I should have been wearing the sexiest, most dazzling thing I owned, with my hair in gorgeous ringlets instead of pulled back in a ponytail. At least my navy blue T-shirt was fitted, and *very* flattering, if I do say so myself. I rocked the fitted T-shirt.

The distinguished gentleman began addressing the room, and I immediately zoned in on his voice, not wanting to miss a moment of this once-in-a-lifetime experience. Peter shrugged and stopped droning on and on. Finally.

"By now all of you know your test results came back favorable, and you have been cleared for this experience. I see you have dressed as we requested. Now, we will view parts of the film on several different screens, but we will be on the move between scenes. I hope you are all ready for the great opportunity presented to you as our test group."

"Test group? What test group?" I hissed in Peter's direction.

A quick glance revealed Peter watching me with a self-satisfied, downright smug grin on his face, but he didn't answer.

My gaze bounced around the room. From what I could tell, the room was sprinkled with younger, fit couples. I stayed in my semi-standing position, straining to see over the seats without being too obvious.

"We will begin momentarily, but are there any questions?"

A thought occurred to me, and my hand shot in the air. But so did everyone else's.

The man chuckled. "Any questions *not* concerning Mr. Bailey."

All hands dropped except mine and two others. He called on me last. I stood.

"Excuse me, but are you saying we will actually, *physically* experience parts of the film?" I swept my hand toward the actors still occupying the stage to my left, somewhat including Mr. Bailey in the wide sweep. "In other words, instead of being able to cower behind my knees and cover my eyes and ears through every single zombie scene"—this elicited a few chuckles, even from Mr. Bailey—"I may, in fact, be running from zombies?"

"Well—not to give anything away—but, yes, that is a possibility."

I began shaking my head, trampling those in my way in my haste to get out of my seat. No way. I'd seen previews. I knew what was coming.

I made my way down the aisle to the conference table. Everyone stared at me. I glanced at Peter. He was turning a dangerous shade of red. I faced the intimidating older gentleman, not daring to look at Gavin Bailey.

"I'm so sorry, but no. No, no, no. I'm so sorry."

I kept shaking my head and repeating my mantra like an idiot. It didn't matter. There was no way I was doing this, Gavin Bailey or no.

The man sighed and shuffled through his papers. "But you have already been cleared, Miss…?"

"Marshall. Candace Marshall."

"Miss Marshall. It would greatly inconvenience our study to have the test group's numbers mismatched."

I continued to shake my head—I didn't even give the guy a chance to finish his sentence before I auditioned for a role whipping my hair for a certain music video.

"Are you quite certain?"

I began nodding my head like a rag doll—jerky, awkward, emphatic. I felt bad, I really did, but not bad enough to put myself through a certain heart attack.

"Candace, sit down and stop making a fool of yourself!" Peter squawked behind me.

My eyes drifted over Gavin Bailey's perfect face as he leaned over and whispered something in the man's ear. They shook hands before I braced myself and turned to my boyfriend. He hadn't stopped talking.

"Don't be stupid. I planned the whole thing. You'll love it."

"*This?* You think I'd love *this?*" I gestured wildly about the room. "No, take me swing dancing, to a Broadway play, Paris—"

"She's not picky or anything," I heard a guy on the front row stage-whisper not-so-quietly. I smirked in his general direction, knowing I was being dramatic. I didn't care. Peter should've known me well enough after five years to know how much I'd hate interactive zombies. I mean, really!

"Or even take me to Scotland!"

I pointed at Gavin Bailey and shot him an apologetic look. He grinned. I snatched my gaze away, my face heating like a child's.

There was no way he'd know I'd always wanted to visit his homeland of Scotland, before I even knew he existed. My brother and his friends and I would dress up in kilts of towels or sheets with sticks for swords and assume Scottish accents, pretending to be William Wallace and his men. I had been a rough-and-tumble tomboy who preferred playing with sticks and racing cars to Barbie or makeup or other stupid, girly things. It had made dates few and far between. None of the guys I knew even considered dating "one of the guys," as they considered me. It wasn't until college a group of girls took pity on me and strapped me down to teach me what a curling iron and mascara were. I still use the stuff sparingly, but at least now I know what it is and how to look presentable. The guys and I made plans to visit Scotland someday but drifted apart during college, too busy to make our dream a reality.

I brought my mind back to the words spewing out of my mouth.

"If you knew me at all, you'd know this is the last thing I'd relish as a *surprise.*"

Peter sputtered, but the man behind me cleared his throat.

"Very well. We do not have much time." He speared his wristwatch with a stern gaze before returning his attention to me. "You are certain?"

I nodded my head again, wondering if I could get whiplash from trying to convince the guy I just wanted to leave.

"Miss Penelope Wilson, will you take Miss Marshall's place?"

"It would be my pleasure," said a deep, sexy voice.

You know those movie scenes where everything goes into slow motion? Like, when someone watches a train barreling right toward them, and all they do is stand there like an idiot and watch?

Yep, that was me at the moment.

Penelope Wilson, the bane of my existence. Only I didn't know it until this very second.

The girl's body matched her voice, and I could only stare with my mouth open as a goddess incarnate floated from her seat and waltzed past me. *Great perfume,* I managed to note through the thick haze that had overtaken my brain. She gracefully lowered herself into my former seat, and stared at me, challenge in her eyes.

I faltered. I didn't do so well with confrontation.

Peter hadn't glanced at me once since Miss Hotshot had come into view. He was practically salivating.

"Um, Peter?"

I hated how timid, how unsure, how blasted tremulous my voice sounded, but there it was. I was a wimp. And I was about to cry. Great.

Peter glanced between me and Miss Wilson, better known as Scum. A myriad of emotions flashed across his face. He was excited, hesitant—he even looked like he felt bad for a second—then resolution took over.

My heart plummeted, right past the floor.

He looked straight at me. I knew right in that second I wasn't going to like what he had to say. At all.

"If you walk out those doors, we're over."

"What?" I laughed. "You're joking."

Defiance lit his eyes. "I'm not."

My mouth couldn't have hung open any farther if it'd wanted to. "But—why?"

He shifted and glanced around. "You're embarrassing me. Again. We talked about this. You act normal in public, then do your little freak-out thing at home. I don't have to date you, you know." He flicked a glance at the woman in *my* seat.

My hands fisted. Oh no, he didn't.

Tension crackled. I stared at him; he stared at me—the theater was an awkward place to be at the moment.

"Well? You gonna stay?"

My hands relaxed. My eyes filled. I shook my head no. I couldn't.

He turned and stuck out his hand. "Peter."

Scum giggled. "Penelope. But you can call me Penny."

Her hand rested in his. He dropped his voice in that deep, alluring way he used when trying to do something romantic for me.

"Pleased to meet you."

Come to think of it, it just sounded creepy.

Miss thing released his hand and snuggled—yes, actually snuggled—into my boyfriend. Wha—? He glared at me, lifted his chin, and draped his arm across her shoulders. My heart froze. She stared up at me in perfect feline satisfaction, as if to say, "What are you still doing here?"

A little fissure cracked my heart's numb surface. I knew if the crack got the smallest bit bigger, I would burst into tears. And I only knew how to cry big, loud. Think wailing. No quiet, delicate sobs for me. Not good.

The theater was eerily quiet. I *so* didn't want to see if I was being pitied or had "that's what you get" looks directed my way.

I snapped my mouth closed and nodded a few times—an annoying habit when I have no idea what else to do—and backed toward the exit. I shot one last glance in Gavin Bailey's direction and nearly shrieked when I almost collided with his broad chest. Dodging him by the merest fraction of an inch, I attempted a smile—my trembling lips wouldn't cooperate—and slammed my eyes to the ground, muttering something incoherent. I spun on my heel and raced out the open doorway, right past the stage and the amused actors.

I had to get to the bathroom before I gave in to the ugly cry.

I glanced behind me, capturing one last picture of Peter and his *date* in my heart forever.

Did she look familiar? Hadn't I seen him talking to her at his job before? I wasn't sure.

Stopping at the drinking fountain, I gulped ice-cold water, trying to grasp what had just happened. Did he seriously just do that? Leave me for a stranger, just like that? It didn't make sense. Water dribbled from my chin, and I absently swiped at it.

Straightening, I vacantly stared at the dark wallpaper and the gold lettering that said "Women's Restroom" with an arrow pointing the way. But maybe it did make sense. He'd always been distant. Embarrassed by me. But did he have to do that on my *birthday*? I sniffled. One hiccup-sob escaped. I needed that bathroom ASAP.

I spun and, this time, managed to collide with Gavin Bailey's strong, muscular, and way-too-handsome-for-anybody's-good chest. I yelped and wrenched myself from his arms, nearly falling over. He caught me. His steadying hands were wreaking all kinds of havoc with my intelligence. I blubbered out a thousand apologies, not allowing him to get a word past mine, and sprinted past him into the ladies' restroom, my cheeks burning.

What was he doing behind me? Waiting for a drink? Trying to

scare the living daylights out of me?

I groaned.

Great. Now two guys thought I was an idiot. Well, more than that, if you counted everyone else in that theater.

I hid in a bathroom stall and took deep gulps of air, but my need to sob had vanished with the scream I'd directed at Gavin Bailey's face. A grin broke through as a tear slipped down my cheek. Couldn't my emotions just make up their mind? But—he'd caught me! Gavin Bailey! *The* Gavin Bailey. The grin melted off my face. Right after I'd been dumped by my boyfriend.

In front of a room full of people.

That did it. My face flushed; my fists clenched.

Now all I could picture was my boyfriend bending down to whisper in his new date's ear, making her giggle, his arm still draped across her shoulders as I fled the room. They'd both dismissed me like I didn't matter, like I was no longer present. Another tear snaked its way down my cheek.

Saying he didn't have to date me. My jaw clenched. You know what? *That* did it. I washed my hands and splashed water on my face. I was not going to cry. He was *so* not worth crying over. I gulped more air, cramming the rest of the tears back down in my chest, and dried my face. Much better.

Thrusting my chin into the air, I marched out of the bathroom as though I didn't have a care in the world. The salty tang of popcorn stung my nose as I took a deep breath. I was just going to leave, start over—

My steps faltered when I rounded the corner of the doorless bathroom to find Gavin Bailey's cut, muscular back, facing me. He must have heard me, because he turned and smiled. Right. At. Me.

"Hello." His deep, gravelly voice ricocheted off my heart and thrilled me right down to my toes.

I opened my mouth to say hi, but nothing came out. He chuckled, and this time, I gave him the dopey grin reserved for times when no other living human being was present. I shook myself right as it got awkward. My mouth was still open. My hand was still half-lifted in some sort of weird greeting.

I needed to salvage the situation ASAP.

"Hi!" I said in my best, nothing-is-wrong, the-world-is-a-happy-place voice as I stuffed both of my hands behind my back. "How are you today?"

I eyed the tinted glass doors leading to outside and freedom. He was standing between me and the exit. I edged around him, trying not to make eye contact, trying only to escape this incredible embarrassment called a day.

"I think a better question to ask is how *your* day is going."

The warmth and concern in his voice caught me off guard, and I glanced up in surprise. My eyes met his outstanding gray ones, and electricity sparked between us. At least, I hoped he felt what I did, and I wasn't just oogling him like a moonstruck teenager.

"My day? Oh, well, I just, I mean, that is to say, it isn't, I wasn't…"

He chuckled. "I get that a lot."

I froze, thankful for his save, humiliated beyond compare. This night was just getting worse, wasn't it?

"You know, I'd like to make it up to you if you'd let me. I hear there's a great little coffee shop not far from here. Would you like to —?"

"Me?"

I pointed at my chest, making sure he was talking to the right person.

He grinned and nodded. "Yes. You."

My mouth engaged before my brain. Again.

"What? Oh no! Absolutely not! No way. I don't think so. That wouldn't be a good idea."

"I think it's a great idea. We could —"

"Oh, I don't think so. Thank you anyway. I'm so sorry, but…"

Movement through the open doorway of the auditorium caught my eye. Couples were getting up from their seats and were strolling toward a large set of double doors on the other side of the room. My boyfriend and sexy goddess-zilla had their heads close together and were chatting away like they were best buds. It didn't help how near they were to each other, either. They'd seemed fascinated with each other. He'd never looked at *me* like that.

Jerk!

My spine snapped to attention, and I stuck out my hand, grasping the rather large hand resting at the actor's side. I pumped it furiously.

"It was so very nice to meet you. I hope you are wonderful, and things go well to you and such, and that you are happy. That you have happiness. And such. Have a great day!"

I threw the fumbling words behind me with a wave and bolted toward the theater's exit, dodging customers who were starting to trickle in for the final set of movies. Clomping down the gradual decline of the theater floor with my combat-sized hiking boots, I weaved in and out of concession ropes.

A rather large swarm of people were leaving, blocking a hasty exit, so I veered toward the front doors, just wanting out. The cords sectioning off the ticket-tearer loomed before me. I hoped I could get through the maze without falling on my face in front of only the world's greatest movie star. I ducked under the last rope and glanced behind me.

It filled me with near panic to see Gavin Bailey strolling in my direction, a mild grin on his face. Did the man ever stop grinning? Didn't he know how irresistible that smile was? I slammed out the theater doors and into the refreshingly cool night air.

I berated myself the entire way to Peter's truck.

How had I not seen this coming?

And why on earth hadn't I gone on a date with *the* Gavin Bailey?

Oh, yeah. I didn't want to make an even bigger fool of myself than I'd been doing all night. It's one thing to claim you'd give anything to go on a date with Gavin Bailey; it was quite another to actually do it.

Still, sometimes it sucked that my automatic response to everything was no. I needed to work on that.

Had I been thinking clearly, I would've gone just so I could say to my boyfriend, "You're sorry? About what? Her? Oh. Don't worry about it! I had *such* a great time with Gavin. You know, he is so much more ripped in person than on the screen. Muscles just pop out under his shirt. We had such a great time, I don't even know what time he took me home!" Childish, yet tempting.

But oh no, I was running from Gavin Bailey and that horrible theater as fast as I could without actually running. I should get a gold medal in speed walking.

I halted next to Peter's truck and smacked my forehead.

"Great. Just great." I threw up my hands and stared at the sky. "Isn't this just great?"

My only ride was on a date with someone else.

I stomped my foot, smacked the dead-beat loser's truck, and glanced behind me.

Gavin Bailey had just entered my row, witness to my little-kid tantrum. I stuck my nose in the air and started my long march into town.

It's not like I would see the man another day in my life.

I just needed to get back to my apartment, bury myself in blankets for the remainder of the evening, and look for a new job in the morning. Preferably in another town. No way was I going back to work with he-who-shall-remain-nameless.

Maybe I should stop for a chocolate bar or a hundred before my place. I nodded to myself. Definitely was raiding the local market before hiding in my room. And I wasn't coming out until I had a plane ticket.

I made my way deep into the huge parking lot, increasing my pace. I looked over my shoulder. Gavin Bailey was still behind me, hands stuffed in his pockets. He grinned and ducked his head when he saw me looking at him, but he kept coming. His soft whistling reached my ears. What in the world? Why was he following me?

My breath started coming in short gasps as I realized no one truly *knows* a person from watching him in movies. Just because he almost always portrayed a hero with strong moral convictions who rescued damsels in distress didn't mean he had those values in real life. People said he was a gentleman, but, I mean really, who knew?

I veered off and cut across a couple of rows. It was quite the walk into town, and my only ride was oblivious to his girlfriend's—make that former girlfriend's—plight outside. Was Gavin Bailey going to follow me all the way back to town?

A grin slipped on my face. Maybe he was protecting me. Looking out for me. The grin vanished. Or maybe he was going to murder me and make it look like a suicide.

I could see the headlines now: "Slighted Girlfriend Commits Suicide after Worst Day Ever."

Okay, maybe it would be more professional than that, but who would ever suspect golden boy Gavin Bailey? It was the perfect crime.

My steps increased. I dug in my pocket for my keys. Hadn't I read somewhere I could rake them across a person's face to defend myself? The keys snagged on the rim of my pocket, and I tugged harder. With a shallow *rip,* my keys flew out of my hands and hurtled through the air, landing on…someone's…boots.

Heavy black boots backed away from a dark purple Cadillac, and the wide door slammed shut, rattling it less than the throbbing music already shaking the car.

My gaze reluctantly traveled from my shimmering keys to the face of the person whose feet I'd just assaulted. I immediately wished I hadn't looked. Tattered and oily jeans hugged beefy legs. A six-pack invaded a finely shaped but massive torso, clearly visible under a so-holey-it-almost-wasn't-there tank top. Dreadlocks spilled over scarred, burly shoulders. But what riveted my gaze was his coal-black eyes, glittering cold and menacing.

I swallowed hard and backed up a step.

Shouting tore my gaze away, and my eyes rested on a sickly pale, skinny dude in slightly more dingy clothes—if that were even possible—leaning over his low-rider pickup's hood, leering at me as I tried to make out his words. His rotting teeth made me cringe, along with the foul innuendos flying out of the man's mouth.

Never mind. I didn't want to know what he'd been saying.

The music lost some volume, and my gaze bounced to a large SUV with five other guys leaning out of the open doors, flinging jeers and catcalls. These were not guys you'd want to meet on a dark night in a deserted parking lot. And I'd done just that. Go me.

Movement from the first guy sent my gaze skittering back to him. He bent and retrieved my keys. Unable to look away, my eyes followed my apartment keys as he tossed them straight up, then plucked them midair.

"Well, well, well. What have we here?"

His deep timbre sent fear crashing through my heart. He strolled toward me and paused in the middle of the lane, not breaking eye contact. The gold on his teeth competed with the gold chains around his neck for brilliance.

Scary dude. I was ready to trade him for interactive zombies. I think.

I raised my hands and backed away, glancing behind me. Maybe a certain hot movie star was still following me? My stomach dropped. Gavin Bailey wasn't there. He wasn't following me after all. Oh, how I wished more than anything he had been! I held out a shaking hand, palm up, and peeked at my keys' captor.

"If you please…my keys…I need those…"

My voice was shaking more than my hand. *Way to be confident, Candace, way to go.*

He chuckled, a low rumble in that drum of a chest of his, and I backed up another step and dropped my hand.

"All alone, little girl?"

My eyes sought the parking lot behind me again, hoping against hope that someone would be there.

Gavin Bailey barreled in my direction, his pleasant grin replaced by a fierce look that would make any warrior proud. Relief washed over me in waves.

"Thank you, Lord," I muttered, my stress apparently taking me back to church days.

I faced the guy, the mantra floating through my head, "Never turn your back on your enemy." Who had said that? My grandmother? Sounded like something she would say…

The guy's chuckle stopped my wandering thoughts. His gold teeth flashed in the garish lamplight. Had he seen Gavin Bailey? I didn't think so, and I wasn't sure if that was a good or bad thing.

"What do you think, boys? Should we give the girl a ride? Show her a good time?"

Bad thing.

Cheers and whistles erupted from the SUV, and he dangled my keys in my face before shoving them into his back pocket.

Oh no, he didn't!

My ears burned, and I forgot all about how scary the guy really was as my temper flared. Marching over to him, I shoved my finger in his chest, thumping it a few times for good measure.

"How dare you? Of all the rude…inconsiderate… If you think for one minute I'm going *anywhere* with you…I absolutely am not. Give me back my keys this instant!"

Leaning forward slowly during my tirade, he gave me a smirk that made me realize my close proximity while simultaneously grossing me out and cooling my temper. I snapped my mouth shut as he leaned forward all the way and sniffed my hair.

"Mmm…you smell good."

What the…? Creepy crawlies exploded down my neck and arms, and I stumbled back a few steps.

"Or you can keep them. I'll just change the locks. No problem."

I spun to leave, but a few of the other guys crowded close behind me, cutting off any chance of escape. The scrawny dude slammed his truck's door with a sneer and started toward me. I backed up two more steps before running out of room, my hands held up in front of me.

"Hey! Where you going? What's the matter, little girl? Scared?" Beanpole slunk toward me, grinning like a fool. He elbowed the scary guy's rock-solid chest, and I almost gagged as his rancid breath floated past me. "She's a pretty little—" He glanced over my shoulder and shoved the burly dude. "Come on, Tyro, it ain't worth it."

He bolted into his superman-blue pickup, and the other guys scattered, roaring away in their dark SUV, not even waiting to see what had spooked the guy.

The blue pickup squealed out of the parking space and screeched to a halt long enough for him to shout, "Come on, man. Let's go! I ain't going to jail again over this!" before peeling out of the parking lot.

Jail? I was going to pass out. I knew it. What had I gotten myself into now?

Tyro hadn't budged, his leer still pointed in my direction. Forget fainting. I spun and dashed toward Mr. Bailey, who'd just made it to the cars behind me.

Reaching him, I started to duck behind him, but he wrapped his arm around my shoulders, pinning me to his side. I threw my arms around his firm waist and tried my best not to tremble like an earthquake. A few heated words penetrated my equally scared and relieved brain before I focused on what they were saying.

"She's with me."

The deep rumble of Gavin Bailey's chest was comforting.

"Don't look like she was with nobody. Why you gotta poke your nose where it ain't belong?"

Gavin tensed. "I suggest you leave now, before security gets here."

"You gonna make me?"

Tyro cracked his beefy knuckles and snapped his neck to the side. A splintering tree came to mind at the loud *crack*. He then jerked his head to the guys behind him—only no one was there.

I glanced up at Gavin. He gave Tyro a tight smile.

"Looks like it's just you and me."

Tyro glared over his shoulder at the two empty spaces. Then he shrugged.

"Okay."

He took a step forward. Gavin shoved me behind him. Flashing lights from a security vehicle pulsed a few rows over.

Tyro paused, then reluctantly backed up a step. "This ain't over, pretty boy." His lips curled as he glanced at me. "Maybe next time, sweetcakes."

My spine stiffened. Sweetcakes? Who was he calling sweetcakes?

He disappeared inside his purple Cadillac, and the raised car squealed away as Gavin pulled me into the row of cars. A flash of gold was the last thing I saw through the heavily tinted windows.

Emboldened, I stepped forward, calling after the car, "And that's what you get! Don't ever come back!"

Tyro slammed on his brakes.

I shrieked and bolted in the opposite direction.

Gavin's footsteps matched mine, but he pulled me to a halt when I reached the edge of the parking lot—on the opposite side from town.

"Look. He's gone."

I glanced behind me, taillights from a lone car lighting up the highway across the massive parking lot.

The earthquake unleashed, and I started shivering like crazy. I may have started blubbering words too, but I chose not to think about that part.

"Hey, it's okay. You're safe. They're gone now."

Mr. Bailey spoke soothing words as he led me right back into the parking lot. I thanked him over and over, my words finally stumbling to a halt when his car came into view.

A flashy red sports car rested between two hulking, black vehicles. They almost looked like sentries guarding the smaller vehicle. Maybe his bodyguards were actually in there. Actors had bodyguards, right? His car's engine purred to life from one click of his keys.

"Wow, nice!"

What can I say? I get distracted easily.

Opening the driver's door, he helped me inside and leaned across me to turn on the heat.

I breathed in deep—it was subtle, I swear—and enjoyed his light cologne. I'd never in all my days imagined I would ever be that close to Gavin Bailey. He smelled just as he should—manly and tantalizing.

Thank God he couldn't read my thoughts. I would die of

embarrassment if anyone knew what I was thinking!

The theater's ancient security guard eked past in his dilapidated security cart, and I did a double-take. He quite possibly was on the run from the old-folks home. I seriously doubted he would've been any help had we needed it.

"Stay here. I will be right back."

"Mm-hmm," I agreed.

I could sit here all day, basking in—

I jerked upright. Alone? I didn't think so! What if they came back? I jumped out of the car and ran after Mr. Bailey, leaving the door wide open and the engine running.

"Wait! Wait for me! I'm coming with you."

He turned, surprise and a touch of dismay etched on his handsome face. He ran back to the car—his baby by the looks of things—and shut off the engine. After making sure all doors were secure and firmly locked, he came back to me, grin wide.

My stomach fluttered. That thing was dangerous, but it looked like he knew that. He dropped his arm about my shoulders once more, and my breath stuttered. I was pretty sure he could hear my wildly racing heart. My arm snaked around his waist, clinging to him for dear life as he led me at a brisk pace back to the theater.

Maybe this night wasn't so horrible after all.

Chapter 2

Scratch that. It was even worse.

"I already told you, I have no idea what nationality the man was! He had long black hair in dreadlocks, gold teeth, a tank top practically ripped to shreds, stained jeans, more gold around his neck than I've seen in my life. And was driving a pimped-out purple Cadillac you can't miss!" I said it all in one breath and paused long enough to drag in some air.

"Put down that he was Latino," the hawkish theater manager directed to the police officer taking the statement. The police officer paused and looked back at me, not sure he wanted to get involved in the verbal sparring.

"And have the guy get away cause I was too scared to ask his origins? Are you stupid? I got that you're rude, but I didn't realize lack of brains could be added to your credentials."

It wasn't the best comeback I'd ever come up with, but apparently my mouth didn't care.

I glared at the middle-aged, stick-thin manager who was rewording everything I said to the police officer. He'd been impossible since Mr. Bailey had convinced him to call the police. I'd been polite, calmly telling the officer every detail I could think of. The entire time, Mr.

Snooty Pants had treated me like a prostitute soliciting customers in the parking lot. I'd taken it as long as I could, but there were limits. I stared him down, daring him to say anything more. To my increasing ire, he smirked. I stepped forward and opened my mouth, ready to tear him to shreds.

"Thank you, Miss Marshall. I think we have enough to go by. I will get an APB out on them right away, just to be safe. If you remember anything else, call me."

The police officer handed me his card, shook Mr. Bailey's hand, and left. I don't think he wanted to referee the knockdown, drag-out fight about to commence on the theater floor.

The theater manager gave me a patronizing smile and walked away.

My fists clenched as I watched him stroll to the box office. The nerve! I started thinking of all the witty things I should have said. Of course, the best ones would hit me at midnight, or just when I was drifting off to sleep.

Gavin Bailey cleared his throat. I spun toward him, flustered that one, I had momentarily forgotten he was there, and two, he had been privy to my many humiliations of the day. A blush heightened the color of my already flushed face.

You would think one would stop blushing once they hit twenty. Not so in my case.

I unclenched my fists and opened my mouth. Not one blasted word came out. Gavin Bailey smiled kindly.

"How about joining me for that cup of coffee? I think we could both use one."

I tried to protest, I really did. I didn't want Gavin Bailey to realize he was talking to an individual who couldn't make small talk to save her life. My mind went completely blank in stressful situations. And, as wonderful as I'd dreamed a date with Gavin Bailey would be, reality just didn't support that dream. He was used to gorgeous, smart, witty, and, well, gorgeous women, and none of those words described me. At least, not when it came to wowing stunning movie stars.

I found myself saying, "Sure, that would be great."

I froze. What? Did I really just say that? His firm hand rested on the small of my back. My steps immediately matched his. Traitors. It would be so much better if they'd run the other way.

I wondered if he'd notice if I just kept walking to my apartment after we reached the coffee shop. I figured I couldn't get away with it, and for the second time that evening, Gavin ushered me to his awesome little red car.

Honestly, the thing might have looked nice on the outside—until you got in. Then luxurious didn't begin to describe it. This time I soaked in all the features. The dashboard and door panels lit with streamlined, dim white running lights. New white leather glistened on the door panels and seats. He pretty much had to speak to it to get it to do anything. I was surprised he didn't go into shock at having to steer the thing himself.

I immediately began playing with all the things I didn't even know they included on the inside of vehicles. After a while, I noticed he was watching me.

I flushed and sat back, remembering my brother wanted to kill me every time I adjusted anything in his car. It didn't stop me from constantly adjusting stuff, but this was a famous movie star, and I didn't want to tick him off. Ever.

"Sorry," I mumbled.

He muttered, "That's okay," and took a moment to put everything back how he'd had it. Then that dazzling smile was back on his face. "What kind of coffee do you like?"

He backed out of the parking space. The sentries looked sad to see the red car go. I chuckled to myself and started talking. Always a bad thing.

"Oh, anything with lots of cream and sugar. And cold—I like cold coffee. But, I guess since it's cooler out, being night and all, I should get something hot, but with all the cream and sugar, like I like it."

My gaze drifted out my window, and I mentally smacked myself. Really? Could I be any more stupid? College apparently hadn't done much for me in the flirting department. Scratch that. I was nowhere near flirting. It hadn't done much for me in the having-a-normal-conversation-with-a-famous-person department. They should offer a class. I tugged on the side mirror and peeked at him in it. I jumped when I saw him grinning at me. My eyes frantically darted around the car, trying to find a topic for conversation.

"So, um, yes, well, what do you do for a living?" This time I actually smacked my forehead. "Oh, how stupid." I turned to him. "I'm so sorry. I'm not any good at this. Why don't you talk about something, and I'll just sit here and listen? The night will probably go a whole lot better that way."

He smiled at me. Again. He needed to stop doing that. It was driving me crazy. I could not be responsible for my actions. Any more smiling at me like that, and I was just going to have to get down on one knee and ask him to marry me. He was walking on dangerous ground.

"I'm actually enjoying myself." Another smile. The guy had no idea what kind of peril he was in. "I understand you probably don't get taken out by actors on a daily basis, but I'd like to change that. What is it that you do?"

I blinked. Did he really just say that? I decided to ignore it.

"Oh, you know, I moved here after college for a job. Now I work here and stuff."

"How did you meet your boyfriend?"

"Um, at the supermarket, or grocery store, or whatever. We reached for the same last bag of chips. He insisted I take it, and couldn't believe it when I did. He thought I would refuse, and he'd have to take it out of kindness. We stood there arguing over the bag until a store worker handed us each a new bag—since we'd smashed the other chips to bits. We laughed and exchanged numbers."

His smile was polite. "Sounds like love at first sight."

"Not really. We both kinda liked each other but drove each other crazy. Not in a good way. So, we hang out and go on dates and stuff, sometimes chur—"

My words hung in the air. My gaze bounced in his direction to see if he'd caught my near-slip.

He chuckled. "I was being sarcastic."

"Oh."

"You go to church?"

I flushed. I wasn't exactly comfortable talking about that kind of stuff with people, especially world-savvy movie stars who might think that kind of thing was quaint and old-fashioned, maybe even a little cute. *Cute* was the last persona on earth I wanted to show Gavin Bailey.

"Yeah."

"Do you like it? Church?"

"Yeah." Part of me was excited he was asking; the other part froze. The second part won. I didn't want to talk about it.

I looked around for something constructive to do with my hands. They were itching to play with the dash again. I settled for drumming my fingers on my knee. The quietness in the car was getting loud. I desperately wished I had something to say. This was so awkward.

"You said you moved here for a job. What do you do?"

I was completely convinced he could not be interested in my boring, uneventful life and was just being polite. I'd much rather hear about *his* line of work. But, he'd asked, so...

"I'm a copy editor at the local newspaper."

"Nice. Do you like it?"

I shrugged. "I'm good at it."

"And Peter?"

I flushed. There was no way to make this sound better. I had moved to this town for one reason alone, and it wasn't about to make me look good.

"He's a reporter."

"Same paper?"

"Yep." I was done talking about him.

"Been here very long?"

"Actually, only a few weeks. I moved here for the job."

"I see. I take it you didn't meet Peter here, then?"

"No, we moved here together. Well, not *together*, together—we both have our own places—but we both got job offers and thought it would be good experience—"

"Do you enjoy living here?"

"It's all right, I guess. Very uneventful. I suppose I thought I'd be doing more with my life. But, well, here I am."

He nodded, respectfully engaged in this boring conversation. The sooner I stopped talking, the better.

"What did you think you'd be doing by now?"

"I have no idea," I mumbled. Telling a movie star your big dreams of becoming a professional photographer is like saying, "Hey! I'm one of those nosy people who wants to follow you around for the rest of your life snapping photos!" Now that I thought about it, I hadn't taken a single photograph since moving to this town. Peter had always been embarrassed by my trigger-happy fingers. Time to change that. I was taking a selfie first thing.

I peeked at Gavin. This was the worst possible night ever to be camera-less. Wonder if he'd let me grab my phone from my apartment so I could take my first selfie in ages with *him*. I grinned. That would be beyond awesome.

My thoughts drifted to Peter as my eyes drifted out the window. Wonder if he were enjoying his zombie "experience" at the movie theater? I hoped a zombie jumped out and scared him so badly he screamed like a girl. I smirked. Impress that young lady. Traitorous leech. Guess I wouldn't be spending much more of my time at that gaudy theater—Peter's favorite place to hang out since we'd moved here.

Our small town, Acción, might have had only one main road labeled "Main Street" trailing past a few buildings that served as our downtown, but they sure could revamp a movie theater. They might not care the rest of their buildings were 2,000-plus years old, but they sure liked their movies. Hey, it was better than hanging out at the factory—the only other large building in the area. Moving to this town had been his idea; now I wondered if I liked my job enough to stay.

"I'm sorry about what happened tonight."

I jumped as Mr. Bailey's softly accented voice caught me off guard. I wondered for which event of the evening he was apologizing.

"That must have really sucked for your boyfriend not to have your back like that. I'm sorry he went with someone else."

"Oh, well." I swallowed hard. It did suck. "It was inevitable, I guess. He just hurried along what was coming anyway." Only I hadn't seen it coming.

"It's quite the drive back to town. How were you planning to get back? Did you drive your own car to the theater?"

I tucked an imaginary strand of hair behind my ear. This night could not be over fast enough. "Um, no. Peter drove me. I was planning on walking. It's not *that* far."

He frowned. "It's a couple of miles, at least. You were going to walk all the way back to town, alone, in the dark, after starting a zombie movie screening?"

I snapped my fingers. "That reminds me! What in the world were you doing at the screening? Were you acting in it? Or just watching it? You don't live around here, do you? Why did you leave? Not because of me, surely." I gasped. "Did they kick you out because I left? Because the test group numbers were mismatched? Was that woman your date?"

Mr. Bailey grinned. "Which question would you like me to answer first?"

I flushed and sat on my hands, which I'd started waving the moment I'd begun hurling questions. I bit my lip, not sure what to say. Mr. Bailey waited just long enough to let the silence stretch into awkwardness before answering.

"I was there because a friend asked me to check out the new interactive features they want to start adding to all films. No, I wasn't acting in it. Yes, I was looking forward to seeing it. I don't live around here. And I voluntarily left because I wanted to get to know the woman who stood up for her convictions, even though I could tell she was scared out of her mind."

I gaped at him. Yep, just like a fish. He glanced at me, then took his hand off the steering wheel long enough to gently tap me under the chin. I closed my mouth with a snap. His fingertip left a trail of heat down my neck that made its way through my body and onto my face. I vowed never to wash my chin again.

We rode the rest of the way to the café in silence.

I settled on the plush couch with my steaming cup of decaf, Gavin across from me. I glanced around, wanting to shout, "Look who I'm sitting with!" Only I was too shy to ever do something like that. I hoped. Fortunately, we were the only two in the dimly lit café besides the employees and a frazzled guy hunched over his laptop. He probably wouldn't care. Oh, well. I blew into my mug and cautiously sipped, soaking in the sight of Gavin Bailey.

Caramel and cream slipped over my tongue, blending exotic coffee with an unsurpassed moment in my life. One thing the café got right was their coffee. I would never be able to drink this blend again without recalling every second of my time with Gavin Bailey.

I was back to thinking it wasn't too terrible a night after all.

I waited a moment before I ventured, "So, Gav—Mr. Bailey, what is your favorite part of being an actor? It surely can't be the awestruck fans." I grinned sheepishly.

"Please, call me Gavin."

"Gavin," I breathed. I was not letting that opportunity pass me by.

He smiled and leaned forward, coffee cup cradled in his hands.

Not gonna lie. I was slightly jealous of that mug.

"I love bringing a character to life. I love being able to make someone laugh or cry, just because I did my job well. It's a lot of work, but I love the satisfaction of getting it right." He chuckled. "And I really don't mind the fans. There are a few strange situations, but nothing a little charm and discretion can't handle."

My smile beamed, inviting him to say more. He didn't hesitate.

We had an amazing night after that. I'm a *much* better listener than talker. As he put me at ease, we actually had a conversation, and he even laughed at a few things I said. Yes, because they were supposed to be funny. I can't remember an evening I enjoyed more.

A lull in the conversation left me smiling—okay, I hadn't stopped smiling—and I sank against the cushions, dreamily mulling over his voice and who I would tell first about our date. Not everything. No, most of this night I wanted to keep to myself. We sat in companionable silence, sipping the last of our now-cool coffee. Glancing at the clock, I was shocked to see how late it was. Well after midnight. I had no idea we'd been here so long.

Gavin casually rubbed the rim of his coffee mug. "So, tomorrow morning, same place, 9:00am?"

I snorted. "Yeah, right."

"No, really."

His eyes met mine. No teasing lingered there, just his question, and —was it possible?—a hint of vulnerability. Was he serious?

I stared at him. Pretty sure my mouth was open again. The intensity of his gaze stole my breath away. I couldn't say exactly what was smoldering there—or maybe I was afraid to—but it made my pulse race and my stomach clench like I was about to take a free fall. He was serious.

"Are you certain?" I asked in a daze. There was no way this gorgeous man could be attracted to me. No way.

His lips lifted in a slow, adorable smile, and he nodded, making me feel as though I were the most important person in the world. To *him*. To Gavin Bailey. I tucked another imaginary strand of hair behind my ear and blushed.

"Okay."

His radiant smile dazzled me. Had I really made him that happy? A grin reached my lips, and I eyed him shyly. This could not be happening. He reached over to shake my hand and held on to it for an eternity. I pretty much melted. Sirens broke through our reverie.

Gavin looked away first, glancing toward the windows. He frowned. My gaze followed his. Emergency vehicles raced past the café. My frown matched his.

"What's going on?" I asked no one in particular. A few of the employees came out from behind the counter, peering out the windows.

Slipping his hand from mine, Gavin rose from the sofa and strode to the windows. My eyes followed his retreating back, then I stared down at my hand. Poor thing. Left destitute. Setting my mug down, I ambled after him. Not seeing anything more than flashing lights glancing off the buildings farther down the street, I let my thoughts wander. Stupid emergency vehicles. Ruined a perfect moment in time. My eyes widened. *Oh!* I flushed. *I hope everything is okay!*

Gavin turned from the window and offered me a smile.

"After you."

His hand swept toward the door. I walked to his car and reached for the door's handle. His arm slipped around me, hovering mere inches from my side, and he opened the door before I could. My eyes widened. There were guys who still opened doors for girls? I may have melted just a little bit more. This was heaven. A whiff of heady cologne teased my senses. Smiling at him in gratitude—okay, maybe a hint of giddiness was in there somewhere—I started to get into the car.

A few more emergency vehicles rushed by, and I paused, my eyes following them down the street. A faint orange glow tinted the sky in the direction they were headed. I sank into the car while Gavin held my door. My head snapped up. The orange glow was coming from the direction of the theater!

I jumped out of the car and raced down the sidewalk. The car door's slam echoed behind me, and Gavin's footsteps rushed to catch up. I took a few turns and came to the edge of my new town, slowing as the last building moved from sight.

Gavin was instantly by my side. I gasped and grabbed his arm.

"The theater! The theater's on fire! Come on. We have to go!" I started to run toward the theater as more emergency vehicles raced past, blaring their sirens.

"Wait!" Gavin's firm grip pulled me to a stop. "We'll take my car."

I nodded and sprinted toward his vehicle. I fumbled with the door handle, but Gavin stilled my hand and jerked it open for me. I jumped in, and he sprinted around the car, sliding in next to me. The engine purred to life. I clenched and unclenched my fists as we waited for several more fire trucks and ambulances to zoom by before Gavin could pull onto the road.

I implored under my breath, "Please, be okay. Dear Lord, please may they all be okay."

Chapter 3 ☣

We yielded to emergency vehicles the entire way back to the theater. The sheer number of ambulances, police cars, and firetrucks racing toward the ever-increasing orange glow filled me with terror. What in the world was happening that took so many emergency vehicles?

I perched on the edge of my seat, willing the already-speeding car to go faster. Gavin reached over and took my hand. I stared at our clasped hands, not understanding. Why was he holding my hand?

He squeezed. "He'll be all right."

I gave him a small squeeze back, expecting him to pull away. He did not.

"You must love him very much," he said in a tight, controlled voice.

I glanced at him in surprise. He studied the road ahead. I thought for a moment before I cleared my throat.

"I can't say we have a future together, not after the way he treated me tonight, but he is my friend. And, as my friend, I would never wish something bad to happen to him." Gavin grasped my hand just a little bit tighter. "I hope he really is all right," I added in a small voice.

Gavin nodded, raised my hand, and planted a tender kiss on the back of my hand. He then concentrated on driving. I guess I can't wash my hand now, either. This night could not get any weirder.

Gavin slowed at a roadblock outside of the theater's mammoth parking area. I noticed the orange glow was coming from behind the theater and breathed a sigh of relief. A policeman waved for Gavin to turn around, but Gavin was already rolling down his window. The officer sauntered over, leaning down to stare into the open window.

"Just turn around and head on back to town, folks."

"What's happening, sir?"

"It seems the factory farther on down the road was set on fire. Must've been dryer than tinder. The whole thing went up in flames. It's too big to put out, so right now we're working on containing it."

"Is the theater in any danger?"

"Naw. We're evacuating folks, just in case. But the factory is a ways from the theater. Shouldn't be a problem at all. You got family at the theater?"

"Friends. We wanted to make sure they're okay."

"Well, now. I'm sure they are. Not sure about those at the plant, yet." He leveled a stern gaze at Gavin, realizing his slip. "Wouldn't say anything about that if I were you. No use worrying folks. The best thing you can do is go on home and let us do our jobs. Don't worry, now. We'll have everyone out of here in a jiffy."

"Thank you, Officer."

"No problem."

They shook hands. Gavin turned the car around and started to drive back toward town. I sat forward and stared at the people in the parking lot. What was wrong with everybody?

People were walking around all right, but no one was getting into their cars to leave, and no one was gawking at the blaze. That's what I'd be doing. They all looked—lost. Confused, maybe? Something was just…off.

"Wait."

Gavin looked my way. He slowed but kept moving. "I can't stop here, Candace."

I thrilled at his use of my name.

"The officer said to go back to town."

"Do you always do what you're told?"

He grinned. "What do you have in mind?"

I nodded toward the cars. "Look. No one's leaving. I thought he said they were evacuating the theater?"

"They're probably using all of their resources on the blaze. My guess is the theater staff is in charge of getting people out. You know how people love to rubberneck."

"No, this was different," I mused. I bit my lip, gnawing on it while I tried to figure everything out. "It looked like people were wandering aimlessly around the parking lot, not looking at the fire, but not trying to leave, either. It was kinda creepy. I wonder if they're hurt?"

Gavin shrugged. "What would you like to do?"

"I want to see what's going on, to see if we—I mean, I—can help." Gavin looked at me, clearly convinced the emergency personnel had it taken care of. "Please, Gavin. I would never forgive myself if there were something I could do and didn't at least try."

Gavin blew out his breath but slowed and turned his car around. Again. "Where's your purse?"

What in the world? I gawked at him. Why would he care? "Uh, Peter told me to leave it home." I grinned. "Guess he didn't want me smacking zombies with it. Why?"

Gavin looked sheepish. "I was just curious. I haven't seen a girl without a bag in a long time."

"Nope, it's just me tonight. But don't worry, I'll have my purse bright and early tomorrow morning," I teased.

"Got anything else with you? Pepper spray? Keys?"

I chuckled. "What is this? Twenty questions?"

He grinned but waited for a reply.

"Nope, just my ID and some cash. Why?" I snapped my fingers. "Oh, no! That crazy guy still has my keys! I forgot to tell the officer. Way to go, me."

Gavin chuckled. "So what should we do? Find a place to park so we can sneak in?"

I glanced at the flat, treeless terrain. He had to be joking, since that was impossible to do in New Mexico. Well, this part of it, anyway.

"Um, no...maybe we could ask the guard again?"

"Are you kidding? You know the guard'll send us packing."

"I know. But, well, maybe we can change his mind?" I finished lamely. Clearly I hadn't quite thought this through.

Gavin didn't look convinced but made his way back to the roadblock anyway. There was no one there. I frowned and peeked at Gavin. He looked as puzzled as I felt. Gavin parked the car after a moment, and we both just sat there. Cracking the door open, Gavin climbed from his seat. I climbed out after he did. He called but didn't get an answer. I wrapped my arms around my middle and shivered. Dread crawled over me. Something was wrong. I knew it.

He turned to me. "I don't like this. I don't like this one bit."

I couldn't agree more. The hair on the back of my neck bristled as a shiver ran down my spine.

"Me neither. But Gavin, I *have* to know if Peter is okay."

He sighed, rubbing the back of his neck. His gaze pierced me. "Are you sure he's worth it, especially after what he did to you?"

I weighed my response carefully. "Yes, he's worth it. Everyone is worth helping."

He stared at me, a slight frown on his face, his head cocked to the side.

I struggled to explain. "If you saw someone in trouble, and you could help that person, would you take the time to find out if he or she was worth saving? Or would you just jump in and save him? All people are worth helping, no matter who they are or what they've done."

He walked to my side of the car and stood close to me. "And what is it that you think you could be doing to help him?" he asked in his best Scottish brogue.

I'm pretty sure I melted into a puddle at his feet. "I...don't... know."

I swayed, wondering if I were about to become the fainting kind of girl. His nearness was intoxicating. He reached out both hands and steadied me. His touch set my pulse on fire.

"Then I think it's best we find out what it is we can be doing."

I nodded and closed my eyes. He was going to kiss me. After a moment, he released me and opened the passenger door. My eyes flew open. I glanced at him, mortified. I'm pretty sure he was hiding a grin while digging around in his glovebox.

I straightened and stomped toward the parking lot. Someday, someday, I was going to grow up and stop doing stupid, embarrassing things!

"Whoa, whoa, whoa! Where do you think you're going?" Gavin jogged to me and grasped my arm.

I pointed at the theater, trying not to make eye contact. Had he forgotten?

"Wait just a minute, lassie. We have no idea what's going on here."

It was then I noticed he held a gun in his other hand. My eyes widened, and I stared up at him. "Do you really think we're going to need that?" My shrill voice echoed around us.

"Don't know. But I do know I'm going to be prepared."

He tucked the gun into his belt, and we made our way past the blinking roadblock, into the theater's parking area.

Chapter 4 ☣

"Where did all the people go?"

"Hmm?" Gavin kept scanning the parking lot.

"People were all over the place just a little while ago. Where'd they go?"

Gavin shrugged and kept himself between the deserted cars and me. We were on the edge of the parking area, working our way toward the theater. Something wasn't right, and it was creeping me out. Big time. I started noticing that a few car windows were splintered and cracked, and there was more trash on the ground the closer we got to the building.

"Gavin," I said in a loud stage whisper. He paused but didn't turn around. "Why are all the trash bins turned over in front of the theater?"

"I think we should go back."

"What in the world?" I ran forward. The glass facing of the theater was shattered in several places, and the theater's lobby looked like a war zone. I vaulted feet-first through a glass-less door and ran inside, my boots crunching on glass and popcorn. Smoke and burnt popcorn tinged the air. I coughed, my gaze swinging wildly in every direction. It was deserted.

"Peter. Peter! Are you in here? Peter!"

Gavin caught up with me, but I sprinted past him to look down the long corridors leading to the individual cinemas. The electronic posters were mostly smashed. Popcorn and broken boxes of candy littered the hallway. The women's restroom sign was even missing some letters.

I headed toward one of the theater's doors. A pounding halted my steps. "Where is that coming from?"

Not waiting for Gavin's answer, I ran down the corridor. I could hear him right behind me. The corridor veered to the right, and there was a door at the end of it, at the very back of the cinema. I assumed it led upstairs to the theater's projectors. The pounding grew louder the closer we moved to the door.

Thud. Thud. Thud.

I paused. It was way too slow and methodical for someone needing help. I glanced at Gavin, suddenly uncertain.

"Every instinct is telling me not to open that door," I ventured.

"It's your decision." He had his gun low but was scanning the halls. I checked. Yep, his safety was off.

I blew out a huff of air. "*And,* right now I would be yelling at my TV screen to get back-up." Gavin looked at me as if I'd lost my marbles. I grinned. "If this were a movie, of course."

"Well, it's not," he snapped.

Touchy, touchy.

I nodded. True. I took a deep breath. The pounding was still there. I reached for the door and tried the handle. Unlocked. The door opened to complete darkness. I felt around for a light switch. Light flooded to reveal a set of stairs leading downward. I stared. Why did the theater have a basement? The pounding stopped.

I headed for the door at the bottom of the stairs before I lost my nerve. It was locked. Glancing up, I saw Gavin watching me from the top of the stairs. Scaredy-cat. I put my ear to the door to listen.

Bang.

I jolted back and smacked my head on the wall behind me. "Owww!" I moaned and grabbed my head.

Gavin sprinted down the stairs to my side. "What is it? What happened?"

I rubbed my head and shook it. I'd whacked it pretty good. "Someone's on the other side of that door." I pointed.

He rattled the door's handle. "Locked."

Brilliant observation skills. "Wait, I've got an idea." I pulled a bobby pin from my hair.

My hair was on the frizzy side, so besides plastering it with enough hair products to make curls and not a 'fro, I could set off metal detectors with the amount of pins securing my stray whispys to my head. Another reason I was constantly tucking non-existent strands of hair behind my ears. Habit from years gone by looking like I had stuck my finger in an electric outlet.

I expertly picked the lock and shrugged at Gavin's surprised look. Another useless talent gleaned from one of my brother's friends. That and cracking small safes. He'd told me it was just a hobby, and I'd believed him. Until he'd gone to jail.

The lock clicked, and I turned the handle. Our eyes met before I swung the door open wide.

I stared with my mouth open at the sight that greeted us.

A group of—*people*—crowded around the door, staring at us with blank expressions and white eyes. Wait. What? *White eyes?* No joke. Their faces were on the gray side, and a few of their heads hung listlessly to the side. Zombies. No freaking way.

A hanging light pulsed on and off in the background, adding to the effect. Talk about eerie.

I couldn't help it. I started laughing. True, it was on the hysterical side, but, I mean, come on. It *had* to be a bad dream.

They lunged, and Gavin opened fire while I shrieked. We moved for the door at the same time. Arms and hands reached out, not letting the door close. They started clawing at the wall. I stared in horror as they tore big gashes in the wall, peeling plaster and wallpaper back. The worst part was the bits of flesh and blood they left trailing on the wall. Bile rose in my throat. This could not be happening.

"Go, go, go!"

I looked at Gavin. What was he talking about? He motioned with his head to the stairs.

"What about you?" I stammered.

"Gee, I would love to stay here and chat, but I'm a wee bit busy at the moment. Get up the stairs now! I'm right behind you!"

I didn't need a third command. I vaulted up the stairs. At the top, I stopped and waited for him. Struggling with the door, he cried out, shoved it hard, and ran. The zombie-like creatures burst through the door, slowly moving after him.

I turned to race out of the theater. I stopped dead in my tracks. More of those—*things*—were standing hunched over in the hallway. If only one of them would grin or someone would jump out and yell, "Gotcha!"

No such luck.

I started jumping up and down and waving my hands like a cheerleader. I was pretty good for having no experience in that particular field.

Gavin burst through the door and slammed it shut. He rolled a trashcan in front of the door, shoving it under the handle.

I was still expressively freaking out in the hallway.

"That won't hold them for lon—" He stopped abruptly.

I started running in little circles, pausing only to jump up and down and point. I babbled incoherently, and my arms were waving big time.

He grabbed me as I made a pass near him and held me down. "Hold very still," he commanded in a low voice.

"Why? So they can walk over here at a snail's pace and eat us for —"

His hand clamped over my mouth. I hadn't realized I was shouting until sudden silence followed.

I stared at them with wide eyes, still bouncing in Gavin's arms. The pounding began at the door behind us.

"Go. Now." Gavin shoved me down the hall.

The door behind us burst open as those in the hall made their move. Gavin followed me closely, shoving me with one hand, shooting zombies with the other. The bullets did nothing. They just kept coming. After getting *shot*. At least the rounds ripping holes in them slowed the zombies enough so we could slip past their grasping hands.

We rounded the corner of the hallway into the lobby. I stopped, and Gavin quit shoving. A rather large group of the things were silently regarding us from outside the broken glass, a few from inside the lobby. Some were dressed as moviegoers and some as factory workers. I could hear the others approaching from the hallway.

"I'm out of bullets," whispered Gavin close to my ear.

"Great. That's just great. You should have saved two for—" My loud voice must have spurred—or should I say shuffled?—them into action. Gavin shoved me once again, but this time toward the ones near the glass.

"Gavin?"

He kicked one down and swatted another away with one of the poles previously holding the partitioning ropes.

While he was defending us, a woman zombie came straight for me —way faster than I liked, too. She looked a tad grungier than the others, with what looked like skin hanging off her chin. The other's eyes were not completely white, with the iris showing through the filmy white, but this dame's were white white. Her nice clothes were torn but vaguely familiar. I stood rooted to the spot.

"Gaaaaaavvvvvviiiiiinnnnn!"

He turned just as the woman reached me and punched her in the jaw for all he was worth. Her head snapped to the side and cracked. Like a gunshot. It stayed like that, bent at a grotesque angle, but she turned and came after me again.

Gavin dove through an opening in the bodies, pulling me behind him. I really had to give the guy credit for doing everything for me.

He took me straight to the box office, shoved me inside, and slammed the door. The lock clicked.

I looked around. The glass was still intact, and we were the only ones inside. Our only problem was there was *one* door, with a virtual army of the undead on the other side.

Gavin tucked me under the box office counter. He shoved his gun into his belt and grabbed one of the chairs at the ticket counter.

"Are you sure we'll be safe in here?" My teeth started to chatter.

"Don't worry. The glass is bulletproof." He secured the chair under the door handle and started piling everything he could find in front of the door. "No one is getting in here."

A loud crash made me jump. Gavin grabbed me and dove under the counter. He bumped right into a soft body.

Gavin yanked the person out from under the shelf, pulling back his fist to punch him in the face. I started screaming.

"Don't hurt me!" squawked a familiar voice.

The haunting *thud* started at the box office door.

Gavin dropped his fist and shoved the guy back. Both of them were breathing hard, and Gavin still looked like he wanted to punch something.

The theater manager clambered back under the counter. "Quick! Before the ones outside see you!"

Gavin ducked beside him. Loud crashes echoed all around us. I could only assume the theater was getting another beating. I desperately hoped no one *alive* alive was still in the theater at their mercy. Vehicles crunched, and car alarms wailed miserably; it sounded like cars were being turned over. The banging on the door to the box office gradually tapered off. Had they really forgotten about us?

"Seems to me you've got some explaining to do," Gavin directed at the manager.

"Me? I'm hiding here like you! Why do you think I've got anything to do with it?"

Gavin pulled back his fist. Oh, yeah, he wanted to punch something, and the manager's face was convenient.

"All right! All right!"

Gavin sat back and waited.

"I might know something about it." The silence—that is, in the box office—stretched on for a moment before Gavin grabbed the man's suit jacket lapels.

"Start talking," Gavin growled.

"It was a test—an experiment! But it was never supposed to be like this."

Something started banging on the glass. I was ready to pee my pants. Gavin noticed I was getting hysterical. Okay, maybe I was beyond hysterical. He released the guy's jacket, scooted next to me, and took my face in his hands.

"Candace, listen to me. I'm going to get you out of this. I don't know how, but we're going to make it. Do you understand?"

My eyes darted around the box office, toward every noise making its way into our sanctuary.

"Candace, look at me."

It was difficult to focus on what he was saying, but he pulled me closer, and my eyes found his.

"We're going to make it. I promise. I need you to keep your head, to stay focused. Can you do that? For me? I'm going to get you out. But I need your help."

My eyes filled with tears, and I nodded.

"Good girl."

He wrapped his arm around my shoulders and pulled me close. I snuggled into him, burying my face in the crook of his neck. I tried to block everything but his nearness. His cologne soothed me, and I took deep breaths, willing my racing heart to calm.

Gavin kept his voice low. "What happened? What kind of experiment?"

I reluctantly looked at the manager but stayed close to Gavin.

The manager's eyes darted everywhere. His fingernails dug into the soft flesh of his hands, causing blood to drip on the carpet. I stared at the red liquid in horror. No one should be so upset they had no idea they were hurting themselves.

I sat up and reached for his hands, trying to soothe him like Gavin had just done for me. He would not be soothed, and I could not pry his hands open. He started talking—babbling, really.

"It was a new kind of movie experience. Sharper images, interactive features involving actors and enhancements—even better than 3D. You don't even need those stupid glasses." His voice faded for a moment. "This isn't right. This was never supposed to happen. We're gonna die!" He bolted for the door.

Gavin lunged for him and pushed him back, pinning him to the floor, out of sight of the many now pounding on the box office glass. The noise was beginning to hurt my head.

"What do you mean? What kind of enhancements?"

"Sensory enhancements, to make the experience come alive."

I looked at the man strangely. We were losing him again.

"Like a drug?" It was a long shot, a jab at keeping the conversation going. I had no idea I was right.

His eyes darted between us. "It's not my fault! It's completely harmless! Just a whiff from a small vial and the images come alive, like nothing you've ever seen before. It was pumped through the air vents. Wears off in roughly three hours. Our test subjects could even drive immediately after the drug was administered. There were no observed changes in the human body whatsoever. It's perfectly safe!"

"Apparently not," muttered Gavin.

"You mean this was tested on more than just our group?" I asked.

He nodded. "On several controlled military groups. This was one of the first civilian groups tested."

"One of the first? Does that mean there're more?" I snapped my fingers. "That woman! The one who attacked me!"

Gavin's look plainly said, *Which one?*

"She was dressed like that Penelope woman. What did the drug do? Did we breathe it? How are we not affected? Where's Peter?"

The man just shook his head. His eyes were starting to glaze over from panic. I had to know. I scooted close to him.

"What did the drug do to the test subjects?"

He focused on me for a moment, but his voice had a faraway quality.

"It was different this time. Everyone was bothered by it, even the actors. They just...died. Started convulsing, and died."

"You killed them?" I shrieked. "You killed Peter?" I jumped on the man's back and put him in a chokehold. I wasn't raised with boys for nothing.

Gavin untangled my arms and peeled me off the man's back.

"You do realize if you kill him, he'll turn into one of them, too?" he whispered fiercely.

I had not.

"I was just gonna teach him a lesson," I muttered into my chest. My head was spinning with questions. I had to understand this. "So... the drug killed a bunch of people, turning them into those *things* out there. But, if they're dead, then how are they walking around? Why do they look like zombies? What do zombies do? Is this for real?"

"Don't you know anything about zombies?" Both men stared at me.

"No!" I roared in the manager's face, even though the question had come from Gavin. The extent of my knowledge came from previews I'd heard from behind closed eyes, not being able to change the channel or leave the room fast enough. Or from snatches of scenes I'd witnessed from walking in on someone else watching a horror flick. That added up to about zilch.

The manager started to cry. "The effects spread from person to person faster than we thought possible. Now they're all dead. They're the undead. Everyone behind the experiment, everyone I ever knew, gone." His voice rose in volume and pitch. "And we're going to end up just like them! It's only a matter of time! What have we done? Oh, what have we done?"

I slapped him as hard as I could.

Gavin's jaw dropped, and he stared at me. It'd worked in the movies, but it didn't faze this guy. He started rocking back and forth. Gavin tried to keep him talking, keeping one eye on me—to see what crazy thing I'd do next, I'm sure.

"You said there were other test groups, but they didn't have the same reaction. How widespread is this thing? Can we get out and get help?"

"You don't understand! They're dead. They're *all* dead. We're all that's left. There's no hope!"

"But—how could it spread that quickly?"

The manager looked at me, but he wasn't looking at me. I shivered. His eyes were vacant. Hollow.

"We're one of many groups tested. All tonight. They all had the same reaction. It's spreading like wildfire."

The toss-up was between crying and beating my head against the wall. I started to cry, and Gavin turned to me. I jumped and gasped as a loud gunshot blasted nearby. Gavin dove on top of me, knocking me over. My head hit hard, but thankfully his hand softened the blow.

I glanced around wildly, my head spinning, my ears ringing, my foggy brain wondering what had happened. I noticed the splattered blood on the bottom of the box office counter and started to scream.

I had always thought myself a levelheaded person, calm in emergencies. This was apparently not the case. Gavin clamped his hand over my mouth and held me close, but that didn't stop me. It took a while, but I finally calmed down enough for my screams to be reduced to sobbing and whimpering. Talk about making a great impression.

Gavin moved enough to look at the manager. He grabbed my face and turned it to the wall, telling me not to look. But I'd seen enough. The manager had blown a hole through his head. Gavin removed the gun from the dead man's grasp and tucked it into his own belt. He turned to me.

"We have to get out of here. Now. Are you with me?"

I looked toward the door and shook my head.

"I know this will be difficult, but we can do it. We *have* to leave now."

I shook my head no again, and he opened his mouth to argue. No way was I going through that door. I pointed at the ceiling. His argument died on his lips as he glanced up.

He grinned. "Good girl. We go by air vent."

He helped me stand and gently turned me away from the body. I wasn't prepared for what I saw. The entire box office window was covered end to end with writhing, churning, undead bodies clawing at the glass. Something odd struck me through the panic swelling in my throat.

"Why are they that decayed?"

"What?" Gavin asked, exasperation painting his voice.

"They've only been dead four, maybe five hours. Why do they look like they've been dead a couple of days, or even weeks?"

"I don't know. You want to ask them?"

"No thanks."

"Then climb."

He stood on the box office counter and braced his other leg on the wall, straddling the air. He held out his hand to me. I looked at the window. Our appearance had excited them. The pounding was almost deafening. I didn't want to get that close to them, bulletproof glass or no.

"I can't stress to you the importance of getting out of here right now."

My eyes widened, and I spun toward the manager's body. I instantly retched my coffee and scones all over the floor. The gore… holy freaking crap. I wiped my mouth and quickly climbed onto the counter with Gavin's help. My shaking hands grasped his tightly.

"Gavin? I don't know if I can do this."

He squeezed my hands. "We've at least got to try."

I nodded and stepped onto his thighs. It wasn't too difficult, for a circus act, but I did feel bad my hiking boots were most likely grinding permanent rug burns wherever I stepped. He directed me where to place each foot, and soon I had climbed onto his shoulders. I easily lifted the grate, and it clattered to the floor.

I made the mistake of looking down. The zombies were frantic, clawing at each other, climbing on top of each other, trying to get to us. I swayed and clutched the rim of the vent above me. Gavin tightened his grip on my legs.

"Um, they can't reach us up here if they get in, can they?"

"I don't know." Gavin's breathing had deepened. "Just hurry."

I reached into the vent, trying to find a handhold. Gavin grabbed my boots and lifted me straight up. I shrieked and lunged into the vent, wildly kicking once he let go. I definitely hadn't been expecting that. I pulled myself farther in, then did a contortion act to turn around. I peered down at him.

"How are you going to get up?"

He grinned. "Just watch."

He dropped lightly to the ground and backed up a few steps. He took two running steps, then jumped. One foot hit the counter's edge. The other foot pushed off the wall. He lunged straight up with the push-off and grabbed the vent's rim.

I squeaked and bumped my head on the top of the vent when he sprang at me.

He grinned up at me, still hanging by his fingertips. "So, what do you think?"

If any critic called him cocky ever again, they were going to hear from me. He had reason to be.

I opened my mouth to say something sexy and flattering but instead shouted, "Look out behind you!" and poked him in the eye with my finger.

The manager lunged, and Gavin swung his legs out of the way. The manager zombie turned and lunged again, this time grabbing one leg. Then he tried to *bite* him. Gavin kicked him in the face, sending him sprawling backward.

I grabbed the back of Gavin's shirt and pulled, almost falling headfirst into the box office.

Gavin grabbed me with one hand and shoved me back. "No! Get back! I'm coming up."

I scrambled out of the way as he vaulted into the vent. I grabbed his hand and pulled, hindering his progress more than helping. He somehow managed to get all the way into the vent in spite of my help.

"Wow, you've got some serious muscles, being able to get up here like that."

He smirked and flexed. As much as I enjoyed the show, I had to roll my eyes. He laughed. I turned my attention to the man below us, all levity falling flat.

The manager snarled and snapped at us, running into the wall and then the box office counter.

I started to freak. "He can't get up here, can he?"

"I don't think so."

I shuddered as I watched his fruitless efforts. Gavin interrupted my growing horror.

"Start crawling."

"Which way?"

We were facing each other. Gavin nodded in my direction. I did another contortion act and started crawling.

"And I must say, you're very flexible."

It was my turn to grin. I appreciated his attempt at lightheartedness. Joking was the best way for me to deal with stress, and right about now I needed an entire stand-up routine. I opened my mouth to say something flirty when my hand plunged into empty space. I pitched forward, but Gavin grabbed my legs.

I could hear the smile in his voice. "Easy, now. Careful of vents leading to other vents. Especially the downward ones."

I rolled my eyes. "Thanks, I'll keep that in mind," I mumbled.

Carefully climbing over the open space, I took my crimson face and humiliated self on down the vent shaft. We crawled in silence for a minute or two.

"I must say, I'm enjoying the view," he quipped.

I flushed and somehow tripped while crawling on my hands and knees. I changed the subject. Immediately. "Why did that guy try to bite you?"

"Oh, probably just upset his dinner was getting away."

"Ha-ha. No, seriously."

"Seriously. I can think of no other reason."

He had to be joking.

"But, but, he tried to *bite* you! Why in the world would he bite you?"

"Candace, zombies like to eat flesh."

"What? But why? That doesn't make sense! Why would they want to eat anything? They're dead—their stomachs don't even work! How does a virus or drug or whatever make a dead body stand up and walk and, and…*eat* things? I don't care how nasty a mutated strain of something is, it doesn't make dead people get up and *walk*."

Gavin sighed. "I don't have any answers for you. I would like to know half of that myself. And, even more than that, I'd like to be out of this vent."

I grumbled and quickened my pace. After a few twists and turns, we finally came to the end of the cramped corridor. I couldn't see through the grate. I tried to remove it quietly, but it clattered to the floor. I cringed and held my breath. Not hearing anything stumble in our direction, I slowly poked my head through the opening. The theater's projection room. I couldn't see past the tall projectors, but I didn't see any flesh-eating zombies. Gross. I so did not need to know that. I took a deep breath and dropped into the room, Gavin close behind. We took a moment to dust off our clothes.

"So, where do we go from here?" I asked.

Gavin opened his mouth to answer, then tensed, his eyes riveted beyond me. I jumped and turned around. One single, shallow-breathing zombie stumbled into view at the very end of the row.

Gavin grabbed my hand. "The roof!" He turned to run in the opposite direction of the dead dude.

"No! The roof is the *last* place you go when someone is chasing you! Even *I* know *that*."

"*Move*!"

I didn't argue further. I darted down the projection corridor while Gavin pulled anything that moved into the aisle behind us, trying to slow the zombie down. I glanced back. A few more had joined him. We came to the door and burst through. I took the steps two at a time with

Gavin close behind, almost trampling my heels.

We slammed through the door onto the roof. Gavin wrapped a chain around the door's handle and stuck a metal rod through it. There was soon clattering on the other side of the door, but the door didn't budge.

"That's great, Gavin, just great. Now what are we supposed to do? Jump off the side of the building? The theater's what, ten stories high or something?"

Gavin marched over to me and grasped my chin. His touch was surprisingly gentle for looking like he was going to smack me down. He turned my face to the other side of the roof. Oh. A helicopter. On a helipad. What in the world? I turned to him.

"What is a helicopter randomly doing on the roof of the theater?"

"It's how I got here."

"Oh. You flew it here?"

"No. But I can fly it."

I frowned at him. "Since when do you know how to fly a helicopter?"

"Since *Living Days*."

My heart skipped a beat.

"I played a military helicopter pilot. Had to learn to fly for the role."

"I know!" I practically squealed. "And you guys were stuck in the middle of the jungle surrounded by guerrillas and you had to get out and the only way you could do that was revamp an old helicopter and go out under heavy fire—and you made it! And—"

"Um, trying to survive here, remember?"

"Oh. Right."

He grabbed my hand and bolted toward the helicopter.

Boy, did I feel stupid. Of all the times to let my rabid-fan side out. None of the fan mags had ever said anything about him being able to actually fly the helicopter in *Living Days*. I'd thought it was all props or green screens or whatever.

Way sexy.

Gavin released my hand, jogged to his side of the sleek machine, and slipped inside. The engine almost immediately grumbled to life. The blades hummed and cut through the air as they gained speed overhead. I hunkered down and scrambled to the other side. I hesitated as soon as I placed my hand against the side of the helicopter. I had never been this close to one before. The sheer power thrumming through my fingers mesmerized me. Gavin waved me in, so I jerked open the light door and clambered in, putting on the headset he handed me.

His voice squawked over the headset. "They haven't refueled yet, but we've got enough to get to those hills over there."

He pointed at the hill line barely visible against the night sky.

My incredulous look seared into him. At least, I hoped it did. "We want to go to those hills—in the dark?"

"We need to stay away from populated areas."

"Sure we do." I wasn't convinced. Surely this was an isolated incident. With every fiber in my being, I clung to the hope that this was a big joke, or nightmare even. I wanted to wake up soon. Before the creepy, dark mountains part.

"Strap in."

"Right." I fumbled with my harness, but apparently I wasn't fast enough. Gavin cinched me in tight, making sure I was secure.

Not gonna lie, I may have enjoyed his help just a little too much.

The helicopter lifted slowly off the helipad, and a feeling of weightlessness gripped my stomach. Just as I started to get excited about this, my first helicopter ride, I happened to glance back at the door Gavin had supposedly secured. Zombies poured through the wide-open door, scrambling for our helicopter.

Gavin took one look at my panicked face, gripped the control stick thingy tighter, and adjusted the pedals, concentrating on getting the helicopter safely off the roof. A couple of metallic clangs resonated through my headset. The helicopter shuddered. I strained to see what was happening. Loud grinding nearly made me deaf, and the helicopter jerked crazily as we went airborne. Red lights flashed on the dash. We went into a tailspin.

"Hang on!" Gavin shouted needlessly.

As if I weren't hanging on already.

The plexiglass front of the helicopter swung inches away from a line of zombies edging the roof. The fact that one of them was still swinging a long metal rod in our direction barely penetrated my brain as butterflies exploded in my stomach, and we dropped toward the ground. The tail crunched against the side of the building. The helicopter shuddered. I grabbed my stomach with one hand and covered my face with the other, just as the mightiest jolt I've ever felt in my life rocked my world.

"Candace? Candace!"

Warm hands caressed my face. I leaned into them. That voice sounded familiar...

"Candace. Are you okay?"

I gasped and jerked fully awake. My chest burned like fire. Gazing at the sand bleeding through the cracked windshield, I wondered why dirt instead of sky was staring back at me. I tried to move. Wasn't happening.

"Hang on. I'll help you get out."

Gavin's comforting presence disappeared, and I started to panic the teeniest tiniest bit. I dangled from my harness, pitched forward at a crazy angle that made my head pound.

I felt him before I saw him. Gavin leaned into my line of sight, his eyes searching my face. His shoulders sagged in relief.

"Thank God. Candace? We've got to get out. Fuel's leaking. Tail's on fire."

I nodded and tried to unfasten my safety belt, pushing past the pain. The clasp refused to release the seatbelt's hold on me. Gavin whipped out a pocketknife and started sawing at the straps. I stared at it, inanely wondering where the thing had come from.

"I'm going to catch you, but I need you to brace yourself."

My arms and legs refused to work, and I fell face-first toward the crumpled helicopter remains. Gavin caught me just in time. He untangled me from the twisted metal and pulled me out. Lifting me into his strong arms, Gavin tore away from the helicopter.

An explosion blasted us from behind. We pitched forward. Gavin threw his body on mine, and we hit the earth with a *thud*. Pieces of burning helicopter landed with alarming crunches all around us. I prayed nothing would land *on* us. Gavin rolled me onto my back.

"Are you all right?"

I nodded, dazed, and stared at him with wide, unfocused eyes.

"Can you stand?" he asked, full of concern.

I nodded and held out my hands. He helped me up, keeping his arm firmly around my waist. Everything took on a dreamlike quality as I tried to focus on something, anything. We were between the theater and the still-blazing factory. There were hundreds of zombies aimlessly milling about in factory uniforms. My head started to throb as I realized the milling would turn to chasing as soon as they caught sight, wind, smell, taste, whatever of us.

"Think you can run?"

I attempted a grin. "Do I have a choice?" My teeth chattered as nerves shook my body.

He let me walk a few steps before letting go of me and grasping my hand. "Here we go." He attempted a light tone. I appreciated it.

We stayed low and scooted behind some large bushes near the theater. After a moment, we raced into the parking lot, using vehicles to shield us from wandering zombies. Scuffling footsteps moved past us endlessly while we hid. Peeking around a badly scratched green convertible, my still-in-shock self took a moment to be fascinated by what a real-life zombie looked like. Deformed. Decayed. Grotesque. Much more disgusting than any I'd seen in any zombie movie I'd had the misfortune of walking in on. Gavin tugged my arm, and I followed.

I wanted to rejoice when we made it to the edge of the parking lot, but I was too zapped of any emotion to care.

We raced to where Gavin's car was parked near the roadblock. Smashed. As in, "I don't think it will ever recover" smashed. My eyes shot to Gavin. He was struggling. Definitely choked up. I could've sworn moisture was lurking in his eyes. I threaded my fingers through his and squeezed. He squeezed back, then cleared his throat.

"We need to find a vehicle." His voice was husky, but I wasn't going to fault him for mourning his way-cool car.

Gavin tried to see if he could salvage anything, then we turned back to the parking lot to search for a non-smashed car. As we neared the roadblock, the police officer—formerly manning the roadblock, now turned zombie—jumped out at Gavin.

Before Gavin could react, I picked up a two-by-four and swung it at the zombie's face. Blood spurted from his nose, and he fell back, unconscious. Gavin gaped at the man, then stared at me with his mouth still open.

"I do all my own stunts."

"No kidding. Let's go."

He put his arm around me and steered me toward the cars. He glanced behind him at the officer. I started to look, too, but he blocked my view with his shoulder.

"Let's hurry before he gets back up."

I assumed he'd already started to, from the way Gavin hauled me down the rows of vehicles.

He twisted around as we passed a black, mid-sized car. I stumbled with how fast he changed direction. I peeked past him to see what had him so enthralled. A Mercedes-Benz, not a scratch on it. He circled it slowly, wasting precious moments gawking. I'm pretty sure there was drool involved. Tragic, how quickly he could forget his other car.

Hmm… I would keep that in mind.

"Nice," he murmured. He tugged on the handles, then checked for a hidden key. He found a magnetic box next to the driver's tire with the tiny slip of metal inside. The door opened with a slight *pop,* but the car wouldn't start.

He opened the trunk and answered my question before I asked it. "Looking for tools. Keep watch."

O-kay…

He was soon back, rummaging around in the vehicle. I started to get in. His head popped up on the other side of the car. "Keep watching. K?"

I nodded once. He disappeared.

I stayed outside the car, crouched down, watching for unpleasant surprises. I wasn't exactly thrilled with my new role as guardian. I glanced in to see Gavin's progress and was shocked to see him hot-wiring the car.

I yanked open the passenger door. "How in the world do you know how to hot-wire a car?"

He grinned. "*Driving Dirty*. I played a car thief who stole expensive vehicles, found out embarrassing things about their owners, then ransomed the cars for a lot of money. Fun role."

Sparks shot through me. I nodded too many times and bounced on the balls of my feet, trying not to make my *Living Days* mistake, desperately wanting to.

Driving Dirty was one of my favorite movies.

And, seriously? The tabloids knew nothing interesting about this guy. Not that I read them or anything.

He paused for just a sec, then resumed what he was doing when I didn't say anything. His smirk was delicious.

"Maybe I'll teach you sometime."

"Uh…th-that would be"—heavenly? Wonderful? The best date night of my life?—"Cool."

The look he tossed my way said he saw right through my monotone reply.

The car purred to life. "See? Nothing to it." He tossed the small case of tools in the backseat. Gavin smiled as he ran his hand across the dash, then tapped it twice. "Beautiful. Full tank too. Get in."

No argument here. We both dove into the car. Okay. I did.

Everything Gavin did was smooth. Me? Not so much.

Gavin eased the car out of the parking lot, lights off. I breathed in the new car smell and relaxed against the headrest, closing my eyes. I was going to block every image from the past few hours if it killed me. Which I hoped it wouldn't. 'Cause those images were hard to block.

We drove slowly along the deserted street, back toward town. I peeked out of my window as Gavin flicked on the headlights. "Where are we going?"

"The turnoff for the desert and those hills is right before we reach town."

"You really think those hills are a good idea?"

"I do."

I snorted, then cackled—a high-pitched, hysterical sound I was *positive* had not just come out of my mouth. People do all kinds of stupid, embarrassing stuff in dreams, so hey, why not? He *had* just said, "I do." Snort.

Gavin raised an eyebrow—something that seemed to happen frequently around me—and shot me a concerned look. "You okay?"

"Nope."

Silence.

"Anything I can do?"

"Nope." *I'll wake up in just a second, thank you very much.*

"Okay."

The shadowed landscape flashed by us for some time before I happened to glance at Gavin's hands on the steering wheel.

He was shaking.

I sat up, dread clenching my stomach. Somehow, that scared me more than anything else. With Gavin in control, not scared, pushing us through this nightmare, I just felt better. I had hope. I knew it was a dream. Now that came crashing around me. The dream wasn't ending. And, if he were scared, this thing was real.

Chapter 5 ☣

I don't know how long we drove, but I woke to daylight illuminating rocky sand sprawled endlessly before me. I squinted and rubbed my face, stretching before I looked around to get my bearings. Solid rock surrounded the rest of the car—even the roof—and it took me a moment to realize we were backed into a small cave. My eyes swung toward the driver's seat. Gavin's head was propped against the headrest, and soft snores drifted out of his mouth.

I couldn't help it. I poked him. I wanted to see if he were real. He stirred, then settled back into sleep. He was adorable. His close-cropped hair stuck out in every direction, and there was a smudge on his left cheek. As I sat there admiring his good looks, the events from the previous day began pelting my memory. All of a sudden, I had to get out of there, out of that dark cave, into sunlight.

I opened the car door as noiselessly as possible and slipped out of the cave. The quiet of the desert soothed me. I closed my eyes and turned my face to the sun, taking deep breaths. It felt *so* good.

My eyes popped open. It was too quiet. Acción was located near a major highway, and, even though the town was small and a good distance from the nearest major city, the constant sound of traffic and semis downshifting was a normal part of everyday life. I listened carefully. Nope, not there. I desperately wanted to hear it again.

The soft *thump* of a car door shutting reached my ears, and I turned to see Gavin stretching outside of our newly acquired vehicle.

He smiled. "Good morning," he mumbled sleepily. Extremely cute.

He ambled my way, his shirt rumpled and his hair mussed. I wanted to run my fingers through it. But first things first.

"Where are all the trucks? Why is it so quiet? How did you know to come here? Are we safe here? Where did your red car come from? For someone who flew here in a helicopter, you certainly know a lot about my town. How did you know where the coffee shop was? Where the highway went? How did you find this cave? What's going on?"

His steps faltered at my barrage of questions. He groaned and dropped his head into his hands, leaning against the hood of the car.

"Too early. Need coffee." He groaned again.

"I need answers. *And* I need to pee. Is the cave safe? Where did all the zombies go? Can they be out in the daylight?"

He rubbed his eyes. "Are you always this high-strung?"

"Ah, no, I, well, I just…" My words ground to a halt, and I glared at him, tears filling my eyes. "How dare you? After all we went through last night, you call me high-strung? I have every reason to be! I need to know what's going on! Aren't you curious in the least? And I need to pee!" I wailed and plopped on the desert sand, my back to him. Then I burst into tears. Oh. My. Word. How humiliating.

I heard him take a deep breath. He was probably counting to ten. When my crying spree turned to sniffles, he ventured, "There weren't any zombies in the cave last night, and the back of the cave is a solid wall, so they can only get in through the front. I'll check again to be safe, but I'm sure you can go to the bathroom back there."

I nodded and sniffled. "That would be lovely."

Slumping over once his footsteps retreated, I grabbed fistfuls of sand and watched the glistening streams run through my fingers. How appropriate. My life was too much like those stupid streams. I mean, I always knew I had a limited time on earth, but I had no idea my time to do anything and everything I wanted could run out so…quickly. I hadn't done one thing I'd wanted to with my life. Not one.

My hands emptied, and my heart sank with the disappearing sand. This couldn't be happening. My fists clenched. I wanted answers.

His footsteps crunched my way. "All clear," he called cheerfully. "There's a neat little pocket of rocks back there, so you'll have privacy."

Standing, I stomped past him without looking at him. My steps faltered when I realized I was blaming all of this on him for no reason. That wasn't fair. None of this was his fault. I turned to him after a moment, regret flaring.

"I'm really sorry for snapping at you like that. You did an amazing job keeping us safe last night, and I'm glad you were able to find this cave. It was a great idea. Please, forgive me for being so rude."

I turned to go, but the light pressure of his hand on my arm stopped me. I waited, not looking at him, self-conscious.

"Thank you for saying that, and you're welcome." He dropped his hand. "You don't have to apologize, you know. I understand."

I looked at him then. "Oh, but I do! I have no right to treat you like that, not after all you've done for me. You've been amazing. I'm really, really sorry."

He tapped me under my chin and grinned. He looked uncomfortable. I offered him a sad attempt at a half-smile and turned to leave once again.

"Oh yeah. There's a newspaper in the car if you need to use it."

I looked at him, expression blank. What was he talking about? I didn't want to read a newspaper.

His tanned cheeks flushed ever so slightly. "You know, since we don't have any toilet paper."

My face flamed, and my jaw dropped.

He ducked his head and moved farther away from the cave, offering me privacy and fleeing the most awkward moment of my life.

If we survived this and the world became normal once again, I was going to carry a backpack with emergency supplies for the rest of my life. And that pack was going to include toilet paper.

"I'm hungry."

Gavin leaned across the middle console and popped open the glovebox. "I found these in here last night."

He pulled out three granola bars. They were the smallest granola bars I'd seen in my life. Why in the world would someone make them that small? My stomach growled.

He grinned and tossed one at me, tearing into the wrapper of another with his teeth. Stale oats and a sickly sweet smell permeated the car. I peeled my wrapping back and took two bites. And the thing was gone. I stared at the wrapper, looking for crumbs I could lick off the packaging. I caught sight of the third lone bar.

We both eyed it.

"You can hav—"

"We could spli—"

We both laughed from speaking at the same time.

"You can have it," Gavin said.

"No, let's split it."

I peeled back the wrapper and pinched off half, handing him the still-wrapped half before I changed my mind and inhaled the entire thing. I tried to chew slowly, staring out my window at the cave wall so I didn't tackle him for the other piece.

"I'm thirsty."

Gavin looked at me, an unreadable expression on his face. I'm not sure if he was amused or annoyed by my needy outbursts. Annoyed, most likely. I'd be annoyed if I had to listen to me.

"No, really. As in 'I will die right now if I don't have a drink of water' thirsty."

I wasn't joking. Whatever was in that granola bar had sucked all the moisture right out of my body. And we were in the desert. Just thinking about that made me want to jump out of the car and run around screaming, "Water! I need water!"

I sat on my hands and started bouncing.

Gavin carefully schooled his features and started searching the car. I joined him, glancing at him every couple of seconds. Did he want to laugh at me or clobber me?

He moved to the back of the car, and I followed. The trunk had nothing but a spare tire and a light jacket Gavin had covered me with last night. The car was so clean on the inside, not a wrapper in the place, I started grumbling at the owner for not having a few spare water bottles rolling around on the floorboards.

I searched the glove box again for no reason, then lifted the middle black cup holder. It was actually the lid for a glass water bottle that fit neatly between the two seats, out of sight.

"Thank you, Lord!" I exclaimed as I screwed off the cap. A pink lipstick stain graced the rim of the bottle, so I turned it away from me and chugged. I sloshed the water away at the last second.

"Oh, Gavin! I'm so sorry!"

I jumped out of the car and handed him the water bottle, barely a sip rolling around in the bottom. I couldn't believe I'd just done that!

He just grinned and downed the last few drops. The man had the patience of a saint. I would have pounded him for drinking all the water had the roles been reversed.

"Seems we need supplies," he drawled in a Southern accent.

I eyed him as he looped his thumbs through his belt loops and struck a cowboy-worthy pose. "No kidding. But how are we gonna get them? I thought you said we needed to stay away from populated areas?"

He shrugged. "We've got to eat. And a roll of toilet paper would be nice."

"And deodorant."

He glanced at me.

"Toothpaste and toothbrush," I quickly added.

"And water." He grinned. "Didn't realize you drank like a fish."

I chose to ignore that comment.

"You're cute when you stick your nose in the air like that," he teased.

I chose to ignore that comment as well.

"So, how do you propose we get these supplies?"

He chuckled before answering. "Didn't we pass a Walmart as we left town last night?"

"Yes, but won't there be people in there? Walmart's 24/7, and there are employees and stockers—will it be safe? How do we know they haven't turned as well?"

"We don't, but it's a chance we have to take."

"Okay..." I said slowly, completely unconvinced. Maybe I could just stay in the car, ready to drive at a moment's notice. But then I would be by myself...

We drove well under the speed limit into town, looking for anything out of the ordinary. I began peppering Gavin with questions.

"Can zombies be out in the daylight?"

"I don't know."

"Are they all slow, like they were last night?"

"Seem to be."

"How are we not affected?"

Gavin shrugged. "Maybe we're immune or something. I don't know."

"Do they really eat people? Were you joking about that?"

"No, I wasn't. That's what I've always heard. That or brains."

My jaw dropped. "*Brains?*"

He shrugged. "I guess."

"Don't you know for sure? Weren't you ever in a zombie film? Haven't you at least seen a zombie movie before?"

He chuckled. "I haven't been in a zombie film yet. Horror movies aren't necessarily my genre. I prefer action, or even romance. I don't mind anything with a good story, though."

"But you've at least *seen* zombie movies before, haven't you?" I persisted.

"I've seen a couple." He chuckled again. "I find it hard to believe you haven't."

"I prefer to sleep at night," I muttered. "But, if you've seen one, then you know what's going on, what's going to happen?"

"First of all, I've assumed up to this point of my life all zombie films were science *fiction,* not capable of actually happening. Right now I wish I'd paid more attention."

"But, you must know something. What happens in the movies? Why are zombies even possible? It doesn't make sense."

He blew out his breath. "You ask a lot of questions. It doesn't make sense to me either. All I know is we both have questions, and I can't wait to figure this whole thing out."

I wanted to shake him. Couldn't he answer even one question? He must know something! "What happens in the movies?" I prodded.

He glanced at me. "Candace, in the movies I've seen, a virus takes over the world. The few that fight it are either turned or spend the rest of their lives fighting it. There's not a resolution."

I crossed my arms. "Well, *that's* not gonna happen."

He turned into Walmart's parking lot. It was completely deserted. Gavin pulled in front of the store and stopped, the car idling. Neither of us moved. He gripped the steering wheel, wringing it until the cover hung limp, millimeters from falling off.

"Let's do this."

I groaned and followed him out of the car.

Chapter 6

Gavin held the revolver, the semiautomatic still out of bullets, as we did a quick sweep of the store. It appeared to be deserted as well.

Gavin pushed a cart at me. "Start grabbing anything edible. Cans, instant soups, chips, anything." He shoved a handful of reusable bags my way. "This will make it easier to load into the car."

He grabbed his own cart and pushed off toward the can aisle. I followed in a daze. He was already throwing random cans into light blue reusable bags.

"At least we're being environmentally friendly, right?" I quipped.

He cast me a sidelong look, then continued loading his cart. "The easy-open lids are best," he replied.

I sighed and picked up a can.

"What are you doing?"

I jumped and spun in his direction. "W-well," I stammered. "We don't want anything with preservatives or MSG, and this soup appears to be high in sodium..." My voice trailed off.

His brow puckered. "Are you serious?"

I put my hands on my hips, shifting my weight to one foot. "You *do* want to be healthy enough to fend off zombies and not fall over dead from a heart attack, don't cha?"

He slowly looked me up and down. I could feel the heat flame on my face, but I refused to look away. He met my gaze.

"I think we're both healthy enough. What I *don't* want to do is die from not having any food. Fill your cart. Now."

We worked in silence, me halfheartedly tossing cans into bags. Beans. Mmm. Canned chili. Yummy. More beans. Woohoo. This was a feast fit for a king. We moved on to canned tuna, peas, corn, carrots, crackers. I picked up a box of rice.

"This would be good with all our beans."

"We might not be able to cook that."

"Great, that's just great."

I put it back. My attitude was quickly declining as I considered the possibility of this being my last time in Walmart. And I couldn't even cook up a box of mac 'n' cheese if I wanted to.

I picked up a box of Honey Nut Cheerios and grabbed some disposable bowls and plastic spoons. I was going to have a bowl of cereal. The electricity was still on, so the milk should be unspoiled. I broke open another box of cereal bars to tide me over till we got to the back of the store. The food made me feel *much* better.

"Okay, where's the other stuff we need in this store?" he asked.

"Don't you ever shop at Walmart?"

He just looked at me.

"Okay, then. Water and toilet paper are back there, and deodorant and stuff is on the other side of the store, near the front. Do we need blankets or jackets or anything? Oh! Camping stuff is in the back right corner!"

A part of me started getting excited. I'd always wanted to fill my cart to the brim with absolutely everything I wanted and just leave—without it being stealing, of course. I'd secretly wished they'd have a sweepstakes allowing that, and I would win. Talk about set for life.

"All right. You get the deodorant and toothbrushes and such, and I'll go check out the camping stuff. I'll pick up the water and TP on the way there."

"Alone? No..." I shook my head, not budging from his side.

He sighed. "Then let's hurry."

I kept up with him and filled my cart as fast as I possibly could.

In the camping section, I tossed survival items in my cart, wondering which items I would be the most thankful for later. Shattering glass threw my heart into overdrive, and I spun toward the noise while diving on the floor. Gavin smashed another glass case, deftly clipping chains with an oversized wire cutter while tugging a few rifles and a shotgun free. Turning to the ammo boxes, he dumped large handfuls into one of the blue bags.

I sat up and rubbed my throbbing elbow. Gingerly picking myself off the floor, I felt a rush of relief he hadn't noticed my little freaking-out episode. I watched him work, his scowl not distracting me from the worry lines on his face. I tried to lighten his mood.

"Walmart guns. Boy, do I feel safe."

He ignored my comment. "Do you know how to use this?"

He handed me one of the handguns—the revolver the manager dude had used on himself. A shudder passed through me as I took it from him with two fingers.

"Don't ever hold a gun like that."

"Right." I adjusted my grip.

"Do you know how to shoot?"

"I went to a shooting range once. Oh, and I've been paintballing several times."

Gavin grunted and shoved bullets into his magazine before slamming it into his semiautomatic. I jumped. His edginess was getting to me. He loaded the shotgun and thrust it at me, making sure his four rifles and my revolver were filled as well. At the last minute, he yanked the shotgun from my hands and gave the revolver back, adding my shotgun to the growing pile in his cart. Would he make up his mind already? I eyed the weapons lining the top of his almost-full cart.

"Don't cha think that's overkill?"

"Not if we need them."

He stalked to the tires nearby. He stacked a few of the tires in the middle of the aisle and dropped a target in front of them. He crossed his arms and leaned against a shelf, studying me. I dropped my gaze to the revolver in my hand. I so did not want to be holding that thing.

"Okay, shoot."

I glanced up, still fingering the revolver. "What?"

He nodded toward the haphazard tire display. My eyes widened, and I stared between him and the brightly colored target.

"In here?" I squeaked. "Won't we get in trouble?"

Gavin gave me a "that's the dumbest thing you've said yet" look, and my face competed with itself for the brightest color it'd turned yet. I cleared my throat.

"I mean, won't the bullets ricochet off the concrete floor and kill us or something? Or won't the loud noise from the guns make us deaf?" I tried to think of other reasons, but those were the only ones I could come up with at the moment.

Gavin threw back his head and laughed. He shook his head and chuckled as he walked behind me. I grew uneasy when I couldn't see him anymore.

"You don't know how to shoot a gun, do you?"

"What?" I sputtered as I craned my neck. He stayed just out of sight. "I *told* you I've been to a shooting range..."

He leaned in to look at me just over my shoulder. I stiffened. He was so close! Why was he so close? He ducked a little so he was eye-level with me.

"Yeah, but did you shoot?" A slow grin spread across his face as the silence lengthened, and I squirmed. "Thought so."

"Watching counts!"

"No, it doesn't. Here."

He handed me a pair of earplugs. After carefully squeezing them into my ears, I lifted the gun and pointed it at the target. Gavin reached around me, grasping the revolver tightly between my hands. My breath hitched, and a delicious shiver ran down my spine. Now I knew why he was taking up so much of my personal space. His arms rested on mine, and his hands engulfed my own. I tried not to melt in to him as he loudly explained the proper way to hold a gun.

"You got that?"

"Mm-hmm," I drawled out dreamily.

He jostled me. "Come on, pay attention."

"I am!"

"Then show me," he said, way too close to my ear.

How was I supposed to concentrate with him all over me like that? I lifted the gun, cradled in one palm, wrapped in the other. Squeezing the trigger gently, I aimed down the sights. The loud *pop* made me jump, and the kick-back was unreal.

"Ow," I moaned. Then I straightened and pointed. "Hey, look! I got a bull's-eye!"

"Beginner's luck," Gavin scoffed as he moved to survey the target. "Keep that thing lowered, will you?" he called behind him.

I nodded and made sure the weapon stayed pointed at the ground.

He made his way back to me. "Again."

I lifted the gun.

"Beginner's luck," I mimicked under my breath. *Yeah right.*

He had me empty the cylinder into the target and reload. The spray of bullets hit just about everything but the target. *So* not cool. Next, he handed me the shotgun. I grinned up at him in unabashed glee as I reached for it.

"This is so much fun!" I squealed.

He grinned at me and held my gaze while we both still held the shotgun. Time froze. His eyes widened, and he looked down at my lips, his grin slowly evaporating.

We moved at the same time. He released the gun. I turned away.

"So," I called, forcing cheerfulness into my tone. "How do you shoot this thing?" I lifted it to my shoulder and looked down the barrel at the target we'd been moving away from with each shot.

"Uh, make sure it's loaded first."

Gavin fumbled taking it from me, then silently showed me how to load and unload the pump-action before handing it back. He never made eye contact. A smug grin crept across my face. I, Candace Marshall, had flustered my favorite movie star. Ha! Then I remembered him staring at my lips. Time to think about something else.

"Like this?" I took a wide stance and held the shotgun away from my shoulder.

"Um, no."

He stepped close behind me, then hesitated. Wrapping his arms around me once more, he tucked the shotgun into my shoulder. I stilled. He was standing much closer than before. I felt his firm chest on my back and wondered if he would think anything was out of the ordinary if I threw the gun and ran.

"Feet shoulder-width apart, weight on left foot."

His husky voice left my mouth dry. I tried to swallow, but, well, I couldn't.

"Hold it close. Aim. Squeeze gently."

Did he seriously think I would be able to function like this? I squeezed the trigger. The butt of the gun slammed into my shoulder.

"Holy freaking crap! Ouch!"

He grinned and stepped back. "Little more kick than a revolver?"

"You think?" I rubbed my sore shoulder and glanced at the target. Another bull's-eye. Not bad.

He chuckled this time. "Try it again."

I took aim and hesitated with my stance, adjusting my grip like five time. He slid into place behind me.

"So…why have you never shot a gun?" he asked.

I shrugged, taking careful aim, trying *not* to think of the gorgeous man with his arms around me. *Me.* I stifled a happy dance.

I overcompensated for the gun's kick and swung the barrel away from the target at the last second. My shot went wide, and I watched a box topple from the top of one of the shelves a few aisles over. *You've got to be kidding me.*

"My dad never let me. The one time I followed my brother and his friends to the shooting range—well, they wouldn't let me anywhere near the guns. I thought they were being mean, but I guess they were just honoring my dad's wishes. Or they were scared they were gonna get shot."

"I can see why," he muttered, probably thinking I couldn't hear him. He raised his voice. "Here, try a rifle."

The low *pop* and mild kick were a dream.

"Geez-Louise. You'd think you would've had me start with this one."

He laughed. "That's just a baby. A 22. Here, try this one next."

He had me shoot all the guns we'd pilfered, loading and reloading. He had me stop only after I started consistently hitting the target. Definitely the most fun I'd had in Walmart. Ever.

Satisfied with my progress and anxious to leave the store, Gavin slung one of his rifles and my shotgun across his back and tucked both of our handguns into his belt. I barely had time to wonder if I would need those before he set off at a brisk pace.

The grin slid off my face as the worried Gavin took the carefree Gavin's place. Reality crashed back in as the warmth from his embrace faded. He was just showing me how to protect myself. Nothing more.

I followed him past the food on the way out. My cart was so full, I couldn't see over it as I struggled to push it. Gavin had no problem with his and kept grabbing food, adding to his teetering pile.

I remembered I wanted milk halfway to the front of the store. "Wait! I forgot something!"

I turned around and jogged to the refrigerated section, passing the doors leading to the stockroom in the back.

Pulling open the fridge door, I grabbed a gallon of organic vitamin D milk. It was my favorite, but I rarely splurged on it because of the expense and the fat content. But I loved the creamy, rich taste and the no-hormones or antibiotics feature. True, the other milk brands *said* they didn't feed their cows hormones, but I only trusted the hippy organic people. They would probably keel over and die if a hormone got anywhere near them—making it safe for me and my overzealous, all-natural tendencies.

My eyes drifted over the other cold-case items as I debated grabbing something else. It would be a shame for an entire fridge-wall-thingy of milk and orange juice to go to waste. Not that anything else would fit in my cart. I glanced up before shutting the door and froze. A pair of white eyes stared back at me, a face half-hidden by the shelving. I let the door drift shut and calmly walked back the way I came, quickening my pace little by little.

Gavin was waiting for me, impatience written all over his face.

"Gavin?"

He raised one eyebrow.

"Run."

The doors burst open behind me, and I took off like a shot.

Slamming into my ridiculously full cart, I strained to get the thing moving. Gavin tugged on my cart and pulled it in front of his.

"Go! Go!" he yelled.

I bolted down the wide aisle, not able to see where I was going, praying I wouldn't run into anything.

Gavin passed me when I slowed to try to see the front doors around my cart.

"This way. Hurry!"

The extra rifles clattered to the floor as Gavin swung his cart toward the doors.

"Leave them!" he shouted, not bothering to see if I would listen.

We raced out of the store as fast as we possibly could. The parking lot was still deserted.

Gavin started the car and popped the trunk. I flung open the back door and my side door and began heaving in bags. Gavin was performing the same feat at the trunk, watching the inner set of double doors.

My gallon of milk fell to the ground, but I kept heaving bags of slightly more important items. The deodorant *needed* to make it in the car. No way was I going to spend weeks or months with Gavin Bailey without it.

"Candace," Gavin warned.

I looked up as the inner doors opened. He slammed the trunk. Five bags left in my cart. I tossed in two.

"Get in the car now!"

"But I just—"

"Now!"

I reached for the milk as Gavin sprinted to my side of the car and shoved me into the passenger seat. He barely had his own door closed before bodies slammed into the car from all sides. He peeled out, driving right through the crowd. A couple of bodies bounced up and over the car. I might have screamed. We made it back to the highway in no time, rapidly leaving the scene behind us.

I could see the deserted carts with a few blue bags still in them and a white jug of milk lying on its side behind the slowly moving Walmart workers.

"My milk," I mourned.

"Your life," Gavin reminded me.

Chapter 7 ☣

We drove without saying a word, both of us breathing heavily as I tried to push panic away. The reality of our situation was starting to sink in.

I mean, really sink in.

We weren't safe. I wasn't safe. I turned on the AC full blast, rotating the vent so the chilled air hit me full in the face. I lifted my bedraggled ponytail off my neck, trying to cool down—calm down. I had to look as much of a mess as I felt.

I glanced in the side mirror. Frizzy hair and smudged makeup surrounding wide, scared eyes stared back at me before I looked away. I don't think I'd ever looked that horrible in my life. The terror in my eyes and strain on my face was not flattering. At all.

Not that I cared anything about that at the moment. I glanced at Gavin, hoping...something. I'm not even sure what. That he would reassure me?

Gavin clutched the steering wheel in a death grip, his lips clamped tight. If the whole thing was bothering him that much, I should definitely be freaked.

"You okay?"

"Fine." His answer was clipped. Short. I didn't think he wanted me to know how much this was getting to him. I was perfectly fine displaying my feelings to the world, but I knew Gavin was trying to be strong. For both of us.

We both just sat there. I took the silence as long as I could, then my fear started pouring out of my lips. "So that's it, then? We're just going to drive—go back to our cave until someone finds us?"

"I don't know."

"Make Walmart raids and live in the desert and never see another human being for the rest of our lives?"

"I don't know."

"We don't even have a plan or anything! What are we—"

Gavin slammed his hands on the steering wheel. "I said I don't know!"

My mouth hung open. It wasn't technically a yell, but Gavin Bailey raised his voice? I groaned. Because of me. I'd pushed him.

Just keep your mouth shut from here on out, all right?

I wasn't sure I'd be able to listen to my own advice, but I was most certainly going to try.

Gavin blew out a loud breath, running his fingers through his hair over and over. "Look, I'm sorry. I shouldn't have snapped at you."

"No, I'm sorry. It's my fault. I shouldn't have—"

"Will you stop apologizing already?"

I snapped my mouth closed and nodded a bunch of times. He gave me a ghost of a grin and a wink. I guess I did say "I'm sorry" a lot…

"This is the first time in my life I have no idea what to do. Where to go. I don't have a script to tell me my next lines." He switched to a whisper. "I don't even know if I can keep you safe."

I swallowed, then attempted a smile. "Don't worry about me. I can look out for myself."

I wasn't sure, but he may have been struggling with keeping a straight face.

It took me a little while to work up my courage, but I finally said, "Thank you for all you've done, Gavin. I mean it. I don't know what I would've done without you."

He nodded, eyes riveted on the stretch of empty road before us.

The miles stretched on, and I realized just how far our little cave really was from town. How did Gavin know where to find it? At least I could be thankful there weren't any staggering undead in the desert on the way. I should know. I checked. Frequently.

Pulling up to the cave's entrance in the side of a hill, Gavin slowed and flipped on the headlights. The cave was empty. Thank God. I felt the prayer rise from my entire being, then instantly felt guilty I only thought of Him in the direst of circumstances. Maybe if I'd paid Him a little more attention, I wouldn't be in this mess.

I glanced at Gavin as he turned the car around and backed into the cave. Or maybe God had put me with the one person He knew could help me. But then what about all those other people? Intense sadness welled within me. They hadn't deserved to die.

The car jerked as Gavin alternately hit the gas and brake pedals too hard. I was thankful for my seatbelt as I held onto the dash. The stuttering car hurt my head just about as much as my thoughts, so I pushed them away.

Once I was safe from Gavin's driving, I started rummaging through the grocery bags in the backseat. I wanted to freshen up. Look better—feel better, get my mind off of everything for two seconds. I pulled out a backpack I'd grabbed in the camping section, putting toothpaste and a toothbrush and, *whew*, deodorant in it.

"Toilet paper in the trunk?"

Gavin rubbed his face, then ran both hands through his hair and settled them behind his head. He took a deep breath and blew it out slowly.

"Yeah."

The dread in his voice was unmistakable. It matched the pulse of fear beating in my heart. But I was going to change that. If I could. Reaching over, I grabbed his knee.

"Hey, you okay?"

He attempted a grin. "Yeah."

"Someone I know told me we're gonna get through this, and I

believe him."

"Thanks."

"No prob. Okey dokey, I am going to brush my teeth! I feel like a scum bucket. *So* glad we were able to get this stuff! Water in the trunk, too?" I barely opened the door, still staring at Gavin.

"Yeah." He still looked miserable. And scared. That had to stop. I was the only one allowed to be scared in this car.

"All righty, then. You should brush your teeth, too. I guarantee you'll feel like a whole new person. Not that you *need* to brush your teeth—" Something slammed against my window. I shrieked and dropped my backpack.

Gavin and I reacted at the same time, pounding on the locks, but my door was still cracked. My door flew open, and two pasty, smelly hands dragged me out of the car.

I stared up into the decaying face of a zombie. He stared back with no emotion. He reeked! No one had mentioned walking dead people smelled terrible! He waited a split second before trying to bite me on the neck. The same person who'd neglected to tell me about the smell also had apparently forgotten to warn me about zombies with vampire tendencies. Thanks a *lot*.

I screamed and dropped to the ground. He missed my neck. I felt it just to be sure. Nope. No zombie teeth marks. He staggered forward, and I tripped him, sending him sprawling. I jumped to my feet. The rustle of fabric and an ungodly moan alerted me to another behind me. I didn't look—I just elbowed it in the face. I peeked just to make sure it wasn't Gavin—it wasn't, whew!—then kicked it down with a powerful thrust of my heel straight back.

My eyes darted around the small cave.

Gavin was having his own karate demonstration on the other side of the car. I wished now I'd actually taken martial arts. Any form would have done at the moment.

The first one methodically got up and turned toward me again. A tremble rippled through my body. This could not be happening.

"Where are the guns?" I yelled.

"In...the...trunk!"

"Great, that's just great," I muttered.

Using the cave wall, I vaulted to the top of the car, hoping it was out of reach of my friend over there. It was not. He awkwardly crawled on the hood and started clambering up the windshield.

I looked around. The tiny cave could only hold a few zombies, but they were all trying to get to us. Gavin was fending off three, and two were focused on me.

Feeling the car dip, I turned to see the other one performing the same crawling act up the trunk.

"Dear Jesus, help!" I shouted, scared out of my mind.

I glanced down at the empty ground next to me. Waiting till their grasping hands almost reached me, I dropped to the ground and bolted into my side of the car.

Gavin got in a few seconds after I did. We both pounded on the automatic lock buttons.

"Drive! Drive! Drive!" I hollered.

The car peeled out of the cave. A body came out of the sky—out of nowhere—and dropped onto our windshield. I was going to be hoarse and Gavin deaf from all the screaming.

It bounced up and over the car, and I spun to see what happened to it. My jaw dropped. Zombies poured over the cave, plummeted facedown on the ground, then staggered to their feet to slowly advance toward our speeding vehicle. I stared after them—my mind a haze of disbelief—as the car swerved crazily through the desert sand.

The tires squealed as the car roared down the small desert road to the main highway. Staggering zombies dotted the desert landscape this time. Lots of them.

Gavin veered onto the deserted highway. Cars, vans, and semis were strewn in every direction. Several semis were on their sides, and cars had been haphazardly run off the road or into each other.

I started to cry. "Gavin, I don't think I can take any more of this! I'm done, I'm through, I want out!"

He cleared his throat. "You want out of the car?"

"What? No! I want out of this horrible nightmare! I want to wake up. Please, make it stop."

"I wish I could," Gavin said in a low, trembling voice.

I hugged my knees and sobbed. Gavin reached over and began stroking my hair. His hand got tangled in the barbed wire that was my hair—I went a little too crazy with all the hair gel and bobby pins to keep the frizz factor down. He opted to rub my back instead. Smart man.

"Dear God, please help us," I whispered through my sobs.

The sky had been tinged pink when we'd left the cave, but now dark purples and lavenders with a hint of orange streaked the sky. Night was falling rapidly. I didn't even want to know what terrors it held.

I cried myself out of tears, then stared out my window.

Cars peppered the highway, and Gavin expertly dodged them all. The occasional zombie, oblivious to my wish to never see another, wandered through the desert, probably belonging to one of the wrecked cars. One or two stood next to a vehicle or in the middle of the road. Gavin just drove around them. They didn't seem particularly interested in us at the moment, thank goodness.

A superman-blue pickup on the side of the road caught my eye. I sat up and pressed my face against the cool glass. Not far from it, a dark purple Cadillac was upside down in a ditch.

"Oh no," I groaned.

"What? What is it?"

I pointed at the cars falling behind us. "Those cars belonged to the guys bothering me in the parking lot." I glanced ahead. "Look! I think that's them."

Gavin slowed and edged around the pair. Tyro and the scrawny dude looked far worse than they had at the theater.

Blood crusted the side of Tyro's face, and his dark skin had a gray tint to it. A festering gash ran the length of his arm. He shuffled along the side of the highway, arms dangling at his sides. As I stared transfixed out the window, his head turned at our car's movement. He stumbled toward us for a second before stopping and staring. Our eyes met. No recognition. No emotion. Just...empty. He started shuffling again after we passed.

The skinny friend didn't spare us a glance but kept walking as we drove by. I leaned forward, trying to get a better view of him. His beyond-pale skin was puckered and flaky-looking. Then his other side came into view. I gasped. He was covered in burns, and his blackened skin blistered and peeled. I jerked back with a cry and covered my mouth.

Gavin looked in the rearview mirror, a mix of sorrow and satisfaction on his face. "Looks like they got what they deserved."

I shook my head emphatically. "Gavin, no! I'd never wish that on anyone. Not even my worst enemy."

Gavin frowned and looked at me for far too long. Thinking. Calculating. "Really?" No disbelief. No censure. Just asking. He sounded surprised.

"Really. Oh, Gavin, this is awful—what are we going to do?"

He shook his head, gripped the steering wheel with one hand, and reached for my hand with the other. He didn't answer.

Our fingers linked. I closed my eyes, not wanting to see anything more.

Not sure when I dozed off, but I woke to complete darkness outside my window and the high beams illuminating the highway ahead of us.

Gavin looked tired but gave me a lopsided grin.

I stretched and yawned. "You need me to drive for a while?"

"Naw. I might take you up on that later, but I'm good for now."

"How are we on gas?"

"We'll need to get some soon."

I peeked at him. "Where are we going, by the way?"

"No clue."

We drove in silence until the glow from the lights of a gas station came into view.

Gavin pulled over at a lone gas station along the side of the highway. He got out to pump while I surveyed the pitch-black beyond the reach of the gas station lights. I so wish we didn't have to stop. My eyes drifted toward the wrecked convenience store and scanned for any pop-up surprises. Even if I weren't much help, at least I could scream a lot and let Gavin know something was up.

All of a sudden, the car was stifling. I wanted out. But I wasn't about to get out. Keeping my door locked, I cracked my window, pushed my face close to the slit to feel the cool desert breezes, and breathed deep.

Moaning, wailing, and guttural sounds emanated from the gloom of the desert. Probably the most terrifying thing I'd heard in my life.

Gavin leaned into the car. "You might want to get out and stretch your legs for a bit. Not sure when we'll be stopping again."

I looked into the darkness warily. "Are you sure?"

"We could also use the restrooms. Not sure when we'll get to use one of those again either."

I just looked at him.

"Don't worry, I'll make sure it's safe. We have to hurry, though."

I didn't believe him, but using the bathroom sounded like a good idea. You know, on any other night when there weren't zombies oozing around. At least the things were slow.

"You coming?"

I gave one swift nod. "K."

I met him at the trunk and helped him get out the guns. He made sure the revolver and shotgun were loaded before handing them to me. I slung the shotgun across my back and tucked the revolver into the waistband of my jeans.

I could do this. I could.

Gavin topped off while I stuffed a few more personal care items into my backpack from the trunk. Dread tried to strangle me as our footsteps crunched toward the convenience store. We did a quick sweep, including the back room and walk-in cooler this time. I'd probably check those for the rest of my life, even when things went back to normal.

I could see it now. *Excuse me, sir; but may I check for zombies in your back cooler before I buy anything?* I snickered.

Gavin glanced at me—yep, you guessed it. Eyebrow raised—then nodded toward the empty, one-room bathroom. I darted inside, making sure the lock was firm and held. I tested it a few more times.

Gavin's muffled voice drifted through the closed door.

"Hurry, Candace."

I nodded, realizing too late he couldn't see me. I smacked my forehead.

"Brilliant, Candace. Absolutely brilliant," I muttered.

Maybe I shouldn't have rattled the door handle so much.

I'd never used a restroom so fast in my life. On the way out the door, I paused to freshen up. Face wipes and a brush do wonders. My fingers flew as prayers darted toward heaven at break-neck speed. I'd left Gavin Bailey standing outside my door, and that's who I desperately wanted to see when the door opened. Not some…some *thing* in his place.

Twisting my hair high to keep it off my neck, I secured it with my trusty bobby pins. Now I was ready to face the world. Well, Gavin Bailey, anyway. I cautiously edged the door open, making sure he was still there.

Relief flooded me. Same gorgeous guy. No one else.

He grinned, and we traded places. I clutched the shotgun, aimed toward the front of the store, praying I wouldn't have to use it. By the time he came out, I was shaking, and my knuckles were white from the death grip I had on the shotgun. I spun toward the sound of the bathroom door creaking open, and Gavin jumped back.

"Wow! Lower that thing, will ya?"

I nodded several times and dipped the tip of my shotgun. Gavin plucked it from my grasp.

"It's okay. It's okay. Just calm down, all right? It's going to be just fine."

He waited until my shaking wasn't noticeable—to him, anyway—before handing it back.

"Don't point that at me, okay?"

I agreed, nodding my head way more than was necessary.

Gavin jerked his head toward the front of the store. "Let's see if there's anything in here we want."

I jammed a bunch of stuff in my backpack, not even sure what I grabbed. Then I headed to the cold-case. I grabbed a bunch of cold drinks, thankful that was the only thing in there this time.

I eyed my loot, particularly excited about Starbucks' ice-cold Frappuccinos. Coffee just made everything better.

"Let's go."

I nodded and followed Gavin.

On the way out, a row of Star Trek Next Gen bobbleheads caught Gavin's attention. He flicked Counselor Troi, making her head bounce crazily. I stopped and stared. She had dark hair piled on top of her head…just like me… I sighed. I was going to stop nodding my head so much. As of right now.

Gavin held open the door, and I ducked past him, embarrassed. Practically running to the car—for more reasons than one—I crawled inside and fastened my belt.

Whistling, Gavin dropped into the driver's seat and started the car. Pulling onto the road, we munched on nutrition-less snacks and downed more coffee than I'm sure is good for anyone in one sitting.

After we'd stopped inhaling junk food, Gavin switched on the radio. I was opening my sixth—or was it seventh?—Frappuccino.

"We're going to have to find another bathroom soon at the rate you're downing those."

I paused with the cool glass touching my lips. I reluctantly replaced the lid and settled it in the cup holder between us. I patted it, silently promising we'd get back together once Gavin wasn't paying attention. He just didn't understand how things were between me and coffee.

Most of the radio stations were static. The rest were silent. The scanner settled on a fuzzy station, then moved on after a few seconds. We both jumped for the knob at the same time.

"Did you hear that?" I shouted, bouncing in my seat.

"Did you happen to notice which station it stopped at?"

Gavin punched through stations, trying to find the one the scanner had just skipped.

"No, but it can't be that many channels away, right?"

I sat on my hands, rocking side to side in excitement. I think those coffees were having a slight effect on me.

"The scanner sometimes skips a lot of channels," Gavin mumbled, concentrating. He kept one eye on the road while he searched. He glanced over at me, and a slow grin lit his face. "You need that bathroom yet?"

I shook my head, pretending I *was* the Counselor Troi bobblehead for just a second. "Nope. Just need to dance. Or run a marathon. Or get out and push the car or something."

He chuckled and shook his head. Much more sedately than I ever had, I might add.

"There!" I shouted, straining the seatbelt as I bounced in my seat and pointed at the radio.

Sure enough, a man's voice was audible through the static.

"If…crazy…anybody…there…please…know…surrounded…out there?"

The channel fuzzed out completely, and Gavin slammed on the brakes. I lurched forward and grabbed the dash, thankful once again for the miracle of seatbelts. He put the car in reverse and backed up a good distance, barely missing a red van parked across two traffic lanes. We finally hit a spot where the man's voice came through perfectly clear. Gavin screeched to a halt. The man on the radio struggled with each word and sounded as if he were close to tears. He had to be exhausted. Poor guy.

"Please, somebody, anybody, can you hear me? If I could just know that there is one person out there listening to me, just one who could hear my voice. Is anybody out there? I'm still here, holed up at the radio station, with those—things—everywhere outside. Is this just happening here? Or in other places? I have to assume it's happening everywhere. No one is returning my calls, texts. Nothing will go through. Please, if you can call me on the landline, the number here at the station is 800-580-7500. Again, 800-580-7500. I don't know if you'll get through, but please, somebody try. I can't reach anyone. I have to know if someone is alive out there. This is KRWZ 80.5, the number-one station in Phoenix, Arizona, the place for all your classic rock hits. And now, here is Aerosmith in 'I Don't Want to Miss a Thing.'"

The nostalgic tune began playing with the guy singing along. Badly. Sounded like he was crying.

I scrambled for paper in the glove box and scratched out the number as Gavin repeated it for me.

"Quick, give me your cell phone."

I reached for it, only to snap my fingers. "I left mine at my apartment with my purse, remember? Where's yours?"

I could now tell when Gavin got embarrassed. He wouldn't make eye contact and would fiddle with stuff, like he was doing now with the radio knob. "Haven't been able to find it since the helicopter crash."

I tried to reassure him. "That's okay. We can always try to find a pay phone. How far away is Phoenix? Where are we headed, anyway?"

"Not sure…is there a map in the glove box?"

I dug around and pulled it out, clicking on the light overhead. "Okay. We're somewhere between Mexico and Albuquerque, headed north. We need to go south, then cut across the rest of New Mexico on highway something or other—what highway is that?—into Arizona."

I squinted at the map as my finger trailed the squiggly line.

"Aha! Highway 10."

I gasped and clung to the dash as Gavin veered off the road. He drove across the rough desert median separating the two lanes and looped around to go back the way we'd come. As my elation from hearing the voice of another human being died down, a sobering thought struck me. I tucked the map away.

"This really is happening everywhere, isn't it?"

Gavin glanced at me. He didn't answer but reached across the middle console and grabbed my hand. I clung to it. We reached the off-ramp for the major highway leading to the even bigger—and therefore scarier—city.

Chapter 8 ☣

"Candace. Candace!"

Gavin, handsome, sexy, and leaning forward to kiss me, instead grabbed my shoulders and started shaking me. Shaking me? My mouth turned down in a pout. I really wanted that kiss.

"Will you wake up?"

I bolted straight up in my seat. "What is it? Is everything okay?"

He grinned at me a bit sheepishly, but a yawn cut off his next words. Finally, the yawn ceased. He looked exhausted. "Do you mind driving? I'm really tired, but I don't think it's safe to pull over and stop."

"Sure! Give me a sec to wake up. Wait. Does that mean we need to switch while you're still driving?"

He laughed and yawned again before answering. "No. But we'll need to switch quickly."

I downed the last Frappuccino. "Okay, I'm ready."

Gavin slowed the car and stopped. He sighed and rubbed his eyes. My eyes darted in every direction. Was it safe? Were we safe?

With a groan, Gavin jumped out and raced around the car. I slid across the seats and locked the driver's door, waiting till Gavin was at the passenger door to unlock his side. I wasn't taking any chances.

Gavin jumped in and locked it. I didn't even wait for him to put his seatbelt on. I jammed the car into gear and squealed the tires in my haste to leave.

Gavin laughed. "You sure you'll be all right driving?"

"Mm-hmm. I'll just run over any zombies in my way."

"You might not want to do that. I would hate to have to run all the way on foot because the car was too messed up to drive."

I gasped. "That could happen? But didn't you...?"

"I wasn't going as fast as you are. Try to drive around them, and wake me if you need anything."

"K. Oh, and Gavin...?"

He was already snoring.

"Gavin?"

Nothing. I eyed the gas gauge nervously. I would need to refuel before we reached Phoenix. I may not have needed gas yet, but I most certainly did not want to run out.

After driving for a few hours in silence—well, except for the occasional mild snore from Gavin—I finally *had* to start looking for a gas station. Signs for Tucson, AZ, sprinkled the roadside. I kicked myself when I saw an advertisement for Old Tucson—a western town built solely for filming movies of the old West. I'd wanted to go, but I'd kept putting it off because Peter wasn't interested. Now there was probably nothing left but destroyed sets.

Taking an off-ramp on the outskirts of Tucson, I passed a large truck stop full of semis and stalled vehicles for a smaller one down the road. It had only one vehicle resting in front of one of the pumps.

I stayed in the driver's seat, clinging to the steering wheel. Terror would not let me move, even though nothing stirred in the stillness of the night. But we needed fuel, and all those coffees had finally caught up with me. I had to pee like a racehorse. I slipped the credit card out of the wallet Gavin had left on the dash. It'd worked at the last station.

I reached over and shook Gavin's arm.

"What? Hmm?"

"Gavin, I'm getting gas. Cover me, okay?"

"Mm-hmm. Sure thing," he mumbled.

I took a deep breath and got out. Every part of me was shaking. From nerves, cold, terror—it didn't really matter. I clenched my chattering teeth, trying to get the card in the slot. I swiped the credit card, my hand hovering over the nozzle. The card was declined several times before the screen flashed, *Please see cashier.*

"Oh, come on! You've got to be kidding."

I huffed and tried again. Obnoxious. It made me almost as angry as it did when that happened to me in my normal, everyday, wonderful life before I'd known there could be such things as stupid zombies. I marched over and tried one more pump, just to be sure. Same thing.

Checking to make sure my revolver was still tucked safely in my jeans, I opened the door and reached for my shotgun. Gavin was soundly snoring in the passenger seat. Some backup.

"Gavin? Gavin! Gavin Bailey, you wake up this instant." I climbed into the car, locking my door. "Gavin!"

I slid the shotgun's strap off my shoulder and set it beside me. Crawling on my hands and knees, I leaned over the middle console.

"Gavin!"

Stretching even farther, I placed both of my hands on his shoulders and shook him. He moved suddenly, and I slipped, landing face-first in the middle of his chest. He wrapped his arms around me in reflex. My breathing shallowed as his arms tightened around me.

"Good morning, beautiful. I must say, this is some way to be woken up." He held me for a few seconds too long before he gently pushed me back and gave me a roguish grin.

My face was on fire, and I couldn't think of anything to say. So I just sat there like a dummy, my mouth wide open.

He chuckled. "Like my Grams used to say, 'You'll attract flies.'"

I closed my mouth with a snap. Straightening, I turned away and started the car. Remembering why I was waking him in the first place, I leaned my forehead against the steering wheel and let out a low groan.

"We need gas?" he asked.

"We need gas."

"Card not working?"

"Nope."

He sighed. "I wondered how long that would last." He eyed the lone car at the pump across from us. "No sign of activity?"

I shook my head.

"Well, we'll just have to go inside and turn on all the pumps. You ready?"

I answered with another groan and grabbed my shotgun. I paused. "You think I can use the bathroom?"

He looked at the abandoned car. "I'm not sure. I don't think that thing will have gone far."

"It's important," I fairly whimpered.

"Okay, we'll give it a go. Let's hurry, all right?"

We rushed to the convenience store, covering each other's backs. Slipping past the unlocked doors, I quickly scanned the small aisles from the front of the store. Gavin ducked behind the counter. It took him a moment, but he figured out how to turn on all the pumps.

"There. That should help anyone else who comes along." He handed me a key. "Looks like the bathroom's out back."

I groaned and started doing the potty dance. I thought only little kids did that. Awesome.

"That bad, huh?"

"Oh, yeah."

He grinned and ushered me out the door. We covered each other once again as we left. Gavin headed around the store, and I followed close behind.

"Hurry!" he whispered after he made sure the one-person bathroom was unoccupied.

I was out in no time, and we rushed back to the car. I started to take off the cap to the gas tank. I jumped when Gavin's hand clamped around my arm. Startled, I looked up at him, then followed his gaze.

Directly behind our car, a good thirty feet away, stood a disheveled being. Long, tangled, dark hair covered half of her face, and her stance was listing to the side. Her breathing was shallow, and her arms dangled at her sides. It was doubly eerie with the gas station's light barely touching her in the darkness. She started stumbling forward.

I jumped into the driver's seat, and Gavin slid across the hood and into the passenger's side.

I peeled out of the parking lot, then slammed on the brakes. I could not leave without getting fuel. We wouldn't get far, and the truck stop would certainly be full of zombies. I gripped the steering wheel, wringing the almost-destroyed wheel cover.

Whipping the car around, I floored the gas pedal and aimed right for her.

"Stop!" yelled Gavin.

I gasped and slammed on the brakes, whipping my head around, staring at him for an explanation.

"What are you doing?" he sputtered. "You can't just hit a zombie at that speed! What were you thinking?"

I glanced at the zombie, then back at Gavin. My eyes darted back toward her. Had the zombie just taken a deep breath? I studied it. No. It'd stopped moving, but nothing else had changed. It was still barely breathing, looking like it would tip over any second.

Gavin grabbed his rifle and jumped out of the car. My jaw dropped as I watched the scene unfold before me.

He aimed and fired. The zombie flew on her back from the bullet's impact, then stood and staggered forward. He fired again. Same thing. The next time, he aimed for her head and blew half of it away. I covered my mouth, gagging and willing myself not to throw up. The zombie stayed down.

He motioned me forward, standing guard a good distance from the still figure.

I scrambled out and started filling the car. I didn't want to look, but I kept stealing glances at the prostrate figure. I had never seen anything so grotesque in my life. Who had this girl been before someone's moneymaking experiment had stolen the rest of her life? Had she just fallen in love? Gotten a new job? Maybe she'd gone out with her girlfriends for burgers and shakes the night before it'd happened. She looked young enough to be in high school. What were her dreams for college? Career? Marriage? Babies? Life?

I stared at the girl, tears filling my eyes. *God, please help me find a way to make this right,* I prayed silently.

No one deserved to have her life snuffed out so tragically, especially over someone else's whim to make a tidy profit. And for entertainment purposes, for heaven's sake!

I glanced around, noticing no other movement, then looked back at the girl. I sucked in a breath, almost choking on the pungent smell of fuel. She was starting to twitch.

"Candace? How much longer?"

I looked at the number of gallons already dispensed. "Nine gallons already. I think we figured this was a thirteen-or fifteen-gallon tank, so not *too* much longer, I hope."

"Hurry."

"Like I can make it pump any faster!" I snapped.

His sharp glance twinged my conscience.

"Sorry," I mumbled.

I started to bounce, willing the liquid to gush from the nozzle. The steady whir continued, totally stressing me out.

Arms and legs started moving. Gavin reloaded and stood with legs spread and the rifle homed in on the stirring creature. The whirring of pumping gas and the odor of noxious fumes filled the air as tension mounted.

"Candace?"

"Almost there."

The zombie groped for a way to stand.

"Candace."

"Not quite."

The zombie made it to her feet, bits of flesh and gore and what looked like pieces of bone hanging off the side of her head. He fired, making her stumble back and sit down hard. She straightened and advanced.

"Candace!"

Click.

"All done. Let's go!" I jammed the nozzle into its holster and flew into the driver's seat. Gavin fired once more and bolted into the car. The last thing I saw from my rearview mirror was her staggering to her feet once again.

We neared the truck stop, and I slowed. A large cluster of trucker zombies crowded the road.

I idled not far from them, wondering if I should plow through them or turn around and take my chances in the middle of the desert.

"Okay, go slowly. Drive to the right of them where there aren't as many. They shouldn't be able to stop us."

"Yeah, unless they pile under the tires," I groused.

I did what he said, though, and crept through them. I only bumped into a couple of them, and they pretty much just slid off of the hood onto the ground next to the car. The rest stared us down.

"Well, isn't this exciting? With this bright crowd, it's a wonder we're scared of them at all."

"Because they overpower a person in great numbers, then eat them. Any more questions?"

"No." I blushed. I didn't mean to complain. Really, I didn't. It just seemed to happen far too often. I was going to stop that, too. ASAP.

I maneuvered the car safely away from the truck stop and eased onto the onramp, for some reason thinking if I went slowly enough they wouldn't notice us or start chasing us or something. A thought nagged the back of my mind. Certain I had pestered the poor man enough, but too anxious to keep it to myself, I finally voiced my concern.

"If there are this many zombies at a truck stop, won't there be thousands more in a city? How are we going to make it anywhere near the radio station, especially since he said he was surrounded?"

"I don't know. We'll figure it out when we get there."

My dark mood returned in a flash.

"Sure we will."

Chapter 9 ☣

I was getting more and more nervous the closer we got to Phoenix. Gavin dozed, leaving me alone with myself. We were not enjoying ourselves.

The tension was building in my neck and shoulders, and I wanted to snap at someone. Anyone. Just give me a drive-thru and a wrong order, and my day would be so much better. The thought of trading a few hundred zombies for a couple thousand was enough to make me want to turn around and disappear in the desert, radio station guy or no. Light tinged the sky as the sun began its ascent. The speed limit dropped, and a few extra lanes widened the highway, signifying we were on the outskirts of the city.

Gavin woke and stretched. His manner was easy, relaxed. In other words, the exact opposite of me.

A lazy grin stretched his mouth. "You ready for me to take over?"

"Yes, please."

I slowed and stopped in the middle of the road. A fuel semi was on its side a good distance before us, and a few cars were piled behind us. It seemed like a good place to stop before the wrecked traffic got heavier.

I stumbled wearily out of the car, stretching and twisting to relieve hours of being cramped in the same position. I met Gavin at the trunk, rummaging through the groceries for something to eat. We took turns pausing and scanning the horizon.

"Tuna sandwiches?"

"Sounds fabulous."

I wasn't kidding. It really did after thousands of granola bars and hundreds of other tasteless snacks from the gas station.

I gasped as Gavin's arms snaked around me and pulled me against his firm, broad chest. I stood frozen as he gently caressed my back and his arms held me captive in a far-too-friendly, definitely-not-brotherly bear hug. He held me tight and rested his chin on my head, probably getting poked in the process.

"You okay?"

"Yeah."

"You sure?"

"I am now," I teased.

No way was I going to let him know how disconcerting his nearness was. I couldn't decide if I wanted to laugh or cry or giggle or squeal or cry or sob at the thought of being in Gavin Bailey's arms. Of course, the endless days of being chased by salivating zombies didn't do much for a stable emotional state. He'd probably leave me behind if I let loose any of the emotions coursing through me.

"How about that sandwich?" My muffled voice wafted up, slightly slurred from my face being plastered on that chest I'd seen in far too many movies. Tension was back in my shoulders big time. A giddy kind of tension.

He pulled back after an eternity, grinned, and tapped me under the chin. He started whistling while he pulled out bread and canned tuna. I wanted to shake him and ask what in the world he'd meant by that hug. But, I was probably overreacting, and he was just being nice. And zombies weren't real. And pigs could fly. And…I watched him suspiciously while we made about five sandwiches each.

Settling on the hood of the car, guns across our knees, we munched on sandwiches and kept a lookout. We sat in comfortable silence, taking time to enjoy the stillness and the yummy food.

I held up some fruit. "Apple?"

"Mm-hmm."

I tossed it at him and kept munching, determined to act completely normal for once in my life.

We finished most of the sandwiches, then downed some Capri Suns. I started gathering our trash to dispose of later when we reached a trashcan. Gavin wadded up his napkins, shriveled juice pouches, and apple core and tossed them on the side of the road.

My mouth gaped open. "What are you doing?"

Gavin just looked at me, a hint of humor sparking in his eyes. "Taking out the trash."

"You can't do that! Pick it up. Right now. That's littering."

"Oh, really? And who's gonna make me? You?" He swiped the trash from my hands and tossed it in the road as well.

I sputtered and jumped off the hood to pick it all up. He threw back his head and laughed.

"You can't be serious! You think the zombie cops will give us a citation for littering when they pull us over to attack us?"

"As long as we are on this planet, it is our *job* to take care of it. And whenever we get it back, which I fully intend to do, I do not want to spend all my time picking up your trash!" I bent to collect what he had lobbed at the ground.

Gavin grinned and rolled his eyes. "Look around you, dearie. There's going to be a wee bit more cleanup than just picking up trash, if that ever happens. You really want to spend your possible last moments on earth worried about some garbage?"

I looked around, suddenly feeling foolish.

"Come on, live a little. I know you want to. Just do it."

I looked down at the trash in my hands.

"Come on! What. Are you chicken?"

I chuckled to myself. Of all the times for another of my crazy quirks to come to light. I grinned and shook my head. I began pitching trash in all directions, strewing it all over the highway. I let my apple core fly in abandon with a loud whoop.

"Wow, calm down there, Princess."

I dug around in the car for all of the other wrappers and drink bottles. A smidgeon of guilt crept up on me, and I flinched. The poor previous owner would be furious if she saw the state of her car now.

I started flinging empty glass coffee bottles all over the road, barely missing Gavin with one of them. He just ducked and watched me with a grin. I flung the last of the garbage onto the other side of the highway, bouncing it off the hood of a truck.

"Now, admit it. That felt good, didn't it?"

My grin was my reply. It did feel good to be footloose and fancy-free. Let my hair down. Shoot the breeze. Stretch out my wings and fly. I ran out of pathetic sayings.

Reluctant to get back into the car and make our way to the city, I took my time rearranging some of the bags, making sure ammo and a few other necessary things were easy to get to and not in the trunk.

Gavin checked our guns, then looked at me. "We should go."

"Yeah."

"We want plenty of daylight to find the radio station."

"I know."

Neither of us moved. With a sigh, he slammed the trunk, striding to the driver's seat. I reluctantly followed, not wanting to be outside the car without him. We made sure the doors were locked, fastened our seatbelts, and waited. For what, I wasn't sure.

"You ready for this?" he asked.

"Not really. What's our plan?"

"Well...we should probably top off. I don't know how long we'll be driving around, looking for the radio station."

"Couldn't we find a phone book or a city map? It should have the address and directions."

"Good thinking. We'll probably want to hide the car so it doesn't get ransacked when we go into the radio station."

"You mean, go on *foot*?"

He smirked. "What, did you think we were just going to drive into the radio station?"

"That's not a bad idea, actually. Why not just call the place and let him know to run out when we honk?"

"First of all, we will try to call him if we find a working pay phone, but we want to draw as little attention to ourselves as possible. Sneaking in there to help him get out is our best option."

"I like the option of the steel frame of a car protecting us."

"And when they rush us, turn the car over, and smash out all the windows?"

"Guess it's better to be on foot so they can eat us on the spot."

"Touché."

He smiled and went on as if I'd said nothing at all. That's the problem with movie stars. They've been in so many action movies, they think they can just boss you around 'cause they know what to do. Not that I had a plan or anything.

"Um, Gavin?"

He kept talking, outlining a shoot-'em-up, take-over-the-world rescue plan or something, which included blasting zombies just so they could get up and chase us again.

"Gavin." I reached for his sleeve, my eyes riveted ahead.

"Just a minute." He had an imaginary floor plan of the radio station in his palm, explaining our best methods of attacking zombies, based on video games from the sound of it. His sound effects would have been hilarious under different circumstances.

"Gavin!" I shook his arm and pointed out the windshield.

A burly, grossly decaying trucker, complete with red plaid flannel shirt and torn jeans, stood in front of the overturned tanker, facing us. My biggest concern was the rifle or shotgun dragging behind him—I couldn't tell which at this distance. All I knew was it was long, pointy, and potentially lethal.

"Um, can he shoot that thing?"

Gavin turned on the car, putting it in gear. "I don't think so."

The zombie swung the weapon to his shoulder, took wobbly aim, and fired right at us. The windshield cracked between us. We stared at it and each other in disbelief.

Gavin shifted in reverse. Tires squealed as he sped backward. We hit the pile of cars behind us with a jolt and a sickening crunch. I gasped and clutched at my seatbelt.

The gun dipped, but the thing hefted it back to his shoulder and fired again. The shot went wide this time and pinged off one of the other cars. Gavin crammed the car into drive and screeched forward.

He sped around the zombie and the tanker. The zombie still relentlessly fired, following our vehicle the best he could. He missed us but managed to blast the tanker full of holes as we drove around it.

One shot ricocheted off our bumper. Gavin's gaze flew to the rearview mirror. His eyes widened. "Hope this works," he mumbled to himself.

Gavin slammed on the brakes and swung the car parallel to the tanker. I whimpered from being jerked around like a rag doll yet again. This was so getting old.

He jumped out and shot a few more holes on this side of the glistening silver tank before aiming for the ground and the rapidly pouring fuel. He shot until a spark ignited the ever-widening circle of liquid. He dove back into the car and took off, swerving until he got the car under control. The fire spread.

I gripped the dash with one hand and watched the side mirror with fascination. The truck exploded, flames shooting into the air and engulfing the zombie. The shock hit our car, and I bounced forward, crying out. Gavin corrected and sped onward, squinting through the cracks in our windshield.

The flames cleared, and the zombie continued to stagger toward us, not caring in the least that he was on fire.

"I *swear* it's a great idea to run them over."

Gavin smirked and shook his head as we left the scorched zombie far behind us.

Chapter 10 ☣

Gavin slowed and carefully navigated through the clusters of cars. I couldn't believe it. The damage was horrendous. Windows were smashed. Signs dangled in front of buildings. Garbage littered every available inch of ground. Anything that could be remotely moved or thrown over was moved and thrown over. We could barely get around the profusion of overturned and wrecked cars.

Zombies milled about aimlessly, apparently running out of whatever things zombies enjoy doing. Our slowly moving vehicle caused a small stir, but they lost interest as we passed.

Pulling next to a gas station, Gavin stopped but left the car idling. He turned to me. "You ready?"

I nodded, swallowing hard. I don't know how he'd talked me into his crazy idea, but he was going to pay if I made it. Someday. Somehow.

I took a deep breath and eased open my car door. I tumbled out and staggered toward the convenience store, trying to look for all the world like a zombie. My slow, rambling gait seemed to be working. A few looked my direction then continued to wander. I made it to the door and pushed it open with my shoulder. So far, so good. Of course, I was shaking so badly my jerky, reeling steps weren't much of an act.

The room looked empty, so I swiped a couple of maps and grabbed a phonebook from behind the counter. I hastened to the front door and took another deep breath. This had better work.

I clutched my bounty as inconspicuously as possible under my arm and started shuffling back to the car. I tried to keep my head motionless while I frantically scanned my surroundings. One of the zombies who'd ignored me earlier stopped tearing newspapers out of a newspaper rack and sniffed the air. Like a freaking dog. He turned and looked straight at me. I froze. Intensity lined his expressionless face as he started stumbling in my direction, making guttural screeching noises. Others started following him.

Gavin pushed open the passenger door. "Candace!" he hissed.

They continued to advance, and I just stood there like a dummy.

Move. Move. "Move!" I finally shrieked to myself.

I bolted for the car, immediately grabbing the attention of every other zombie in the vicinity. I wriggled out of one's grasp as it clutched at my arm, then I jumped into the car.

Gavin peeled out before I had the door closed. At least, he tried to. The zombies swarmed our car. He tried to drive through them, but their sheer number made it impossible. We couldn't see past them.

"Gavin?" I clutched the dashboard.

He put his arm protectively across my chest. "Hang on."

He squealed the tires in reverse. But we were surrounded. The teeming mass pushed back, surprisingly stopping the progress of the car.

"Gavin?" I whispered, my voice catching.

He removed his arm long enough to shift, then revved forward. Nothing. I gasped as the car was lifted on my side, then dropped. Gavin held me back. The car jerked and shuddered as it was pushed from all directions.

Our already-cracked windshield began to splinter even more as zombies piled onto the car, trying to get to us. Gavin stopped spinning the tires for a moment, then slammed his foot on the gas. The car lurched forward, dislodging a few of the zombies. I could only hang against Gavin's arm and pray we made it out alive.

The unexpected lurch forward gave Gavin the opportunity he needed to plow through the bulk of bodies. We couldn't see where we were going, but Gavin kept his foot plastered to the gas pedal.

Just as we cleared the press of zombies, we slammed into a pole and pitched forward. Gavin's arm was the only thing that kept me from smacking my forehead on the windshield. I groaned as my head spun and pain slithered through my body.

Gavin unlatched his belt. He quickly crawled across the middle console and pushed my door open. He tumbled out and scooped me into his arms. Stumbling away from the car, he bolted toward the nearest building as the stampede reached our car. When he'd cleared the bodies, he set me on my feet and turned to run. My legs refused to work, my eyes riveted on the mob swarming our car. He jerked to a halt.

"Candace! Come on. You with me?"

I tore my gaze away and tried to focus on Gavin.

His eyes darted around us. He tried to pull me farther away from the zombies piling all over our car. They'd not yet noticed we were no longer in the car and were trying to tear the car apart. Literally.

"Candace, I need you with me now more than ever," Gavin whispered, his voice hoarse as he tried not to draw attention. "Do you understand? Can you hear me?"

He tugged my hand. I stumbled into him, almost falling.

I couldn't move. I couldn't think. Functioning was not an option at the moment. And the ones not currently tearing apart our former vehicle were starting to notice us.

Gavin gently took my face into his hands and pulled me close, touching his forehead to mine. "Candace, I need you."

My eyes shot open as his lips covered my own in the best kiss of the century. He deepened it then wrenched back. My own shock was mirrored on his face. He took a moment to run a roughened thumb over my cheek, his eyes drifting to my lips. Dropping his hand, he claimed mine once more.

As he hauled me down the street, realization streamed through my body. Gavin Bailey had kissed me. Really, truly kissed me.

I looked up at him, awed and fully satisfied with what had just happened. He peeked at me, admiration in his gaze. Movement caught my attention.

I only had a split second to act. I pushed him out of the way, and the zombie grabbed me instead. The zombie shoved me to the ground and tried to bite my face. I writhed and bucked, barely missing her decomposing face and gnashing teeth.

The zombie was lifted straight up into the air and tossed to the side. Gavin shoved another zombie aside, grabbed my arm, and pulled me up. We dodged and fought and pushed, barely eluding grasping hands.

We finally broke free from the heaving swarm and bolted down the street. We left the massive congregation behind us but constantly had to dodge and fight off others milling about. It was ridiculous. They just kept coming. No relief.

When I thought I could run no longer, Gavin pulled me behind a short brick wall and sank to the ground. We slumped against the brick, gasping for air.

We heard shuffling on the other side of the wall, and Gavin slowly peeked over it. I checked out our hiding place. An alley with a row of squat houses on both sides peeked at us through backyard fences. Gavin waited until the shuffling faded before sinking beside me once more.

"Best kiss ever!"

He grinned unabashedly. "Glad you liked it."

"Like it? That was the best kiss of my entire life!"

"So you said." Smugness tinted his tone.

"Oh my gosh, where did you learn to kiss like that? Do they have kissing classes for actors? Sign me up!"

His grin slipped. I could tell by the way he was squirming he was getting uncomfortable. "Moving on…" he mumbled, more to himself, but definitely loud enough for me to hear.

But I was embarrassed and thrilled and excited and scared and kept right on talking like an idiot.

"But, seriously, why did you do it? Why did you kiss me? I know I'm not a hot model or anything like you're used to, so it probably wasn't a very good kiss from my end, but wow, that was an amazing kiss! So good!"

He got up and walked away. I could tell he was angry from the set of his shoulders. I groaned. Good job me. I never knew when to shut up.

I ducked my head and scuffed my toe in the dirt. Way to ruin a perfect moment. I kept my head down and felt tears sting the back of my eyes. I blinked rapidly. I was not going to add crying like a baby to the truly most embarrassing moment of my life.

I heard his footsteps crunch back in my direction. His boots paused before mine. I tucked my chin further onto my chest. He hunkered down in front of me. "Candace, look at me."

I shook my head no and continued to stare at our boots.

"Candace, baby, look at me."

My head shot up. My gaze slammed into his as I stared at him in amazement.

"I kissed you because I wanted to. I've wanted to for a while now."

My mouth dropped open. I snapped it closed and leaned forward, wrapping my arms around my legs. I tucked my face behind my knees.

"I don't get it," I mumbled to my knees.

"What don't you get? That you are fun, drive me crazy, and are so beautiful you take my breath away?"

"No. Never mind. I don't want to talk about it."

"Candace…"

"No, seriously, what's our next move?"

He waited so long, I wasn't sure he'd answer. He finally blew out his breath and stood. I kept my face hidden, not daring to look at him.

"I don't know."

I gazed up at him then, fear and uncertainty dancing across my face. He hunkered before me and cupped my cheek. I leaned into his hand.

"We need to get out of the city." He dropped his voice. "But I don't know what to do from there."

From the display of emotions on his face, the sensation was new to him. I moved to comfort him. Wrapping my arms around his neck, I gently held him.

"It will be okay," I whispered, desperately trying to believe it myself.

Chapter 11 ☣

I peeked around the other end of the alley. "So they *can* be out in the daylight!"

"Candace…" Gavin warned.

I could tell it was the last thing he wanted to talk about at the moment. What? I like to be informed.

"You can finish your research on the attributes of a zombie at a later time. Right now we need to focus, okay?"

"Got it."

Gavin scanned the street around the corner, and I looked behind us. Something caught my attention. A good-sized piece of paper tumbled down the alley. I had an overwhelming feeling we needed that paper. I chased it down, snagging it with my foot. I walked back to Gavin, smoothing out the wrinkles.

"Ha!" I shoved it triumphantly under his nose. "Look, a map!"

Gavin rolled his eyes and muttered, "Well, that was convenient."

I scrunched my nose. "Huh?"

"Never mind." Gavin spread the detailed tourist map of Phoenix on the wall we were hiding behind and gave me a brilliant smile. "Perfect."

He pointed out our spot on the map after checking a precariously tilted street sign not far from us. He folded the map and handed it back, studying the wandering zombies once more.

"There don't seem to be too many," Gavin mused to himself. "I don't see any undamaged vehicles. But if we're careful, we might be able to reach the outskirts of the city before it gets dark. We've got to find a car or some kind of shelter."

"What about the radio guy?"

Gavin glanced at me then returned his focus on the few zombies between us and our way out of the city. "The last thing I want to do is get stuck in the radio station tonight."

"It might be the safest place, since he's made it this far," I urged.

Gavin studied my face for a moment then nodded. "Let me see the map again."

I spread the crumpled sheet of paper on the wall. His eyes traced the streets again.

"The most direct route takes us through the heart of the city. I want to go here." He pointed. "On the outskirts, with as many shortcuts as possible. Think we can figure it out?"

"We've got to try," I said with a fake smile and false encouragement. Locking ourselves into a nuclear shelter seemed a more viable option at the moment.

Gavin's smile was tender. Apparently the man could see right through my façade. I was trying oh so very hard to be brave, but it *so* was not working. Just about anyone else in the world would have been a better choice for Gavin's partner. I started to say just that, but his lips covered mine in a gentle kiss. Before I could even comprehend what was happening, he turned away, peeking around the building's corner.

My fingertips caressed the last place Gavin's warm skin had touched. I wouldn't get used to Gavin Bailey kissing me for as long as I lived. Which I hoped would be for a long time. That is, living as a person, not a zombie. Alive, alive. Not dead alive. You know what I mean. Anyway…

Our guns were gone, mine having fallen out in our now-destroyed car. Gavin wasn't sure where or when he'd lost his, but now we needed to rely on stealth and evasive maneuvers more than ever.

I folded the map, leaving our route on the outermost page. I didn't want the crinkling of a stupid map getting us into trouble with zombies while we were trying to sneak away.

"Now! Let's move."

I followed him out from behind the protection of the building, and we ducked behind an overturned car. None of the zombies milling about noticed us. Yet. We ducked and weaved, bobbed and hid behind vehicles, buildings, posts—anything big enough. We made it several city blocks without being noticed. Whew.

I started to get excited when we successfully made it out of the heart of the city, and the buildings became shorter and farther apart. Gavin cleared a loading dock and parking area of a big distribution warehouse. I followed close behind. We rounded a pile of garbage dumpsters and froze in front of a group of zombies feasting on what looked like the remains of a deer. They stopped tearing into the carcass and stared at us, clearly wanting more.

"Run!" Gavin placed himself between them and me.

I dashed away. Following the path of least resistance, unfortunately, led me straight back toward the city. "Gavin?"

"Keep going!"

I did. Rounding the corner of a towering office building, I immediately reversed direction, stumbling back a few steps. Gavin slammed into my back, nearly knocking me over. A horde of hunched corpses, arms dangling, faces void of life, faced all different directions. At our appearance, they crowded forward, forming a semi-circle around us. I could hear the ones behind us closing in. There was nowhere to go.

They surrounded us, waiting. For what, I don't know. The suspense was palatable.

Something inside me snapped. As terrifying as this was, I was not going down without a fight. I take that back. I was not going down. Period. I fisted my hands and eyed the buildings on either side of us. Solid wall met my gaze.

"What do we do now?" I ground out.

Gavin's arm slipped around my waist, and he squeezed. "Don't get separated," he directed in a low voice.

A moan rose from somewhere, and they moved forward as one. The smell was outrageous, the guttural sounds enough to make me want to pass out and never wake up. Not to mention their grotesque, horrendous, twisted, gaping faces. Walking dead people are downright ugly. Good luck ever sleeping again for the rest of my life.

I fought with everything I had in me, yelling like a crazy person. I punched, shoved, and clawed my way through them, seeking escape. Their sheer numbers began to shift us apart.

"Gavin?"

"Stay with me!"

My steady resolve started to splinter and crack as I fought to stay beside Gavin. As he started to drift away. He was my last link to normal. I could not lose him. I could not.

A zombie spun me around. I shoved it away and glanced behind me. He wasn't there.

"Gavin!"

A zombie clamped on to me from behind. I bucked as I strained to hear Gavin's voice over our brawling. I couldn't tell what he was saying, but his muffled voice drifted farther away.

"No! Gavin!"

I struggled to find him, but I couldn't see him. Jostled from zombie to zombie, each one tried to get a piece of me. One crazy aggressive zombie was unwilling to let go of me as her companion tried to drag me away. I wasn't exactly hyperventilating, but I was getting pretty darn close.

Sharp pain tore through my arm, and I looked down, my mouth frozen in a silent scream. What had just happened? Blood swelled and ran red fingers down either side of my arm. I stared at it in shock before I started screaming bloody murder.

I heard a commotion and muffled *oomph's* and groans. Gavin appeared next to me—crawling on the ground—and stared at my arm in horror. He threw off the zombie still trying to drag me away and lifted me in his arms.

Gavin barreled through the mass of zombies. He somehow slipped through them all and bolted for the nearest building. He ducked around a corner, leaned against the wall, and sucked in every breath with desperation.

Tears streamed down my face. I clung to his neck, unwilling to let go. I'd almost lost him.

"Oh, Gavin. What are we going to do?"

We both jumped when someone else said, "Psst! Over this way!"

Bright sunlight gave way to pitch black as Gavin, still holding me, ducked through the doorway an older gentleman—a normal-looking, older gentleman—held open for us. We followed the guy through a maze of hallways until we reached a door barred with chains and heavy furniture. He slipped through a path I couldn't see, moving furniture in place behind us. The door opened at the man's coded knock. We entered to find five other people staring at us, mouths open, eyes wide.

"Peaches, get the first-aid kit."

A skinny blonde whose clothes had seen better days tore from the room and soon came back with a well-stocked kit. The guy motioned for Gavin to put me down and began cleaning my wound.

I watched him with wide eyes. He looked up at me and winked. "Don't worry, girlie. I'm a doctor. I'll take good care of you."

"Am I gonna turn? I'm gonna turn, aren't I? Am I gonna turn?" I demanded, hysterical and not trying to calm myself in the least. "I don't want to be a zombie!" I wailed.

"There, there, now," soothed the doctor. "You will be just fine." He bandaged my arm. Someone handed him a glass, and he passed it to me, smiling. "Drink this, now. You'll feel much better. I promise."

I downed it without a thought and swiped my mouth with the back of my hand. My eyes darted to each of the people crowding around me. There were so many. How did—?

Anxiety fled as tiredness slammed into me. I drooped, wondering how to keep my eyes open.

I realized as I was falling asleep they'd probably drugged me so I wouldn't eat them all before they could get me back outside. I struggled and let out a whimper before all my muscles relaxed.

Gavin's arms slipped around me as I fell into oblivion.

Chapter 12 ☣

I woke up on a pile of old blankets, muffled voices floating in from the other room. I sat up and squinted into the shadows surrounding me.

Was it safe? Where was I? How long had I been here?

From the slant of the light streaming in the room from the high, squat, barred windows, it had to be the next day. And it was mostly over.

I stumbled off the mound, promptly tripping and landing on my face.

"Ack! Seriously, Candace? Seriously?"

My voice echoed in the barren chamber.

Covering my face with my hands, I took deep breaths. Maybe the medicine hadn't worn off yet entirely or something. Groaning, I rolled onto my back, glad there was no one to witness such a humiliating moment. A soft chuckle reached my ears. My head shot up, and pain sliced through my head as my eyes darted in search of the person who dared laugh at me.

The man who'd bandaged my arm walked into view with a smile on his face. A fake cough covered another laugh, and he wordlessly held out a hand. I took it. He helped me to my feet.

"I was wondering when you were going to wake up. How do you feel?"

"Like I just tripped and fell flat on my face with an audience."

"It can be our secret." He winked at me. "And how is our patient's arm today?"

I tested it. As in, I poked it. Not a good idea. Firm bandage in place, it only stung a little. "Much better, thank you."

"Good, good. Wouldn't want you feeling poorly now, would we?"

I blinked, realizing I hadn't been left in the street outside. "So… does this mean I won't turn into a zombie?"

"Doesn't seem like it."

"Thank heavens!" I breathed in relief. "Gavin?"

"In the room with the others. Shall we?"

"Oh, yes, of course."

We entered side by side, and the conversation vanished, all eyes on me. I squirmed. So not cool. Gavin jumped up from a table and wrapped me in a very long, very uncomfortable hug.

"How are you feeling?" he asked, his voice full of concern.

"Fine, just fine. Really hungry. But good. Yeah, I'm good."

"I'm glad."

His nearness was threatening my intelligence again. Must think of something witty to say. ASAP. Edging away, I tried to act nonchalant.

"How are you? You know. Since you've been here."

I winced. My brain somehow missed the witty memo.

He chuckled.

I glanced at him sharply, only to find his eyes dancing in merriment.

"I'm better now I know you're okay."

I may have melted just a little. How sweet!

"Okay, okay, move it. I'm not gonna stand here all day," said a young girl's voice behind him.

He kissed my cheek and stepped to the side, letting said young girl shove a recently microwaved, previously frozen dinner my way. She grinned, clearly enjoying interrupting us—clearly enjoying my discomfort.

"Yes, well, introductions," the doctor inserted. "This is Sara." The girl, probably fourteen or so, smirked in my direction. Her hand was still outstretched, holding the most unappetizing dinner I'd seen in my life. I lifted the limp cardboard tray from her fingers and mumbled my thanks.

"Karl." A skinny beanpole of a man lifted a half-wave as he focused on deciphering obnoxious squawks from a transistor radio. He didn't even look my way.

"Matt. He keeps our weapons well-stocked and in good working order."

My face flamed as Matt's gaze traveled over me. His eyes lit with interest. From what I could tell from his seated position, he was a well-built, good-looking guy. In other words, hot. I edged a step closer to Gavin. Matt noticed and smirked. I could very nearly hear him think, *Challenge accepted.*

But then again my imagination was overactive, and I needed to focus on the good doctor.

"Peaches." I did a double-take. Yep, he'd really said Peaches. This time and the last. The bleached-blonde with dark roots nicknamed Peaches—at least I *hoped* that was a nickname—grinned at me, snapped her gum, and offered a little wave.

"And Sam. She's our ragtag group's leader. It would be hard to find a more competent person to guide us." A rough-looking, could-possibly-be-pretty-if-she-didn't-look-so-severe woman barely spared me a glance.

"Nice to meet you all." My voice barely penetrated the room.

"There are a few others—Chris, Scott, Jeff, and Trevor—and I think Jenifer is around here somewhere..."

"Back here, doc." A mildly pretty brunette waved from the back of the room, busy placing little red and blue pins in maps covering the back wall.

"Ah, yes, of course. The young men should be back soon. They're scrounging for supplies."

"We had a ton of stuff from Walmart in our car," I offered.

Sam jerked upright and speared me with a glare. I flinched. She and the doctor exchanged glances.

"Where?" Sam demanded, eyes back on me. I wanted those violent-looking orbs directed elsewhere. ASAP.

The doctor leveled a warning look in her direction. "Sam…"

I answered her unspoken command, only stuttering a little. "I-I'm not sure where we crashed it, but last I saw, zombies were tearing it apart."

Sam and the doctor immediately started talking.

"They've probably lost interest by now."

"We could salvage something."

"It would be smart to check it out."

"We should leave the moment the others get back."

"We should leave now, before it gets dark and even more supplies go to waste!"

The doctor spread his hands wide and spoke in a soothing, placating manner. "I'm not comfortable with so many gone at once. How will we know if something happens to you? At least right now we've got visuals on the team that's out."

"Who's in charge of this group?"

"Geez, Sam, it's a democracy, not a dictatorship," cut in Sara.

"Thank you for your opinion. Didn't ask for it. Don't want it."

"You're welcome," Sara called out over her magazine.

"Besides," continued the doctor. "They don't even know where they left the car."

"I think it was on Georgetown Street, near a market of some kind, if I remember correctly," offered Gavin.

Sam leveled a glare at the doctor. "See? Georgetown Street. Matt. Peaches. You're with me."

Karl bolted to his feet and opened his mouth.

"Not now, Karl. My decision is final. Sit down."

Karl clamped his mouth shut and slumped into his chair, dejection in every line of his stance.

"Jenifer."

"Yo."

"I need eyes."

"Georgetown? I won't have eyes on you the whole time. Street cameras are out Hayes through 9th."

"Give me what you can."

"Gotcha."

"Let's move, people!"

Everyone scattered to do Sam's bidding. I could see why. Sheer terror of the woman would make me do anything she said.

"Oh, yeah, you two."

I shrank back when I realized she was addressing Gavin and me.

"Don't touch anything. I'll deal with you two when I get back."

And she was gone.

Before she could even see me nodding like an idiot.

Gavin broke the tongue-tying spell of her departure. "Kind of like the Tasmanian devil. Don't know what hits you till it's too late." Gavin grinned, clearly enjoying the peppy dictator.

"You got that right," I mumbled into my rapidly cooling plate.

"Hey! Lay off of her! She's a great leader!" Karl jumped out of his chair and glowered at us, fists clenched.

"No one said she wasn't, Karl. Just give them time to get used to her. They'll warm up to her eventually," the doctor interjected.

Karl plopped into his chair and muttered to himself. "She's a *great* leader. A great woman. How could anyone not like her?"

I raised my eyebrow, and Gavin and I exchanged glances. His eyes sparkled. A half-grin touched my mouth.

"If you'll excuse me? I have a few things to take care of." The doctor turned to leave.

"Wait!"

The doctor glanced back at me.

"You never told me your name."

"David. My name is David." He gave me a slight bow before striding from the room.

Sara flipped through her magazine, and Karl fiddled with his radio. I pushed the now-cold food around my plate while Gavin watched me. Microwaved food never stayed warm for long, but this was ridiculous. I stuck my finger in it, just to be sure. Yep, the center was a solid chunk of ice.

"Care to sit?" Gavin indicated a table nearby.

"Sure."

The food wasn't too bad, for a cold pile of indecipherable mush. I choked down a few bites while holding my breath, guzzling tepid water after every bite. Was it even safe to ingest?

Gavin stretched and lazily reached for a folded newspaper resting on the table. He flipped through it while I squinted to read the tiny print on the front cover. One week old.

"Hey! I saw that paper at my doctor's office. He's a big Cardinals fan. Can't believe it's been a week since my appointment."

Gavin lowered the paper and gave me a sympathetic look before disappearing behind it once more.

I gulped down a few more bites before deciding being hungry was better than eating slop. I pushed the plate away and fiddled with the fork. Gavin stayed sequestered in his literary world. Bored, I pulled the plate toward me once again. Discovering the goo stuck together surprisingly well on top of the rock-hard frozen base, I started seeing how fast I could make a sludge castle before it oozed back onto the plate. I heard the paper rustle but was too intent on my building project to notice Gavin watching me.

"What are you doing?"

I jerked, and a blob of the goo landed on the table with a *slurp*.

"Uh…eating."

He leveled an incredulous stare in my direction.

I squirmed before saying, "Kind of."

"That's disgusting."

I snorted. "No, eating it is disgusting. You should try it sometime."

He shuddered. "Already did."

I gave him a cheeky grin before returning to my project.

The paper rustled a few more times before Gavin slammed the paper on the table. I jumped, destroying yet another delicate piece of art.

"Please, just stop. You're making me queasy, thinking I put that in my stomach."

I gave him a devilish grin. "What, this?"

I shook the glop in his direction. He deftly plucked the plate from my fingers and hefted it into the nearest trashcan. I laughed and leaned back, hooking my hands over the bench-like seat. "Nice shot."

"Thanks," he grunted, looking slightly green.

"So…what's next? Are we going to stay here with these people?"

Gavin rubbed the back of his neck. "I guess we'll find out when the team leader gets back."

"You think it's safe?"

"I sure hope so. Seems to be, with how long these folks have been holed up together."

I cocked my head, my brow furrowing. "How long has it been?"

Gavin folded his hands on top of the table and dropped his head. A soft blast of air left his lips. "About a week."

I had to strain to hear his soft words, but they hit me like a blow.

"So," I choked. "That paper is two weeks old now?"

He looked up at me, eyes tired. "Give or take a couple days. Yeah."

"Wow."

"Yeah. Wow."

We sat, lost in our own thoughts, before I ventured a question I'd been mulling over for some time now.

"Isn't…isn't there…what I mean to say, can't we just? I mean, it might work…"

"Spit it out, Candace."

My eyes shot up to his in shock, but the grin playing about his lips made me feel sheepish instead of offended. I took a deep breath and plunged in. "Can't we just kill them with a silver bullet to the heart?"

I waited, half-proud of the zombie knowledge I'd remembered from somewhere.

Gavin dragged a hand down his face. "No, that's how you supposedly kill werewolves. Ancient lore."

"Oh." I frowned. "What about using garlic somehow?"

Gavin's lips twitched, and he rubbed his jaw. Was he trying to keep a straight face?

"Vampires."

I nibbled my lip, not sure I wanted to display even more of my lack of knowledge. But I was sure I had one of these right. "Wooden stakes?"

"Candace! You can't be serious."

I threw up my hands. "I am! I have no idea about any of this stuff."

Karl huffed and rolled his eyes, pulling his hat down over his face. He shook his head before turning his chair around so he wouldn't have to look at us. Me, specifically.

I dropped my voice. "Then, how in the world *do* we kill these things?"

Gavin opened his mouth, but the door burst open behind him.

"Oh my gosh, you guys, these things are great!" Peaches sauntered through the door, heaving several of our blue bags onto a nearby table. She flipped the bags over one at a time and spilled the contents as the others tromped in after her.

Wow, they were fast.

Gavin stood and relocated next to Peaches, rummaging through the cans and boxes sprawled on the table.

I recognized two of the people who entered and tried to remember everybody's names as they crowded around the supplies. Four guys I didn't recognize carted in the rest of the reusable Walmart bags. Matt made his way over to Gavin, slapping my revolver into Gavin's open palm.

"Yes! Thanks, man."

Gavin pumped Matt's hand, then Matt handed him his rifle and my shotgun. Gavin got even more excited when Matt pulled Gavin's handgun from a holster on the small of his back.

Gavin reverently lifted it from Matt's grasp. He dropped the magazine and slid open the chamber.

"Where did you find it?"

Once again, I wished someone would look at me like that.

The rest of their conversation was lost to me as I tried to blend in with the faded wallpaper. I was pretty sure I'd succeeded until I noticed Karl eyeing me. I shifted and dropped my gaze, hoping he would leave me alone.

"Do you have a nickname, Candace?" Karl warbled in his high-pitched voice, calling across the subdued commotion once the groceries had been sufficiently manhandled.

I froze, not wanting to be the center of attention. All activity halted as every eye in the room swung in my direction.

"Yes, sometimes," I hedged.

I did not like the glint in his eyes. It had been a while since someone had made fun of my nickname, but I was certain that was about to be remedied.

"And what would that be? Can't expect people to walk around calling you 'Candace' all the time."

I glanced behind me at Gavin. He just smirked and continued cleaning his gun. Everyone seemed to be waiting, and I hate making people wait. I also don't stand up well under pressure. The tension crackled in the room, every eye on me. I mumbled a reply, hoping he wouldn't catch it.

"Candy? As in, 'I want Candy'," he crooned in terrible pitch, completely off-key.

The woman I'm pretty sure they called Sam smacked the back of his head. "Don't be an idiot, Coffey."

I sent her a grateful look. She stared back at me. No smile. The grin died on my face. Karl Coffey tossed a can of beans in the air and caught it, then moved away from her, humming the tune of "I want Candy" under his breath.

"So, here's the thing," Sam began without preamble. "You're welcome to stick with us as long as you're an asset. The moment you slow us down, or do something stupid, you're on your own."

I began nodding my head. I'd agree with anything this woman said just to get her away from me.

"And stop nodding your head so much. You look like a freaking bobblehead."

My face flamed as laughter erupted. Gavin coughed and ducked his head, clearing his throat a few times to make it sound less like a laugh. I dropped my head and slunk to the nearest corner, perfectly happy to wait for them to finish dividing provisions without me.

Gavin caught my eye and winked. The floor could not swallow me fast enough. Remembering a movie scene Peter had shown me where zombies clawed their way through the floor, I instantly took it back.

Chapter 13 ☣

Sam paced as she issued orders. She had to practice in her sleep. I yawned and rubbed my eyes, just wanting to crawl back into my nice, warm sleeping bag and give the whole sleep thing another go.

I definitely hadn't slept well last night.

Jenifer snored, Sara kicked, and the guys in the other room—the room across the building, by the way—had been worse than little girls at a slumber party. It'd sounded like they were cracking jokes and wrestling, their loud guffaws and even louder bangs on the walls enough to keep me wide awake while Jenifer and Sara slept through it all. Even Sam's "*Goodnight*, gentlemen," had only settled them down for a couple of minutes.

I glanced at Peaches. A wide yawn split her perfectly makeuped face. So glad I wasn't the only one kept awake. I eyed the guys as Sam barked instructions, pleased they looked somewhat tired under all those self-satisfied grins.

"We need to get out of this city. We already know there aren't any other survivors here, so we need to move on. Coffey has deciphered a code from a military base not far from here, asking for any still living to converge on their location."

"Huh?" Sara's face twisted with the question as her eyebrows scrunched.

Sam glared at her. "To meet them there."

"Oh. Got it."

"And you trust it?" asked Jeff, his voice incredulous.

"Yes, I do."

"But they're the ones who started this whole mess in the first place!"

"I want answers, and we aren't going to get them sitting on our duffs in a locked room. This is our chance to find out what's going on and how we can stop it." Sam waited till the objections settled. "We need a bus of some kind—school bus, church bus, large van, something—anything that can hold all of us and is still working. We'll take shifts driving. It's about a full day's drive from here, nonstop."

I interrupted. "Um, we came here because we heard a man on the radio asking for help." Sam looked bored, like she couldn't wait to start talking again. "KRWZ 80.5. Does anyone know where that station is?"

"Already been there. The guy's been turned. I need a couple two-to-three man teams to locate any working vehicles and—"

"What? How?"

Sam's annoyance flashed. Maybe interrupting her again wasn't the wisest choice…

"By doing some reconnaissance and bringing back the working vehicles, topped off with gas."

"No, how was he turned? How did they get to him?"

She sighed. "Do we really need to discuss this right now?"

I crossed my arms and stood, facing her defiantly. "Yes, we need to discuss this. Right. Now."

She eyed me with a newfound appreciation. It was brief, but it was there. "They finally broke through the bulletproof glass and tried to eat him. Apparently they killed him too soon, and he's now one of them. End of story. Moving on. Perhaps you would be willing to raid the local drugstores for medical supplies?"

I nodded, sinking back into my chair, keeping my arms crossed for good measure. Great. That should be fun. Now they'd all get to see how well I handled zombies.

"Mr. Bailey, I need you to go to the three helipads in the city and see if there are any working aircraft."

"Wait! You're *the* Gavin Bailey?" Peaches stared at him with her jaw dropped, a fat wad of gum visible in her wide-open mouth.

Gavin gave her an easy smile and leaned one hip against the desk in the room. "The one and only."

"Get outta here!"

She continued to stare at him in wide-eyed fascination. Not that it bothered me, but, well, it did.

Gavin grinned at her and flexed with his arms still crossed. I rolled my eyes, slightly less amused this time.

She squeezed his arm and giggled. "I found my partner."

I glared at them both. Fine. That was just fine. If he wanted to do the town with the underaged drama queen, what was that to me?

Matt sidled up to me, trying not to look too eager. I nodded at him, and he nonchalantly beamed. Matt was on the short side—taller than me, but still, nowhere near Gavin's 6'2" height—stocky, fit, and far too good-looking. But I'd gotten used to and taken for granted the fact Gavin was with me throughout this hellhole. Apparently he'd only been with me because I was the only other living, breathing thing in the vicinity with no desire to kill him. Not till now, anyway.

I turned to Matt, eyeing his semi-automatic. "You do know how to use that thing, right?"

He grinned at me. "No worries, mate. You're safe with me."

My eyes widened. Australian. This wasn't going to be too terrible after all.

I glanced back as we were leaving the room to find Gavin staring after us with an odd expression on his face. I grinned wickedly and gave a two-fingered salute before we disappeared around the corner. I hope Miss Drama Queen turned zombie and tried to eat him.

I was growing angrier by the second. I seriously wanted to punch something. And I never wanted to punch things.

Matt and I had dodged zombies, gotten two packs full of needed medicine and bandages from a pharmacy, and returned without being chased or followed. We had done exactly what we were supposed to do and returned with what we were supposed to get.

Gavin and Peaches, on the other hand, had returned empty-handed, but they had battled zombies together. Each spewed glowing reports about the other person's bravery. They were telling the story, finishing each other's sentences, talking on and on about how wonderful and amazing and incredible the other person was. It was sickening. Really.

My fork rang sharply against the side of my tin dish. Matt eyed me with concern.

"You okay?" he asked in a low voice.

"Yeah," I whispered back, my voice full of misery.

Matt glanced between the merry couple and me, then silently went back to eating. They went on and on and on, Peaches taking every opportunity to brush up against Gavin or rub his arm. I could stand it no longer. I jumped to my feet, my loud voice echoing in the room.

"Anyone want me to do their dishes?"

Everyone went perfectly still as they stared up at me from their seats. Peaches mouth was open, story interrupted mid-sentence.

"Sure."

"I'm not gonna argue."

"You're just glad to get out of dishes duty tonight."

"Yeah, I am. Quick, give her your plate before she changes her mind." Karl jumped to his feet and started grabbing half-full plates. Sam glared at him, and he changed direction mid-snatch to take someone else's plate. A couple of people shoveled a few more bites into their mouths before Karl swiped their dishes.

Apparently the only thing more interesting than a zombie attack was getting out of kitchen duty. Well, I'd take it. I stomped into the kitchen with a pile of dirty plates.

I'd never considered myself to be the jealous type, but here I was, seething with envy over the stolen, misplaced, misguided, whatever, affections of a movie star. A movie star, for pity's sake! I could die any second, and I was acting like a besotted fan delusional enough to think her crush had been interested in her. It was just a kiss. Well, a few kisses. And one rather passionate one, at that… It didn't matter. It was *over*. And I was an idiot. What had I been thinking?

I heard the door swing wide behind me.

"Just put 'em there." I indicated with my head. "I'll get to them in just a moment."

I hoped the person intruding on my pity-fest wouldn't bother talking to me. I wanted to be alone. If that two-faced *actor* ever talked to me again…

"I thought I could help."

I spun around. Gavin held a few more plates, grinning at me as if he hadn't just committed high treason. Sudsy water dripped from my hands onto the floor. I spun back around, scraping off another dish and plunging it into the warm water.

"Just leave it on the pile there."

"You wash, I'll dry." He said it like there would be no argument. As if.

"Just leave it," I said through gritted teeth.

He took the dish I'd scrubbed and dipped it into the second tub of clean water. He dried it with a towel, whistling a cheery tune.

I wanted to strangle him.

"You're angry."

I rolled my eyes. *You think?* "That's ridiculous. Why would I be angry? What possible reason could I have for being angry? Huh? *Maybe* because Peaches is the world's biggest airhead and can't keep her hands off you? Or *maybe* because I fell for a couple of lines from the world's greatest actor and thought he might possibly be interested in me? But oh no! Find the first bimbo, and it's all a lie. A big, fat, stinking lie!"

I plunged the dish into the tub, and water sloshed. All over me. As in, completely drenched. I gasped as the warm water streamed down me from chest to toes, then stared at Gavin, mouth open. He was trying to be serious, but his eyes were starting to crinkle at the corners.

He could *not* be cute while I was mad at him!

"Great! That's just great."

I pressed the sopping dishrag against my middle in reflex, further soaking me. I have no idea why I thought that stupid thing would dry me off. I groaned and threw it into the bucket, spinning to find a dry rag. And slipped on the puddle of water I'd made. Gavin caught me as my feet flew out from under me.

We both noticed our audience at the same time.

"Show's over, folks!" announced Matt as everyone else scrambled back to the other room. Well, at least to the other side of the door, where they could still hear what was going on. I would, anyway.

I launched myself out of Gavin's arms.

"Let go of me!" I demanded needlessly, considering I was already standing a few feet away from him. I turned to march from the room.

"Wow! Hold on there, sister." Gavin grabbed my wrist. I wrenched my arm away.

"Let go of me! Right this very moment. I am warning you!"

I tried to break away but just couldn't. All of those bulging muscles really worked. He waited until I stopped struggling. He had my other wrist by then.

I stood perfectly still and said in my most calm voice, "What is it that you wanted to say?"

"That's better."

He pulled me to sit beside him at a table. I bolted the moment he let go. He quickly grabbed me and plunked me on his lap, turning me to face him.

"Eek!" I shrieked. "Let go of me! I can't sit *there*! It's indecent! Let. Me. Go!"

"What are you, twelve?"

My anger exploded, and I tried to wrench my arms away again, causing me tons of pain and Gavin, none at all.

"I'm not letting go until you listen to what I have to say."

I continued to struggle. I fought until he pulled both of my arms straight out, and I fell face-first into his chest.

"Will you listen?"

I listened to his heartbeat and breathed in his amazing scent. I was weakening. I turned my head slightly and mumbled into his chest. "Only if you let me sit next to you."

I shrieked again as he lifted me and set me next to him as if I weighed nothing at all. He pulled me close to his side and kept his arm around me. I sat straight as a board and tried not to melt into him. He felt so good…

"Now, if I had to guess, and my guesses are pretty good, I'd say you're angry with me because I was Peaches' partner today, instead of yours?"

I opened my mouth, but he kept talking.

"And perhaps because of recent events, you feel somewhat betrayed by me because someone else recently betrayed your trust, is that it?"

I opened my mouth again, but nothing came out. Dang it. He was right. I slumped against him. "I wondered why I freaked out so badly after one lousy kiss."

He wrapped both arms around me. "Oh, so it was lousy now, was it?"

I elbowed him in the side. He kissed my forehead.

"I just want you to know nothing happened."

"It didn't sound like 'nothing' happened," I teased, a bit petulantly. I wasn't going to give in *that* easily.

"Well, nothing happened like what's been happening between you and me. I meant what I said."

"That I drive you crazy?"

"Most definitely. And I want to get to know you better. Much better." He held me for a while before asking, "Are we good?"

"Mm-hmm." Staying angry just wasn't working. I was enjoying being held by him so very much. I never wanted it to end. "Just as long as I don't have to hear anything more about your wonderful, glorious, amazing day with Peaches the magnificent."

I could hear the smile in his voice. "Agreed. Are you going to freak out if they pair me with Jenifer or Sara tomorrow?"

"Most definitely." He pulled back and looked at me askance. "But mostly if you are paired up with Sam." I lowered my voice. "She's the scariest person I've met in my life!"

Gavin grinned at me. "You run a close second when you're mad." His usually jovial face turned serious, and my heart dropped as I waited to hear what he had to say. "By the way, I wanted to say how impressed I am with you."

"With me?" I squeaked, not daring to believe those words had just come out of his mouth.

"Yeah. Matt told me how well you did today, and I haven't had a chance to tell you how well you fought when we first found this place. I was impressed you fought instead of falling to pieces."

A stupid grin stretched my mouth wide. Praise from Gavin Bailey? I could die a happy woman. I mean, live. I could *live* a happy woman.

I lifted my bandaged arm before I got too giddy. "You mean, before this happened."

"Yeah, well, that was kinda understandable." He stood to leave, then sat back down next to me. "Oh yeah, one more thing. The way to handle Sam? Don't back down. Get in her face when she gets in yours. I think you'll soon earn her respect."

I nodded, my serious look matching his. *Fat chance, buddy.* If she didn't act like an irate pit bull every time I got near her, I might give that a go. But at least I tried to look like I was considering it.

His signature grin crawled back across his face. "How about one little kiss? You know, to prove I'm not mad at you for ditching me for

Matt?"

"Oh! You!"

Reaching behind me, I sloshed the wet rag out of the dishpan and onto Gavin's neck. He jumped up and caught me before I could escape. He doused the rag in the water again and squeezed it over my head. I squealed and giggled—yes, giggled. I'm not proud of it, but it happened.

He pulled me to him and dropped the rag in the bucket. All mirth evaporated as he held me close and stared into my eyes, then at my lips. He lowered his head and gave me the sweetest, lingering kiss, then pulled away.

"It looks like we need a shower."

He stepped back and peeled off his wet, clinging T-shirt. He gave me a saucy grin before he turned and strode toward the door.

My eyes went huge. I tried not to salivate, I really did, as his perfect form walked away from me. He disappeared, and I squeezed my eyes shut. I wanted to follow him so badly. I plunked onto the bench, clinging to its edge until my knuckles turned white. No way was I going anywhere near that man and a shower together.

Chapter 14 ☣

"Come on, Candace. Sam's called another emergency meeting."

I stopped slathering Doc's ointment on my finally-healing arm and looked up at Sara's reflection in the mirror. She hung halfway into the ladies' shower area from the doorway.

"Emergency meeting as in, 'Zombies are breaking down the door—grab your weapons,' or, 'I'm power-tripping and want to boss you all around again'?"

Sara grinned and popped a sticky pink gum bubble. "Ding, ding, ding! And the winner is option number two!"

I laughed. "Thanks, but I just might skip this meeting." I waved to the mirror. "Tending my wound and all or something. Tell her what you like."

"No can do, buckaroo. Sam says we all have to be there."

"Fine." I sighed after Sara disappeared behind the door. I started wrapping my arm.

"Lookin' good!" Jenifer punched my shoulder lightly as she marched out of the room.

Sara popped her head back in. I jumped.

"Oh! Gavin said he needed to see you in the kitchen first. Something about something or other."

My heart skipped a beat, but I laughed anyway. "Something or other?"

She shrugged and snapped another bubble. "Wasn't paying attention." The door swung shut after her.

I laughed and shook my head, my stomach twisting itself into knots. Gavin and I hadn't spoken much since the shower episode—I wasn't avoiding him, I swear—but I could still barely think straight each time I saw him. It didn't stop him from taking a moment for me each time I saw him, no matter what was going on. Sam kept everyone busy.

But some alone time? I couldn't wait.

I grinned at the mirror as I pulled a long-sleeved shirt over my tank top. I couldn't wait to see him. Maybe he would kiss me again? I darted out of the room.

I stood outside the kitchen door. Should I knock?

Or would he think that was weird? Doubts pelted me. What if Gavin wasn't alone in there? What if he hadn't actually wanted to see me? What if he'd just asked how I was doing, and Sara took it as an invitation? Should I go in?

"Oh, for pity's sake!"

I pushed open the door.

No one was there.

My shoulders drooped. Must have been a prank. *Thanks a lot, Sara.*

An arm wrapped around my stomach as a hand clamped over my eyes.

I shrieked.

The person winced. "I thought I should've covered your mouth instead."

"Gavin?" I tried to turn, but the muscular arms wouldn't let me.

"Don't look. I have a surprise for you."

He pushed me to the far end of the room, toward a cluster of tables rarely used. I knew because I'd had to clean those suckers too many times.

He stopped. "Ready?"

For him to take his arms away? Never. "Sure."

He chuckled and dropped his hand. His arm stayed where it was.

I gasped. A birthday cake. Full of candles. I counted. Twenty-four. My eyes filled. "But, it's not even my birthday anymore."

He moved away and shrugged, lighting each one carefully. "I heard you tell Sara it all started on your birthday. I hadn't realized." He quirked a confused smile at me. "Even though Sara weaseled Peter's breakup out of you, even though he broke your heart on your birthday, you still didn't trash him. Why?"

It was my turn to shrug. "Wasn't right."

"Did you love him?" He sounded hesitant, as if he wanted to hear my answer, yet didn't.

"No. No, I didn't." My answer shocked even me. "I guess I was"—Desperate. Lonely. Afraid no one else would want me?—"I don't know. But I didn't."

Relief flooded his face. "But you didn't tear him to shreds. Why?"

"Guess that's how I'd want to be treated were the roles reversed."

He shook his head. "I don't understand you."

My eyebrows shot up, and I bristled. "Why? Because I didn't want to relive the most humiliating and terrifying night of my life? Because it still hurts like crazy Peter would dump me for no reason? That I believe you shouldn't talk bad about someone behind their back, no matter what? He's dead, Gavin. I will never get to ask him any of it. Why he even dated me in the first place. Did he actually even like me? Why he wanted me to move to that godforsaken town if I *embarrassed* him so much. What on earth Scu—Penelope had that I didn't."

Gavin moved toward me and kept trying to break into my tirade. I jerked away when his hand landed on my arm.

"Everything's happening so fast. I can't keep up. I don't know what we're doing here. How long we have to stay. Sam won't stop sending us, well, you guys, mostly, out on recon missions or whatever. Is this all it's ever going to be? I just want to go home, but I don't even know where that is."

Gavin caught my wildly flailing arms and pulled me to him.

I burst into tears. Started babbling. As usual. Oh, man. "I'm sorry. I shouldn't have said that—or, at least I shouldn't have yelled..."

"Shh. I'm the one who's sorry. I'm the one who shouldn't have said that. Here I was, trying to make it better, but I only made it worse."

I shook my head and hiccuped. He rubbed my back and shushed me with beautiful Gaelic words until I calmed.

I felt like an idiot. A big, fat, stinking idiot. Gavin was just being nice, and I totally went psycho on him. What was *wrong* with me?

"Happy birthday, Candace."

I laugh-sobbed.

"Sorry I ruined round two."

I pulled back, my eyes going wide. "You didn't ruin it. I did! I'm sorry. I shouldn't have freaked out."

He shook his head and grinned. "Maybe we can stop apologizing to each other and eat some cake? At least before it catches on fire."

I smacked his arm and eyed it. It was starting to tilt a little. But that wasn't from the candles, right?

"I made it myself."

"Really?" I squealed and threw my arms around his neck. "It's perfect! I love it so much. Thank you for thinking of me, Gavin."

He pulled back and stared deep into my eyes. "Here's to a wonderful twenty-four year old. May the rest of your birthdays be many, and far better than this one." His gaze drifted toward my lips.

I nodded and inched toward his lips. I wanted that kiss.

He leaned toward me. My eyes drifted shut.

The doors burst open, and I jumped, my eyes flying wide. Sam stood in the doorway, glare firmly in place. Seriously? *Now* of all times?

She grunted, hands on hips. "There you guys are. I called a meeting. Let's go."

She slammed into the doors on the way out, and I jumped. Again.

Gavin kissed my cheek. He trailed his fingers down my arm and clasped my hand tight. "Shall we?"

I groaned. "I guess."

"Blow out your candles first?"

My wish was simple. For the world to once again be normal. As in, yesterday.

He tugged on my hand, and I sighed as we made our way to the "conference" area. Sam's emergency meetings were getting old.

Sam pointed to the map littered with blue and red pins. "Here is the bus." She pointed all the way across the map to the edge of the city. "This is where we are." Her finger then indicated the heart of the city. "We need to get to the bus. We will split into two teams…"

"Are you serious?" I interrupted. "You've got to be joking."

Annoyed and curious glances—Sam sporting the most outraged, although Karl tried to match it—swiveled my way, but I pressed on.

"Why is the bus parked all the way over there, instead of out front? Didn't you say you wanted the bus refueled and brought *to* us? Not left halfway across the city, where we'll have to avoid thousands of creatures that want to tear us to shreds?"

"First of all," Sam returned. "There are over a million of them in this city—four million, if you're counting the surrounding area…"

I started to babble incoherently, but Sam talked right over my blathering.

"And second, there is no way we could make it out on a bus swarmed by millions of zombies."

"But—but we can walk out of here with millions of zombies chasing us?"

She needed to be admitted to a place with padded walls.

"We have a chance."

Sam turned her back to me and continued outlining our plans. Make that their plans. They could come get me after they had saved the world.

Matt's quiet voice rose out of the crowd when Sam took a breath. "I think we need to stay together as one group, Sam."

Sam paused and turned from the board. "Why do you say that?"

I stared in awe at the hint of respect in her tone. I didn't think she was capable of that particular emotion.

Matt shrugged. "Lessens the chance of leaving one group behind."

Sam stared at him, waiting for him to say more.

"Also, we're stronger together."

Sam nodded thoughtfully. She was actually listening to Matt? I wanted to throw my arms around him in a grateful hug—God love him.

Sam continued. "What if we moved through the city in smaller teams, staying together but making ourselves less noticeable that way?"

Matt stretched back and rested both hands behind his head. "That might work."

"Hey, wait a second! What about breaking up so at least one group has a chance of escaping if the other is captured? It's how we've always done it," Karl whined.

I wanted to shove that pen he was clicking down his throat. Matt interrupted my murderous thoughts.

"We should stick together for this one, watch each other's backs. We need to make it to the bus at the same time. If we did break into groups, the group who got there first might not be able to wait for the others. We don't want to leave anyone behind."

It was the most I'd heard the quiet, observant Australian say, and I had to admit, I could've listened to him all day. Common sense mixed with an Australian accent? Delicious.

Gavin must have noticed the dreamy look on my face. He elbowed me and waggled his eyebrows, looking between Matt and me. I blushed hotly and stuck my nose in the air, pretending to ignore Gavin. Unfortunately, when I turned away from him, my gaze rested on Matt, whose ears and neck were tinged pink. He apparently had seen our little exchange. I wanted to die. Well, actually, I didn't. Why did so many of my go-to phrases have to do with death or dying? I was going to think of a few new ones, as soon as I had time on my hands for frivolous stuff like that. When I wasn't so focused on actually *not* dying.

"Bailey, you and bobblehead are together." Sam nodded in my direction. "Jeff and Jenifer, stick with Karl." Both nodded, but Karl looked as if he were going to blow a fuse. He tried to get on Sam's team any chance he got. Sam ignored his sputtering. "Chris, Scott, Trevor. Doc, you're with Peaches, and Matt, you and Sara with me. We stick together. Keep your eyes on one of the other teams at all times."

Sam continued to direct how we were going to move through the city in small groups, all staying together, and somehow stay completely invisible to the millions of zombies we'd be walking past. Right…

I did not like this. Not one bit.

Here we had this safe, secure, un-zombified shelter, and everyone was so freaking eager to leave it and our zombies and go fight other zombies. How did any of them know this military base thing was a good idea? They had all kinds of technology. Let them find us.

A bunch of heavy-duty canvas packs were distributed, and everyone started dividing food and necessities, loading supplies into the packs. My bag hung limp in my grasp as my gaze traveled the room, watching everyone else work.

"Marshall! Load your bag! I have no problem leaving you here."

Karl and Peaches sniggered, but Sam smacked Karl. I wasn't sure why, considering how she treated me.

Unwanted tears stung my eyes. Overwhelmed by everything, I sniffled as I grabbed a few things and shoved them in my sack.

Matt grabbed my hand as I was tossing in the fourth or fifth can of beans. He shook his head, glancing around the room to make sure he didn't further embarrass me.

"Too heavy. Here."

He handed me a box filled with a diverse supply of provisions, casually emptying my backpack of the beans. He returned to his bag without another word.

Gratitude filled me as I saw the assortment, including toothpaste, deodorant, shampoo, and healthy foods I enjoyed way more than beans. I couldn't believe he'd picked up on that.

Gavin slammed his bag next to mine, making me jump. "Need help packing that?"

"Uh, no, I've got it. Thanks."

He spun a chair away from me and straddled it, watching me shove stuff haphazardly into my sack.

I grew more and more uncomfortable the longer he watched me, saying nothing. Hand frozen midair, I stared at him. He didn't say a word, just grinned and stared back.

"Is there something on my face?"

"Huh?"

"What are you staring at?"

"You."

What in the world? If I wasn't flustered before, now I was. Big time. My hands fluttered to my throat, then helplessly tried to find something constructive to do—except packing.

"Well, that's stupid," I mumbled.

"Come again?"

"I said that's stupid. Why in the world you'd want to stare at me…"

"Why? I'll tell you why." He leaned forward and draped crossed arms over the back of the chair, a lazy grin lighting his face. "I like looking at the most beautiful girl in the room."

My mouth hung open, mid-objection. Gavin stood and moved close, crowding my space. I backed up a step, bumping into the table behind me. He ran his hands up my arms, settling them on my shoulders. Gooseflesh followed the trail of heat left by his hands, and I shivered.

"I love the way your eyes light up when you have an idea or think you've figured out a solution. The richest chocolate in the world couldn't compete with the color of your eyes. Then your lips..." His thumb grazed my bottom lip. "Full and lush like a peach, and so ripe I want to taste them." He dropped a light kiss on my lips as my mind raced. Was he serious? "And your hair."

He tugged my ponytail loose, pulling out the bobby pins one by one. Self-conscious, I grabbed at my hair, once again bemoaning the fact I no longer owned hair products.

"A cascading waterfall of winding, curling black silk."

They did not pay this guy enough, that was for sure. He needed a raise. And to write his own script. It was romantic fluff, all lies, but I didn't want him to stop.

"Someone so small—you barely come to my chin—but such a fighter. Sure, you scream like a girl, and cry like one too, but you aren't going down without a fight. Maybe that's why I want to stare at you."

My jaw dropped, and a giddy smile lifted the corners of my mouth. I was sure my face was a few shades redder than it'd ever been in my life. I buried my face in his chest, embarrassed and speechless. He chuckled and wrapped his arms around me.

"Marshall!"

I jumped at the volume of Sam's voice, inches from my ear. I spun toward her, and Gavin released me. My foot caught on the table leg as I grabbed my chest and stumbled back. Gavin's hands steadied me, keeping me from falling over.

"I thought I said to pack."

"I was—I am—"

She grabbed my bag and shoved it at my midsection. A poof of air left my lips, and I hunched over, nearly dropping it.

"Fill it. Now."

She jabbed a finger in my face, then turned to make someone else's life miserable. The pack slid from my fingers and hit the floor with a soft *thump*.

A few were staring openly, looking back and forth between Sam and me. I got a couple sympathetic looks, and that did it.

Karl, at the next table over, was reaching for a can of creamed corn when I snatched it from his grasp. Hurling it with all my might, I launched it at an old computer monitor that was part of the room's décor. The most satisfying crunch of shattering glass followed, and I immediately held everyone's attention in the room.

Sam spun toward me, "What the…?"

Matt reached for the gun at his hip, ready for anything. Shock registered in his eyes when they met mine. Gavin, behind me, dropped his hands on my shoulders, but I shrugged them off. I glared at Sam, my chest heaving and my fists clenched.

Biting back a snide remark—it would have been brilliant had I been able to think of one—I spun on my heel and marched through the swinging door, heading for the bathroom.

"Marshall, get back here!" Surprise and concern tinted Sam's commanding tone.

Once the door whooshed back into place, everyone start talking. I heard the door open behind me, and I picked up my pace. I made it to the bathroom and clicked the lock, just as whoever was following me reached the door.

I slid to the floor and hugged my knees to my chest, burying my face in my arms. Everything caught up to me—being scared out of my mind, not fitting in, Sam's rudeness, Gavin's completely baffling attraction to me… I gasped in huge gulps of air as I tried desperately not to cry like a baby. Tears slipped down my face as I told myself for the millionth time it was all just a dream. Why couldn't it just be a dream?

"Candace?"

I said nothing, though I was surprised Jenifer was on the other side of that door.

"Candace, you okay?" She waited a moment. "Look, I know Sam's rough around the edges, but she does mean well. I'm sorry she yelled at you like that." Another pause. "Hey, can I come in?"

I wasn't sure I'd had a good enough cry yet, but I felt bad for keeping her locked out of the bathroom when she clearly wanted in. I mean, what if she really needed to use it or something? The guilt built until I finally reached up and slid open the lock. I scooted out of the way of the slowly opening door and buried my face again.

Jenifer closed the door and sat beside me, saying nothing. I took several deep breaths—almost gagging on the scent of bathroom cleaner—and slowly blew out the calming air. I was so sick of crying over every little thing, but, well, it was how I coped. *Deal with it,* I thought rebelliously as Sam's disapproval echoed in my head. I heard rustling and glanced at Jenifer. She held out a small pack of tissues. I sniffled and took two, loudly blowing my nose.

"Better?" she asked.

"Uh-huh."

"Good. Let's get you back in there and get your bag packed."

We got up, and she handed me a few wet paper towels. I blotted my splotchy face. I took a couple of deep breaths, willing my face to return to normal instead of shouting to everyone, "Hey, I've been crying!"

"Do you really think Sam would leave me here?"

"Naw. Her bark is way worse than her bite. She really cares about keeping us safe, which is why I think she gets so testy. She honestly doesn't want to lose anyone else. Don't worry about it."

"I'm not, actually. I was kinda thinking it was a good idea..."

My voice trailed off as we left the bathroom to find Sam and Matt arguing, Gavin throwing in a word when he got the chance. Matt was upset, Gavin concerned, and Sam just looked irate. I shrank back from them all.

"Um, I think I'll just go back to the bathroom now," I mumbled and headed that way.

Jenifer propelled me forward. The girl had the grip of Tarzan.

"I'm not going to..."

"Do it, now! You..."

Sam and Matt stopped bickering as all three of them turned toward me.

Jenifer pushed me up to them and stopped, dropping her hand from my back. She stayed close, though.

Probably to make sure I don't go anywhere, I grumbled to myself.

I glanced at Gavin. Concern crinkled his forehead, and his eyes searched my face. He opened his mouth to say something, then snapped it closed, glancing at Matt and Sam.

Matt was angry, but his face softened when I looked his way. He didn't seem to like how Sam had treated me, either.

I glanced at Sam, but at her glare, my gaze bounced back to Jenifer and the guys. The silence stretched on until I wanted to scream. Jenifer cleared her throat. I looked at her, wondering if I should apologize. I opened my mouth to do just that when Matt and Gavin pushed Sam at the same time.

"All right, all right!" Sam scuffed her boot on the floor and didn't quite look at me. "Maybe I was a little harsh in there..."

Matt snorted, Gavin grunted, and Jenifer muttered, "A little?" under her breath.

"Yeah, a little. We aren't gonna make it out of here alive by being whining, sniveling little girls..."

Matt bumped her shoulder—rather roughly, I thought.

Remembering what Gavin had said to me earlier, I crossed my arms, shifted my weight, and stared at her, silently daring her to say what I thought she might be trying to say.

"But, well, that is...what I mean to say is, I probably...maybe... shouldn't have been quite so harsh on you."

My eyes widened, but I managed not to fall over. Did that really just happen? Maintaining eye contact, I raised an eyebrow and tried to look fierce. Not back down. Show the pit bull I wasn't scared of her.

A slight smile crept across Gavin's face, and he nodded his approval. I almost beamed at him, then snatched it back at the last second. Probably not the look I was going for.

"Thank you."

The words came out more clipped than I intended, but Gavin was right. I needed her to think I had more backbone if I wanted to earn her respect. If I could fool Gavin, I could certainly fool Miss Nazi USA.

"Fine. Are we good here? Let's go." Sam marched away. "Of all the stupid, ridiculous..." Her voice trailed behind her as she stomped from the room.

Jenifer and Gavin grinned broadly, and Matt smirked.

"I don't believe that just happened," I mumbled to no one in particular.

Jenifer shook her head, patting my shoulder before she left the room.

"Me neither, mate." Matt gave me a little salute before following Jenifer.

Gavin and I chuckled, then fell silent. "You okay?" he asked, once again full of concern.

"Yeah. I just want this to be over."

"I hear ya."

Chapter 15 ☣

One by one, small clusters of our team trickled out of the building, staying within sight of each other. Karl, Jeff, and Jenifer filed out in front of us.

"You ready?" Gavin whispered into my ear.

Shivers ran down my spine, and not exactly from his nearness. I gave an abrupt nod, and Gavin took off. I rushed to keep up with him, barely making it to his post before he bolted again.

This time when I reached him, he hissed, "Eyes behind! Eyes behind!"

I frantically looked back to see the doctor and Peaches catching up. I turned just in time to see Gavin take off once again.

"Good grief," I muttered as I trailed behind.

We kept up the ridiculous game for quite some time—dodging cars, racing around buildings, sprinting across streets—until Gavin halted behind a large, overturned garbage bin. I made it to his side, gasping for air. I almost ran into him when he didn't move right away.

"What—ah—what is it? Is—whew—are they moving?" I dragged in long gulps of air, resting my hands on my knees. And I thought I was in shape.

"Don't know," Gavin muttered. "Come on, come on!" he groaned to the group ahead of us, although they couldn't hear him. "Don't get separated from the rest of the group!"

I looked back at David and Peaches, who had questioning looks on their faces. I shrugged and turned my attention back to Gavin.

"What do you see?" I asked.

"They aren't moving. Why aren't we moving?"

Gavin was itching to go find out what the problem was. As much as I didn't want to stay here, just waiting to be discovered, I didn't want to rush into trouble, either.

I checked on the team behind us just as two gnarly, ashen hands reached around Peaches and pulled her from sight. My heart nearly stopped as her screams echoed around us. The doctor spun to help her, running around the corner.

Gripping my shotgun tighter, I bolted in their direction. Gavin passed me, sprinting around the corner before I could. Sam had warned us not to fire our weapons until we reached the bus, if at all possible. I heard two loud *thuds* as I rounded the corner and saw Gavin using his rifle like a club on two zombies latched onto David. Where was Peaches? My eyes riveted on a trail of blood leading into a cluster of bushes.

While Gavin was helping a badly wounded David, I clutched my gun and inched toward the shrubbery. Heartrending, guttural noises sickened me, and I pushed the blood-smeared branches aside with the tip of my shotgun, bracing myself. The noises stopped, and my eyes darted around someone's deserted backyard. Blood was splattered everywhere, but no Peaches. I hesitated, not sure whether to follow or run.

Just as I'd made up my mind to find her, she flew at me—her hands closing around my throat. I didn't even see her coming. I shrieked and dropped my gun, my hands covering hers. Blood streamed down her face, and her eyes were starting to glaze over. I stared in horror at her gnawed-up throat and shoulder, unable to look anywhere else.

We struggled. She was wild, trying with everything within her to get her teeth into me. With a cry and an unbelievable surge of strength, I threw her off and lunged for my gun. I yanked it up. She sprang at me. I pulled the trigger. She jerked back and disappeared, falling through the bushes.

I spun and bolted for Gavin. She'd be back any second. Gavin defended the doctor with all his might, trying to get him away from the two maimed dead people. I staggered to a halt. Something was wrong. David didn't look right.

Gavin downed the two zombies again and bolted for the doctor. He lifted David's arm around his neck and hurried him in my direction. I lifted the butt of my gun to smash the doctor's face, only it never made it. Gavin shoved my gun away just before I hit David.

"What the heck are you doing? Have you lost your mind? You could've killed him!"

Gavin's agitated voice buzzed in my ears, but my eyes stayed fixed on David. His head lolled to the side. When it rolled in Gavin's direction, he took one look at Gavin and opened his mouth. I raised my gun to try to hit him again, but, as Gavin blocked my weapon, he actually looked at the doctor this time.

He had only a second to react. He shoved the doctor's face away just in time. The former Peaches tackled me from behind.

I collapsed forward, then rolled to the side, dislodging her from my back. Gavin and I stumbled next to each other, putting our backs together to face each of our attackers.

Two loud shots resounded, and I cried out and dropped onto the cement. Both Peaches and the doctor sprawled on the ground next to me.

Jeff yelled, "Hurry!" and we bolted to our feet and ran. Jeff fired a few more shots while we caught up to Jenifer and Karl.

Karl was flipping mad. "Thanks a lot, guys! You just had to go help them, didn't you? Once they're attacked, you know they're as good as gone. Now we're miles away from the rest of our team, stuck in the middle of this God-forsaken city!"

Gavin punched him in the face, hard. Blood spurted from his nose as he fell back.

"What the—what did you do that for?" Karl yowled from the pavement while he held his nose.

Jeff stepped over Karl to speak to Gavin. "There's nothing to be done?"

Gavin shook his head and wiped his eyes, his shoulders drooping. "No, they've both turned."

"Hey, man, it's not your fault." Jeff grasped Gavin's shoulder. "You with me?"

"Yeah. Let's find our team."

Karl stumbled up from the ground as Jeff hurried down the street in what I hoped was the right direction. Karl scurried after him, Jenifer following. Gavin nodded for me to go next.

I took off after them, just as they ducked off the street onto another.

I rounded the corner to find Jeff, Jenifer, and Karl taking turns firing and swinging their firearms at advancing zombies. Gavin dove into the fray.

"Oh, come on. You've got to be—"

I never had the chance to finish. One staggered out of a building on my right and launched himself at me, his full, dead bodyweight nearly taking me down. I shrieked and wiggled out from under him—still on my feet—and whacked him as hard as I could with the butt of my gun. I lifted it again. Gavin grasped my weapon midair and jerked me away.

"Come on! There's an opening."

I bolted after him.

We twisted through the city, desperate to find the rest of our team. Gaining distance from the zombies, Jeff ducked into another alley, losing our attackers. He pulled up short, pointing ahead.

Chris, Scott, and Trevor were just ahead, their backs to us as they peered around a corner at the other end of the alley. Scott looked back as Trevor started to run. With a low shout, Scott called him back and waved for us to join them, his movements full of urgency.

The three guys took time to hug Jenifer and clap Gavin and Jeff on the back. Karl got a nod. I got ignored.

"Where's the doc and Peaches?" Chris asked.

Jeff sorrowfully shook his head. Scott doffed his hat, lifting it to the sky then covering his heart. We all stood in silence for a moment.

"Sam, Matt, and Sara?" Gavin broke the silence.

"Just ahead." Trevor nodded in their direction. "If we hurry, we can catch up."

Trevor waved for Jeff and Jenifer to head out first. They nodded, checked to see if they were clear, and took off, Karl scrambling after them.

Next, Trevor motioned for us to go.

"Are you sure?" I asked in a small voice, remembering what'd happened to the last group who'd been behind us. Not that it made me *want* to be the last group.

I think it was the first time Trevor or any of the guys on his team looked at me. Well, except for a brief perusal when we'd first been introduced. A hint of compassion entered his expression, and he nodded.

Gavin touched the small of my back and was gone. I raced to stay with him. The dodging, chasing, sprinting, running, feeling like I was going to hurl game started all over again. Just when I thought I was going to die—er, I mean, spew breakfast everywhere or something—I saw our entire group clustered ahead. We reached them, Scott, Trevor, and Chris not far behind.

After our joyous, totally stressed-out reunion, Karl asked the obvious. "So, where's the bus?"

Sam scowled at him. She turned her back on us all, looking over the debris we were huddled behind, and conferred with Matt in hushed tones. Hushed voices or no, I heard one phrase abundantly clear.

"It should be around here somewhere..."

"What? What do you mean, it should be around here somewhere? Don't tell me you lost the bus! How can you lose a bus?" Gavin clamped a hand over my mouth as my voice rose. He kissed my ear and waited.

Sam scowled at me. "We didn't lose it. It just isn't exactly where we thought it would be. No problem."

"What she means is—we're lost." Sara snorted.

I wiggled free from Gavin's embrace. "Don't you have a map?" I screeched in a hoarse whisper.

Without another word, Sam got up and bolted, her team close on her heels. Jeff's team followed, and Gavin nodded at Trevor to head out with his guys.

Gavin ran his hands down my arms and pulled me into a strong hug. He leaned back just enough to give me a really good kiss. I mean, a toe-curling, foot-popping, only-in-the-movies kind of a kiss. I melted into him, letting his nearness and strength calm me.

He pulled back far too soon, in my opinion, and gave me a devilish, I-know-I'm-amazing grin.

My wide smile answered his. Yep, I was falling for this romantic, incredible-looking movie star in the middle of a war zone, where more important things were happening at the moment…I just couldn't remember what they were.

He leaned in to kiss my neck and whispered, "We should go."

My eyes had been sliding shut, but they flew open at his words. Oh! Right. Zombies. I jumped up and ran past him—in the wrong direction.

"Whoa, whoa, whoa—hold on a minute." He lunged for me and grabbed my arm. "This way." He pointed behind him, a slight wrinkle on his brow and confusion in his eyes.

"Oh!"

I bolted past him, trying to find the group who'd left us mere seconds ago, though it now seemed like an eternity. He kept changing my direction, showing me the right way. Blast that man and his kisses! He had me so mixed up and turned upside-down, I couldn't remember which way the team had gone. And I'd watched them leave!

How am I supposed to be on the alert for zombies, I fumed. *If he has me sighing and simpering like an idiot?*

I plopped down behind our stalled group once more, my face flaming red. Once again, I'd acted like a two-year-old in Gavin Bailey's presence.

Gradually, the muted tones of our team penetrated my fuzzy brain. They sounded worried. Very worried. Fear overwhelmed their expressions. I turned to see what was wrong.

Directly before us—between us and where the bus was "supposed" to be—was a giant, milling mass of the undead. They were agitated and acting sporadically. I looked to Gavin with a million questions churning in my mind and ready to spew forth, but his gaze was riveted on the spectacle.

"We have to get through there," Sam insisted.

Jeff's look was incredulous. "There's no possible way around?"

Sam huffed and pointedly looked down the street to our right and left. "And risk getting lost again? There might be, but we have to go through herds of zombies either way. Plus, finding another way would take too much time. We don't have the daylight for that. The bus should be right over there. I'm not comfortable looking for another way when the bus should be..."

Sam thumped the map a couple of times. I craned my neck to see. A haphazard X splashed across several city blocks. The center looked like it was in the middle of a shopping mall. What in the world?

She kept talking. "We need to get there. Now."

"Should be?" Jeff prodded.

Sam bit her lip, worry scrunching her forehead.

"Guys, they know we're here."

We spun at Matt's voice. Sure enough, they were getting more and more agitated, searching, milling, bumping into each other. It was a matter of seconds before they found our huddled position.

I caught a glimpse of a familiar-looking jacket. I tugged Gavin's sleeve. "Gavin look! The zombie from the gas station!"

Gavin looked where I was pointing then back at me. "What?"

"The girl you shot a bunch of times so we could get gas!"

He looked again, searching longer this time. "Couldn't be. There's no way she'd be way over here."

"I'm serious. That's the same jacket the girl zombie from the gas station was wearing. Same hair, same face—everything! Could she have walked all this way?"

I strained to locate where I'd last seen the jacket.

Gavin sighed and turned me toward him. "Would it matter if it were? I doubt that zombie would have come this far, but yes, I suppose it's possible."

I looked back, trying to find the familiar jacket. It had disappeared. If that zombie had come all this way, there had to be a reason. Something didn't add up.

Sam's voice interrupted my frantic searching. She pointed. "Over there. We've a good chance of getting past them over there."

My eyes followed her finger. The sidewalk running parallel to the street was relatively bare. A wrought-iron fence separated it from the street filled with rambling creatures. Only a few zombies wandered around in the gated area, and Sam was sure we could clobber them as we ran by.

Yeah, that or get trapped in there with them.

I eyed the main thoroughfare once more. The other side didn't have a fence, so with a few hasty nods and grunts, Sam took off for the sidewalk, crossing the main road. Matt and Sara covered her back; Jeff and Jenifer followed close behind.

Karl hesitated, looking unsure. "That's not a very high fence..."

Gavin grabbed my hand, and we ran. I heard footsteps behind us and could only assume the four other guys were matching our frantic pace.

The zombies went wild. They clambered to the fence, trying to get over it. It was more a decorative fence than anything, and several of them fell over the chest-high barrier. Stumbling to their feet, they advanced, many of them too far behind to be a threat—at the moment, anyway. The loud report of gunshots echoed all around me, and the zombies on our side of the fence fell away as we sprinted past.

I could not take my eyes off of the pressing stampede of zombies. They gnashed their teeth, spittle flying as they savagely tried to get to us. The fence groaned as it started to twist and warp from the weight pressing against it.

Running down the length of the sidewalk, we rounded the corner onto another main road. The crush of zombies, now free of the barricade, hurried after us in a frenzied attempt to reach us.

We ran as fast as we could, gathering more pursuers the farther we went. Sam, still in the lead but barely, pointed to another road, and we veered toward it, the zombies behind us advancing, flanked by more and more zombies. The map flew out of her hand, whipping in the breeze and settling far behind us.

"Just leave it!" Sam shouted as we pressed ahead.

I started gasping for air, wondering how much longer I could run.

"The bus! I can see the bus!" shrieked Karl, bolting ahead. We matched his stride.

Screams echoed behind us.

"Don't look back! Keep running!" Sam ordered.

I couldn't help it. I looked back. Chris and Scott were nowhere to be seen. They'd disappeared into the crowd of rotting corpses, their cries cut short. Were we really going to leave them like that? I slowed. Gavin must've known I would. He was at my side, shoving me forward, not allowing me to slacken my pace. My heart dropped at the sheer number that'd joined those chasing us. I heard Jenifer cry out from my other side. I spun in her direction. In that split second, I watched the swarm swallow Jenifer into their midst. I immediately turned to help her.

Gavin spun me around and threw me over his shoulder. Straightening, he ran faster. How did he have the strength for that? We'd been running for what seemed like hours. Bouncing crazily, I tried to locate Jenifer, my discomfort nothing compared to the ache from losing three more of our team.

"Gavin, stop! We can't—we can't just leave them!"

Bolting on the bus, he dropped me onto the front row of seats.

Sara sat across from me, crying. Gavin grabbed an extra gun from Matt and blew away a zombie trying to clamber onto the bus. Karl slipped on before another zombie slammed into the open doorway. Karl fell into the front row of seats on top of me. Talk about disgusting. I didn't want scrawny, sweaty Karl Coffey on me—ever!

I shoved him hard, sending him sprawling as Gavin grabbed a bar conveniently located above the open door. He pulled himself up and kicked an advancing zombie in the chest, sending it and several others reeling backward. Trevor dove onto the bus, and Sam swung the doors closed with a *whoosh*. Grabbing the huge steering wheel, she punched the gas.

Exhaust fumes filled the bus as we swerved down the mostly open road before us. I jumped up and dashed to the back of the bus, staggering crazily down the moving aisle, straining for a glimpse of those we'd left behind.

Thousands of zombies swarmed after the bus, but an even greater number surrounded the area where our three comrades had fallen. I tasted bile as I watched the creatures pile on each other—claw at each other—shove others out of the way, trying to get their share.

I could only watch, horrified, as we left the teeming masses of the undead and our fallen teammates far behind.

Chapter 16 ☣

Jeff's frantic gaze tore around the bus. "Jenifer?"

Uncomfortable silence stretched between us, Sara's quiet sobbing and the roar of the bus engine the only other sounds. I didn't know what to say.

Jeff started looking between the seats, searching the bus for her. "Where is she?"

Tears streamed down my face as I recalled the way she'd disappeared into the crowd of zombies, my mind playing it over and over again like a feverish nightmare. Jeff looked at each of us. Gavin steadily met his gaze. Trevor wiped his face, dropping his head into his hands. I could see Sam watching us in the bus's oversized rearview mirror.

Karl wouldn't meet his eyes. Jeff grabbed his shirt's collar, yanking him out of his seat. Karl's feet dangled in the air.

"I said, where is she?" Jeff bellowed.

Karl opened and closed his mouth, but nothing came out.

"Put him down, man," Matt commanded in a low voice.

After too long a moment, Jeff shoved Karl back onto the seat. Karl stumbled and slid to the floor.

With an anguished shout, Jeff grabbed something—it looked like a baseball—off one of the seats and threw it at the window, cracking it. He slumped into a nearby seat and dropped his head into his hands. Tortured sobs filled the bus.

I looked over at Sara, who was bawling with her knees pulled to her chest and her arms clamped around them. Sniffling, I staggered across the aisle, plopped next to her, and wrapped my arm around her shoulders. She leaned into me and sobbed. She was going to have a major snot-and-tear-soaked spot on the top of her head from me to match the one she was currently applying to my jacket.

Sam and I locked gazes through the rearview mirror. She turned her focus back to the road ahead and swiped her eyes with her sleeve, not looking back again.

A dip in the road bounced me awake. I conked heads with Sara, who groggily rubbed hers and went back to sleep. I looked around the bus. Rapidly passing still-working streetlights lit the interior of the dark bus at intervals. Gavin sat slumped near the back, a scowl on his face as he stared out the window.

Jeff, a few rows in front of him, stared out his window with no expression. He hadn't moved since I'd fallen asleep.

I slipped Sara's head off my shoulder, and she settled onto the bench, curled into a ball. I stood and stretched, taking a moment to wake up. Hitting my shins on just about every single seat I passed, I stumbled back toward Gavin. There were going to be major bruises. I briefly touched Jeff's shoulder, but he didn't flinch or look my way. I gave his shoulder a squeeze, then moved on.

I glanced up, and my eyes connected with Matt's. His gaze was steady, asking me a question. I gave him a half-smile, hoping that answered whatever he wanted to know. I needed to get to Gavin.

I sank next to Gavin. Gavin didn't look at me either.

Settling against the seat, I waited, wondering if I should say something, take his hand, snuggle into him, something. Not that I was brave enough to do any of that. So I just sat there, longing to comfort him.

I jumped when his hand found mine. My gaze darted toward him, but he continued to stare out the window. My heart swelled with sympathy as I watched him struggle. Leaning against him, I wrapped my other arm around his waist. He pulled me close and held me tight.

I woke to daylight and a motionless bus. Gavin, snoring softly, still held me in a vise grip.

Lifting my head off his chest to look around the bus, I couldn't see anyone else. I didn't want to disturb Gavin, but I started freaking out just a little. Where had everyone gone?

Muffled voices reached my ears, and I strained to look out the window, still trying not to wake Gavin. I saw the top of Sara's head. Her arm shot up, and she caught a baseball, swiftly bringing it down and lobbing it back to the person who'd thrown it.

I wiggled out of Gavin's arms. He sat straight up and looked at me. I offered a sheepish grin, and he immediately turned and curled into the most uncomfortable position I'd ever seen a human being twist themselves into. He once again started snoring. Loudly.

Chuckling, I stretched and left the bus. Shielding my eyes from the bright sun, I arched my back and scanned our surroundings.

We were in the middle of nowhere. Sand and scrub brush stretched as far as the eye could see. Voices from the rest of our team reached me from the other side of the bus.

I sneaked around the bus, not wanting to be seen. Peeking around the front bumper, I watched our team play a lousy game of baseball. They were using a two-by-four for a bat. Sam had even been roped into the game, and Karl was trying, as always, to impress her. It wasn't working.

Jeff was the only one not participating. He was sitting on a crate under the awning of a dilapidated building, fingering his handgun. An old-fashioned gas pump rested behind him.

"Head's up!"

I ducked, and the ball slammed into the bus where my head had been.

"Sorry!" Sara called with a wave and a grin.

I returned a half-wave, slowly straightening.

They kept staring at me. I looked around, hoping there was something way more interesting than me they were looking at. No such luck.

"Oh, for the love!" Sam rested her fist on her hip and shifted her weight. "Think you can throw the ball back, genius, or is that too much to ask?"

I looked around, wishing I had the courage to throw the ball at Sam's face. I spied it next to the bus's wheel. I picked it up and halfheartedly tossed it. It fell not far from my feet.

Sara's smile slipped. Sam rolled her eyes and shifted her weight to the other side. The guys glanced at each other, then tried to look anywhere else but at me.

I picked up the ball, tossed it the air, and threw it as hard as I could at Sam. She plucked it from the air, a slight smile on her face. "Now, that's what I call a pitch." She tossed the ball to her other hand, shaking her hand to show it stung.

She jerked her head, and I ran to join them.

I was really getting into the game when Trevor hit the ball hard and fast too far above me. I lunged, but there was no possible way to catch it. I braced myself for the sound of splintering glass from one of the bus's windows but instead heard the firm slap of the ball hitting someone's palm.

The rest of our team was in front of me, so I spun to see who'd caught the ball. Gavin grinned at me, tossing the ball in the air and catching it. "You're really good."

"Th-thanks," I stuttered, still not entirely comfortable with his compliments.

"But how good?"

He reared back and threw the ball.

My arms and legs became a tangled mess of adolescent awkwardness. And I was *so* past that stage. I tripped while stumbling after the ball, and my face ended up where my hand should have been. With a loud *crack*, my world went black.

"Dude! That was the most awesome thing I've ever seen in my life! Did you see her head snap back? I've never seen someone out that fast."

"Shut up, Coffey, and get some ice."

"I'm going, I'm going! But seriously, you have quite an arm. That should be on America's Funniest Home Videos or something!"

"Yeah, the zombie edition," sniggered Sara.

"Karl..." The warning in Sam's voice was lost on him.

"Ha-ha! I won't forget that as long as I live!"

Karl droned on and on, and I wondered how long it would take for the pain to subside so I could hit *him* with a ball traveling at the speed of light.

"I knew it! The doctor should've at least stayed. We obviously still need him."

"Shut your mouth, Coffey."

"Like he had a choice," Sara muttered.

Huh? That didn't make sense...I must've been hit harder than I thought.

A slight moan escaped my lips as whoever held me shifted.

"She's waking up! Candace, baby, can you hear me?"

I should've known Gavin would be holding me.

Another groan escaped, and I slid my eyes open, squinting at the worried faces above me. Matt appeared with some ice. Sam plucked it from his hands and gently held it to my head. Even she looked worried.

I mumbled, trying to get my mouth to match my thoughts.

Gavin leaned close. "What was that?"

"Now I know I'm dreaming. Sam's being nice to me."

Relief flooded the faces above me, and everyone laughed.

"Thank God, she's going to be okay."

"Yeah." Karl snorted. "Even though you tried to kill her."

Embarrassment flooded Gavin's face in deep tones of red, and he hugged me to him gently.

I peeked over his shoulder. Trevor shoved Karl. "Take a walk, Coffey."

"But I just—okay, fine! If that's how you're gonna be about it." He walked off, grumbling something about how no one could take a joke.

Sam patted my shoulder and spoke to Gavin. "Let me know if she needs anything, K?"

"Sure thing."

The rest of the team trickled away, after making sure I really was alive and conscious. Matt's gaze lingered longest. I wasn't sure what to think about that.

I watched Jeff as he walked away. Though my brain was still foggy, I'd been reassured to see concern on his face, since he hadn't spoken or reacted to anything since he'd lost Jenifer.

He took up his post on the crate, fingering his gun once more. His face emptied of emotion, and his eyes took on a faraway look. Not good.

Gavin eased me to the ground. I looked at him to find tears pooled in his eyes. "Candace, I am so sorry. I never meant for that to happen."

He opened his mouth to continue, but I cut him off.

"Gavin, please, it wasn't your fault. I totally should've caught that ball. You had no way of knowing I'd fall over like a klutz and get smacked in the face. It's not like you were aiming at me. Forget about it."

He touched my face, slowly tracing my cheek and jaw with one finger. If nothing else snapped me out of the haze, that did the trick.

I sat up, dislodging his hand. Everything started to dip and spin, and Gavin grabbed me as I started to pitch over.

"Whoa! Hold on there! Take it easy."

I let my head clear before trying to sit up again. Gavin gently helped me, propping me against him while he leaned against the bus's tire. Resting my head against him while enjoying the bus's shade from the warm desert sun, I continued to watch Jeff.

"Do you think he'll be okay?"

Gavin took a moment to answer. "I don't know. I hope so."

"I didn't really see them together much. Were they—a couple?"

"Jenifer was his sister."

"Oh, man! That stinks. How did…?" I paused mid-sentence, my mouth hanging open. I faced Gavin. My head throbbed, but I pushed past the pain. "Gavin." I clutched his shirt. "Gavin…" My mouth opened and closed a few times as I tried to form the words.

Gavin's eyes widened, and he jumped up, pushing my feet apart and gently forcing my head between my legs. "You're white as a ghost! Take deep breaths. Breathe slowly. That's it, in and out, in and out."

Tears trickled across the bridge of my nose, running down my nose and dripping off the tip into the sand. "Gavin!" I gasped.

"It's okay. I'm right here. Just stay there until your head clears."

"It's not my head."

I tried to sit up, but he held me in place. He apparently wasn't taking any chances on me passing out. I struggled for a moment, then started to sob, hiccuping a few times.

"Gavin…my brother…what happened to my brother?"

With a groan, Gavin dropped next to me and eased my head onto his shoulder, holding me tight. "He'll be fine. You hear me? He's just fine. We're going to find him, and when we do, he will be perfectly safe."

"But, how do you know? How can you promise me that?"

"I just do."

"What about my parents? What if they…oh, Gavin!" I buried my head into his shoulder and sobbed harder. "Everything's been moving so fast…I didn't think…I never stopped to think…I just assumed they were okay!"

"Shh..." He buried his face in my hair and shushed me a few more times, adding a few strongly accented, Gaelic-sounding words. I had no idea what they meant, but they were comforting all the same.

I silently berated myself. With everything happening lightning-fast, one thing after another, I hadn't once thought about *my* family. How lame was that? "What—what about your family? Do you have any?"

"No." His clipped answer was interrupted by footsteps crunching in our direction.

"Hey, is she okay?"

Gavin nodded, misery filling his tone. "Her brother."

"Oh." Matt hesitated.

Jeff abruptly stood and marched into the shack.

Sara stared after him, then got up from her perch on the curb near Jeff's crate. She strode after Jeff, determination marking her footsteps.

Gavin nodded at Matt, and after a few moments, his footsteps moved away. Much slower this time.

Gavin rubbed my back until I calmed.

"Dear God, my brother...my family..."

It was the only prayer I could utter, and I repeated it over and over in my head.

"You'll see them again, lass, and they'll be safe. I know it," Gavin murmured against my hair.

I knew he was just being nice, but his words helped. They really did. I pleaded with God my brother would be safe, and His peace filled me. I don't know how, but I believed Gavin. It was going to be okay.

Chapter 17 ☣

We relocated to the shack as the desert heat grew more intense. Sara, looking worried, sat next to Jeff on a matching crate.

"How are you feeling?"

I looked up in surprise at Trevor and flushed. This made a grand total of two times the guy had ever spoken to me, and I was not thrilled at being the center of attention. Again.

"Um, fine. Yeah. Fine."

Matt approached me next, and I wondered if I could hide before the next wave of well-wishers assaulted me.

He pulled out an old chair, motioning for me to sit. I did so gingerly, hoping the thing would hold my weight. How old was this chair, anyway?

I jumped and sucked in my breath as his fingers found my goose egg. I stared at him with wide eyes, horrified. What was he trying to do to me?

He grinned apologetically. "Sorry, my bedside manner ain't the best, mate, but it'll have to do. Let's take a looker."

With that, he proceeded to poke and prod to his heart's content. Just when I was getting ready to tackle him to the ground and beat the living daylights out of him, he smeared cool, wonderful-feeling gel on it and lightly pressed gauze and medical tape to my forehead. If that didn't scream "wounded," I didn't know what would. Next, he grabbed a flashlight and shined it in my eyes, switching it back and forth between my two pupils rapidly.

I wanted David back, for more reasons than one.

"She'll be fine," he pronounced loudly.

"Glad you're here to tell us these things," muttered Karl from across the room.

Matt ignored him and kept talking, directing the next bit to Gavin. "I'll wake her up every fifteen minutes tonight for a couple of hours to make sure she doesn't have a concussion, but no worries after that. The swelling should go down in a few days."

"I'll do it."

I glanced at Gavin. I hadn't heard that particular strident tone to his voice before.

Matt shrugged. "Just make sure you do."

Gavin nodded, and Matt moved away to check on the weapons, looking relieved to be done with his role of doctor. He wasn't the only one. My head couldn't have taken much more.

I started to look around, once Matt was a safe distance from me. Some of our bags had been moved into the shelter, and Trevor had convinced Sara to join him at the decrepit ping-pong table in the corner. They were having a time of it, trying to get the collapsed, cracked ping-pong ball to sail between them, but they were making a valiant effort and laughing in the process.

The place looked like it'd been abandoned years ago, before the person who'd implemented sensory enhancements into movies had even been born.

The room was a mix of…everything. Dried tobacco lined the floor and wall near an ancient pot-bellied stove. I could picture old codgers sitting around it in rocking chairs, spitting and spinning yarns about the biggest rattler they'd killed yet. The ping-pong table was most likely constantly surrounded by young-uns traveling through with their parents on vacation.

A table crusted with years of use sat near the stove, probably having served hundreds of meals to hungry travelers. I'd like to think so, anyway. A thick booth that reminded me of a shortened bar from old Westerns served as a checkout counter, with snacks still resting on top of it.

"Wow," I muttered and moved toward it. The old-time candy wrappers were incredible. I hadn't seen packaging like that except in antique stores. And the old register was to die for. I mean, was to enjoy greatly while still alive. Forever. Not dying.

I started pressing keys, enjoying the fantastic ringing. I started fiddling with it, trying to get the old wooden drawer open. A musty smell drifted out of the register as the drawer slid open a smidgeon of an inch. I tried to pry it open the rest of the way with my fingertips.

The corner of a notebook under the counter caught my eye.

Abandoning the ancient cash register, I tugged the notebook from its hiding place and flipped through it. It was completely blank.

"Yes!" I said to no one in particular.

I tested seven or eight pens from the mug sprouting with them next to the register before I found one that worked. I started scribbling away.

"Whatcha working on?"

Gavin propped his elbows on the counter across from me and leaned in to see what I was writing.

I didn't even look up. "Writing down what happened so we can tell our kids how we won the first and *last* zombie war. Ever."

All conversation ceased, and I jerked my head up and stared at Gavin, horrified. His cheeks and neck were a dusky red, but a grin tugged at the corner of his mouth. My face erupted with heat.

"Oh! Not…not *our* kids…just…kids in general," I stammered. "You know, when people start having kids again, and the world is normal, and they want to know what happened and all of that…"

Glancing at everyone staring right at me, I buried my face in my notebook once more and slumped behind the register until I couldn't see anyone. Or better yet, until they couldn't see me.

Conversation gradually resumed—with laughter I *knew* was directed at me—and I pretended to write. Open mouth. Insert foot. As always.

Gavin leaned farther over the counter and dropped a light kiss on my cheek. I tried to ignore him while I pretended to be busy—scribbling nonsense without being able to write one blasted, coherent word. He straightened and ambled over to Matt and Jeff, striking up a muted conversation with Matt.

Karl abandoned his transistor radio and hovered at the end of the bar. I raised my chin, pointedly ignoring him, dreading what he was inevitably about to say.

"Hey, Candace," he whispered hoarsely, and none too quietly.

I ignored him.

"Candace! Hey, so you wanna make bobblehead Bailey babies?"

My fading face took on new life as it went neon red. Sara laughed aloud from her side of the ping-pong table. I stared at her in shock. Traitor. She looked ashamed—if only slightly—and coughed a little.

"Uh, sorry 'bout that." She focused on the deformed ball and rickety table before her.

I heard a *smack* and turned to Karl. Sam was walking past him to join Matt and Gavin on the other side of the room. Karl rubbed his head and stared gloomily after her before slinking back to his radio.

I grinned and ducked my head, praying I wouldn't utter one more stupid, ridiculous thing in Gavin Bailey's presence for the rest of my life. I traded the notebook for playing with the cash register. It could get me into way less trouble.

Sara laughed again when their warped ball crumbled into pieces. "Well, that was fun." She grabbed an apple from her bag and hopped on the table, making it sag and groan dangerously. And she was tiny. "What's the plan, Sam-I-Am?"

"First of all, if you call me that again, I'm going to shove that apple up your nose."

"Sure thing, Sam-I-Am."

Sam lunged for her, but she rolled off of the table backward, popping up on the other side. She laughed and kept crunching her apple when Sam made no move to follow.

"Second, we're going to stay here, hopefully only till tomorrow, until Coffey figures out where the base is."

"Wait, we don't know where the base is?" I stopped messing with the cash register to stare at her in shock. "I thought Karl had deciphered the location already."

Sam rolled her eyes. "I thought so, too, but the position seems to have changed when Coffey checked it again."

"Changed? How can the position of a military base change?"

"The base never changed, stupid, just where the transmission was coming from." Karl glared at me, not happy about being called out in front of everyone.

Trevor explained. "Karl was basing the location off of where the message was transmitting. Well, apparently what he thought was the origination point was the transmission bouncing off yet another tower, giving us a wrong location. Now he's trying to muddle through and find the right location."

"Didn't the base give its location? It was a repeating message, after all."

Karl glared at me. "Would you like to give it a try, hotshot?"

"No, thanks," I mumbled, returning to my way-cool register. Only now I'd lost interest in it, wanting just to be gone from this awful place to somewhere truly safe and, well, normal. "It's just..." my voice trailed off. I hadn't meant to say anything out loud.

"'It's just' what?" Gavin asked when I didn't continue.

I tamped down the rush of invading embarrassment and forced myself to meet his eyes. "Well, shouldn't the base be on a map? Or have signs leading to it or something? It just doesn't make sense."

Losing a bus, then a base, wasn't exactly strengthening my trust in the leadership capabilities of this group. Looks were exchanged before Sam spoke up. I wished they'd stop doing that.

"This isn't a base that's on a map. Most likely, we won't even know we're on it when we get there. It's a top-secret military base, and probably has some kind of front—a small town, a hospital, nothing but desert, something."

I looked around. "Like this place?"

Everyone stared in amazement at each other, all bolting into action at the same time.

"Sara, you check out…"

"On it."

"Gavin, look at the…"

"Already done."

"Trevor?" Sam looked around, but everyone had already scattered, testing walls, floors, the counter, everything. Gavin and Trevor headed outside.

Jeff remained on his crate. "You know it's not going to do any good."

"Even if this isn't the base," Sara called from under the table. "It won't hurt to look."

"That's not what I meant. Even if we find the base, it won't change anything. It won't bring her back."

Sara scooted out from under the table, moving toward Jeff, but she froze when he lifted his loaded gun, safety off.

"It's just a matter of time before we're all turned."

Sara's eyes went wide, her face white, as he slowly turned the gun toward himself. I'm pretty sure my face matched hers.

Sam marched up to Jeff and smacked the gun away from his face. He gave no resistance as she easily lifted the gun from his fingers.

"If you're going to shoot yourself, have the decency to do it outside and out of sight of the kid," she snapped. "We don't need a freaking zombie in our refuge."

She slapped the gun into Gavin's outstretched palm. I hadn't noticed when he and Trevor had come back in.

"Find anything?"

Gavin shook his head, still watching Jeff. "No. If this is a base, then it's definitely well-hidden. My guess is they would've received a signal from Karl and come out already if anyone were here."

"All right. Then our plans are still the same. Coffey tries to locate the base by finding where the signal originates, and we stay here for the night. Tomorrow we move, whether we find anything or not."

"Is it safe here?" I asked timidly.

"Safe as anywhere."

Sam nodded at Matt, and he stood near Jeff, keeping an eye on him. Gavin lounged against the wall, staying near Jeff as well.

I looked around. Sara had disappeared. I hurried outside, not wanting her to be alone. I circled the building but couldn't find her. I started to panic, then glanced at the bus.

Cautiously opening the door, I poked my head inside. I didn't see her, but I decided to look around anyway. Tentatively, I climbed the three steps and started down the aisle.

I heard muffled static the closer I got to the back. She was sitting hunched over on the back row, headphones blaring, angrily flipping through a magazine.

"Hey, you okay?"

She didn't respond. I nudged her with my foot. She jerked and looked up at me, surprise and fear lighting her face.

"Are you okay?"

She shrugged and pointed to her earphones, shaking her head and returning to her magazine. I tugged them from her ears. She lunged for them, but I pulled them out of reach.

"I said, are you okay?"

"Yeah, why wouldn't I be?" She stared at me defiantly, daring me to contradict her.

"Liar."

I plopped into the seat next to her, waiting for her to speak. Her confidence slipped, and she stared out the window.

"It's just—it's—I've never seen someone try to shoot himself before. I was—I was so scared he was gonna pull that trigger." She sniffled, and I rubbed her back.

"I watched someone do that recently."

Her head jerked toward me, her eyes huge. "You did? When?"

"The first day I found out about the zombies. A manager at the IMAX Dome Theater where I'm from—or, where I'd been living—the town I'd been temporarily staying at?"—her look said, *Move on*—"shot himself. Gavin tried to keep me from seeing it, but I saw enough. It was awful."

"Wow, I bet."

"I'm so glad you didn't have to see anything like that."

"Me too."

I waited a fraction of a second before venturing, "Especially someone you really care about."

"Yeah."

"Someone you…I don't know…like, maybe?"

Sara gave me a suspicious, sidelong glance before a sheepish grin broke through. "Yeah."

I thought so. The girl followed Jeff around like a puppy.

We sat in companionable silence. I really liked Sara. I didn't have to try to be friends with her. She put me at ease, something no one else on this trip could do. Except maybe Gavin. When we were alone, that is. Well, and only part of the time at that. When I wasn't making a complete idiot out of myself. Then I was perfectly at ease with him. Which was almost never.

"You like him a lot, don't you?" Sara interrupted my thoughts.

"Hmm? Who?"

"Don't 'who' me. Gavin. You get that dreamy look on your face every time he looks at you."

"No, I don't. What look? I don't even know what you're talking about."

Sara sighed and rolled her eyes. "Puh-lease. That look. That one right there. The one currently plastered all over your face."

She popped open a cracked compact and passed it to me. I stared into it, even though I didn't want to, but the only thing I saw was a blush-stained face covered with dread that a teenager was questioning me—a recently graduated college student—about my love life. I snapped it closed and handed it back.

Gavin poked his head through the still-open door. "There you guys are. Everyone was worried." He jogged up the steps and ambled toward us. "Whatcha doing?"

Sara giggled and poked me. My bright-red face flamed even brighter. Could this day never end? "Two can play this game," she whispered.

"Don't. You. Dare." I threatened, barely moving my lips.

Gavin paused a row in front of us and leaned his hip against the edge of the seat, crossing his arms.

"Nooooothing," drawled Sara, giggling again.

"Oh, I see how it is. Girl secrets."

"Maaaaaybe."

Gavin shook his head. "I don't think I want to know."

"We were just admiring your"—*cough*—"stamina while fighting, and bravery in the face of certain peril."

"That's it." Shoving to my feet, I tried to leave, but Gavin's body effectively blocked the entire aisle.

"Really? Tell me more." The grin on his face showed how much he was enjoying himself. At my expense.

"That really isn't necessary," I mumbled as Sara waxed eloquent.

"Oh, you know, Candace was just sharing with me how cute she thinks you are, and how much she loves your ripped muscles and your tight a—"

"All right! That's enough!" I hollered as I tried to push past Gavin. I did not need to hear any more of this. Gavin's ego didn't need to get any bigger. Nor did my humiliation.

Sara laughed and hopped over the back of the seat. "See ya."

She waved as she disappeared. Gavin still wasn't letting me past him. And, boy, was I trying. He leaned toward me, spreading his arms on either side of me, hands resting on the backs of the seats.

"So...you think I'm cute, do you?"

"Yes! I mean, no. Let me by!"

"No? Well, that's a shame, 'cause I think you're pretty cute yourself."

I stilled. "You—you do?"

He nodded and leaned closer. The stubble on his chin came into focus, and wowza, did it add to his charm. Scruff on a strong jawline? I sighed. Yep, I was pretty much head over heels for this guy. The dreamy look slid off my face as three words popped into my memory: bobblehead Bailey babies. I tried to push past him again.

He leaned in all the way, closing the gap between us and smothering me with a kiss. He stepped closer and wrapped me in his arms, deepening the kiss. My arms slipped around his neck.

As passion flowed between us, panic gripped my insides. I hadn't felt this way about another person before—not even Peter—and it scared the crap out of me. I had to get out of there. I turned us around and pushed him into the seat. Surprise and pleasure flickered across his face, and he reached for me. I kissed his cheek and darted off the bus, scared by the depths of my feelings for this guy.

Chapter 18 ☣

"You awake?"

I sighed. "Yes."

"Are you ever going to fall asleep?"

"Not with you asking if I'm awake every fifteen seconds."

Gavin shifted in the seat across from me and propped his head on one elbow. I had no idea how he managed to lie down in such a tiny seat.

"Doctor's orders. I can't believe it takes you so long to fall asleep."

"Oh, believe me, it's impossible to sleep, anticipating your questioning me every couple of seconds."

"Every fifteen minutes."

"Whatever."

I sat up and jammed my bag between the seat and window, using it as a pillow. I dropped my feet onto the seat in front of me. Trying to get comfortable, I wondered how long it would take my back to protest my sitting like the letter V.

Gavin took my seated position as an invitation to join me. He snuggled up to me and whispered, "I have the most interesting idea of how to wake you up."

Any hint of tiredness evaporated. Thoughts of my brother hiding snakes and spiders in my bed filled my mind, though I wondered if Gavin had something a bit more…enjoyable…in mind.

"Oh?" I asked nervously.

"Mm-hmm. And I can't wait to try it."

He leaned closer and nipped my ear. I scooted closer to the window. It wasn't that I didn't like it—I did—but all this romantic stuff was making me uncomfortable. I was enjoying it too much. And I had standards. Boundaries. Too much more ear nibbling, and I might just forget what they were and jump him.

Gavin leaned across me, bracing one hand against the wall of the bus. He bent close and stared into my eyes by the moonlight. My lips parted in their own invitation.

His lips met mine, and I began to lose myself. His kisses were so heady—so heavenly. He pulled my legs from the back of the seat and wedged me underneath him.

I bolted straight up, shoving him off me. I hadn't even let my boyfriend do that, and we'd been dating a year and a half. My shove didn't budge Gavin an inch, but he rose off me in concern.

"Are you okay? Did I hurt you?"

"No. Yes. I mean, no. I'm fine."

"Well, then, what is it?" Genuine confusion filled his eyes.

"I can't—I mean, I don't think this is a good idea."

His ever-ready grin was back. "I think it's perfect."

He leaned in for another kiss, but I held him at arm's length. He was never going to speak to me again, but he had to know how I felt.

"No."

"No?"

"No. Gavin, I don't do stuff like this. I like to think the man I'm going to be with will respect me enough to wait till we're married to get me pregnant."

Gavin pulled back. "You aren't on birth control?"

I flushed. 'Cause that came out exactly how I meant it. "N-no, I'm not, but that's not what I meant." I sighed and ran a hand down my face, not wanting to say what I needed to say. "What I guess I'm trying to tell you is I'm one of those crazy girls who wants to save sex for after I get married."

I cringed, waiting for the familiar "get up, leave, never speak to me again" routine. Well, except for joining Karl Coffey in making fun of me every day for the rest of my life. However long that was going to be.

Peter had just barely kept dating me after I'd told him the same thing. Probably the first warning sign he was going to ditch me for someone a bit more…easy?

Gavin sat up a little more and ran his fingers through his hair. "Okay, I guess I can respect that."

My attention snapped back to Gavin. *Really?*

A rustling noise from the seat in front of us made me freeze. Sara's head popped up over the back of the seat. "Oh my gosh, you're dating a nun."

I blushed and stammered, my words coming out more defensively than I intended. "Sara, you don't have to be a nun to wait to have sex with a guy who will fully commit to you by getting married first."

"Good on ya, mate," Matt called from the front of the bus.

I flushed as I realized we had an even bigger audience than I'd thought. Or wanted.

Sara rolled her eyes. "Whatever. All I know is, if Justin Bieber ever propositioned me in the back of a bus, I wouldn't hesitate."

I wasn't sure what to say. "Oh, well, that's sad," I finally mumbled.

Sara gave me a strange look before slinking back to her side of the seat.

Guess my grand total of allies had gone from two to zilch.

I picked at a loose string on the shirt I'd pilfered while we were still in the big city, not wanting to see Gavin's reaction.

"Hey."

"Yeah?" I still didn't look at him.

He leaned close and forced my gaze to meet his. "I can't say I understand, but I do respect it. I mean what I said. I want to get to know you better. And if that's so important to you, well, then it's important to me, too."

"Really?"

"Really."

I still didn't quite believe him.

He laughed. "I mean it. Stop looking at me like that."

The man could read me like a book. "Wow. Okay. Thanks?"

"Yeah, I'm awesome like that."

I punched his arm, giggling. Again. This had better not become a habit.

"One more goodnight kiss?"

I raised my shoulder in a half-shrug and lifted my face to meet his. Cupping my cheek in his palm, he lowered his lips to mine and gave me the sweetest kiss yet. He pulled back, then gave me one more before sliding back to his side of the bus.

I settled into the bus's seat with a sigh. That had gone much better than expected.

Karl muttered from near the front. "Thank God that conversation is over."

"No kidding," mumbled a tired-sounding Sam.

I think that was the first time I'd ever heard them agree.

Just as I was starting to doze, Gavin asked, "You awake?"

"Yes!"

Sara prodded me awake. I sat up, groggily checking my surroundings. I groaned when I saw I was still on the bus. I'd been dreaming I was at my parents' home the day my brother and a group of his friends had hog-tied me and put peanut butter all over my feet. Then they'd held me down while our dog licked it off.

Sure, it'd been kinda funny, but what was even more hilarious was sewing my brother's pajamas to the bed while he slept like a rock. He couldn't even get out of the bed or worm his way out of his pjs. He'd been furious. Best comeback ever. My parents hadn't exactly been thrilled with the big holes in the mattress—and his clothes—from his finally tearing himself free, and I wasn't exactly thrilled with being thrown in our neighbor's pond, but hey, it'd been worth it.

Determination to see my brother again swept through me. No zombie was going to keep me from it.

"Come on, sleepyhead. It's your turn to watch for zombies."

Dread filled my stomach as I stumbled after Sara.

She stopped and stared at me. "You might want your gun."

"Oh!" I ran back and grabbed my shotgun and revolver, strapping my newly acquired gun belt to my waist. Tugging on a sweater, I rushed back to Sara. I did a double take as we passed Karl. His butt was in the air and his mouth, open, drool dripping off the seat and pooling on the floor beneath him. Disgusting.

We stepped outside. The chilly night air was refreshing after the stuffy bus, but I still pulled my sweater tighter around me.

"Any chance I can use the restroom first?"

Sara sighed. "Fine. But hurry, please. I'm beat."

I rushed by Sam, who stood, then sat back down when I didn't replace her.

Stepping out of the restroom with my gun raised, I hurried around the building. My eyes widened. Matt was waiting for me?

"I hope you don't mind, but I told them I could handle it till you got back."

"No problem. I was wondering who was gonna be my partner tonight."

He grinned and sat at the makeshift lookout positioned in front of the bus. The bus had been moved away from the old gas station so zombies could be spotted from most directions.

"Did Karl figure out where the base is located?"

"He thinks so."

I laughed. "I still don't understand how a base with a message, asking to be found, is impossible to find."

Matt shook his head. "Me neither, mate, me neither."

We sat in silence, both of us scanning the horizon in all directions. Occasionally, one of us would walk in a wide arc around the shelter, making sure the desert was clear in that direction, too. Most definitely my least-favorite part.

After one of my laps around the building—no way was I walking slowly, by myself, around a deserted building in the middle of nowhere—I hurried back to Matt, trying to act as if I hadn't been running.

He shook his head as I settled next to him, and I tried to pretend I normally gasped for air as though I'd been running a marathon.

"I have something for you." My eyes widened as he picked up a large hunting knife that had been resting on the seat next to him and handed it to me. "It might come in handy."

I took it reverently. It was beautiful. Running my finger down the wide part of the blade, I admired the craftsmanship before slicing the loose string off my shirt that had been bugging me for days now.

"Thank you. This is perfect."

He laughed. "That's not exactly what I had in mind, but it works."

"What did you have in mind, then?"

I tried to stick it in my belt without stabbing myself, but it was too long. Then I tried to stuff it in the holster with my handgun. Not gonna work.

Matt stayed my hand and passed me a black case and strap, lifting his pant leg to show me the one strapped to his ankle. He bent down to help me fasten it.

Nervous energy coursed through me. His touch was partly embarrassing, partly thrilling, but mostly just plain awkward. I shook the feelings from me. Peter's outrageous jealousy was not going to dictate how I treated other guys. Especially a guy who'd been nothing but a perfect gentleman since the first day I'd met him.

Guilt made an appearance. Peter may not have been the world's best boyfriend—and I may've had a friend in college who'd told me over and over again to ditch him—but I still wished he hadn't died. How sad.

I peeked down as Matt's fingers tightened on my leg. He pulled the strap taut and stuck a finger in the loop, making sure it wasn't too tight.

Man, was I thankful I'd gotten a chance to shave yesterday. In scary movies, the girls were always glamorous. Great hair, perfect makeup, still able to wear a tank top after days of no shaving…well, so I'd heard. I was beyond thankful I'd been able to shower just about every day since joining these guys. Showers were intense and short—no one wanted to be caught naked during a zombie attack—but thank God they'd been available.

"You know, in case you need to use it on one of the creatures."

"I don't think stabbing them will work, Matt, especially if bullets do nothing—" I squirmed under his penetrating gaze. "What?"

"Candace, you can only truly kill a zombie by cutting off its head."

He bent once more and showed me how to unbutton the strap with my thumb and yank out the knife without cutting myself.

"What?" I choked out. "Please, tell me you're joking."

Matt just looked at me.

"Oh, come on! Seriously?" I unbuckled the strap and shoved the knife into his hands. "Nuh-uh. No, sir, that's not happening. No way."

Matt sighed and gently passed it back to me. "I hope it never comes to that, but keep it with you, just in case." He stood. "I'm going to walk around the building again. You check the bus."

I darted around the bus and came back to our spot, not wanting to be alone in the dark. Thank goodness for bright moonlight. I tapped my foot, not-so-patiently waiting for Matt.

Although he didn't tear around the building like I did, I started to worry when he didn't show up right away.

"Uh, Matt?" I edged closer to the building, not wanting to leave my post or get too close to the dark shadows. "Matt? Are you there? Come on, dude, I really need you to answer me right about now."

He didn't answer. I inched forward but stopped. What if he were using the loo? That would be embarrassing. For me. But I hoped he would've had the decency to tell me he was going to be busy for a little while instead of leaving me alone, outside, in the dark, watching for nasty creatures.

"Matt, I mean it. Answer me right now!"

I heard pounding footsteps. I started backing up. Matt appeared around the corner, running full speed. "Get on the bus! Right now!"

I stumbled backward, then turned and bolted for the bus, running smack-dab into someone. I looked up. Make that something.

I shrieked and stumbled back. Tripping, I plopped onto the sand. Where had it come from? I'd just been around the bus and had seen nothing. No one had been there. I would swear to it. I glanced past the creature. A few more grotesque figures stumbled away from the desert toward our bus. I glanced back up.

The creature stared at Matt, then slowly dropped its gaze to me. Scrambling back, I slipped my handgun from its holster and aimed at the zombie. Without a change in expression, it dove on top of me. I fired three times, but it continued its assault, doing nothing more than jerking crazily with each bullet ripping through it.

I struggled, pushing its face away time and time again. Pinning my arms at my sides, the creature pressed away from me. I bucked and wriggled, but the thing was strong. My hair started to fall out of its ponytail, something that never happened when it had gallons of hair gel in it. It looked at my shoulder and opened its mouth. Just as it started to bite me—and I was too pinned to do anything about it—Matt kicked its face, and it flew back.

Grasping Matt's extended hand, I vaulted to my feet, and we dashed to the bus. Matt pounded on the door, and a groggy Karl pulled it open for us.

"Hey, guys, what's going on?" he slurred, stumbling a little.

Matt dove in the driver's seat and reached for the keys. "Where are the keys?" he shouted.

Heads popped up all over the bus. "Keys?" mumbled Sam.

"Yes, keys! You know, the things that make the bus go, so we aren't eaten alive by zombies!"

His rant was punctuated by smashing glass. The rest of the team dove from their seats, pulling their weapons. The large window in the back shattered, and the side windows began splintering and cracking as zombies grabbed rocks or tried to claw their way into the bus with their fingertips.

A frantic search for the missing keys began.

"But where did they come from?" I hollered. "There were absolutely no zombies, then, *bam*, there they were, like they'd popped out of the sand or something!"

"Just look!" called Matt. He was on his hands and knees, searching under the steering wheel. "Sam?"

"I left them in the ignition!"

The guys and Sam were busy playing "bop a zombie," trying to keep them from clambering through the windows. Sara and I searched everywhere. I reached up and held on to the door handle. That's when I noticed it moving. I looked up. The zombies were trying to peel off the bus's door.

As I held the door handle with all of my might, something glistening on the dash caught my attention. "Matt! The dash!"

Matt sprang toward the console, knocking off all kinds of papers and maps. The keys tumbled off the dashboard—right next to the grasping hands invading the bus's door.

Matt, Sara, and I looked at each other. I was the closest one, the lucky one blocking the other two from reaching the keys. Matt seized the door handle, nodding at me to get the keys. "You can do it, Candace."

Lightheaded, I inched toward the zombies. Their ghastly faces reflected the moonlight, and they grew more frantic the closer I got.

Sam yelled from the back, "I don't think we can keep them out much longer!"

The door started to splinter and crack. I leaned closer, finally diving for the keys. I grabbed them, but a zombie seized a handful of my hair, which had fallen completely loose from its ponytail.

"Ahhh!" Painful didn't even begin to describe the excruciating spasms wreaking havoc in my head, but I stretched my arm back and handed Matt the keys anyway.

He couldn't see what was happening to me as he still struggled to hold the door. "Sam! I need you to drive!"

Great, just great. I was about to leave a clump of my hair and probably half of my scalp behind.

"Um, busy at the moment," Sam called.

The zombie reacted in what I can only describe as glee as it pulled my head closer, opening its decaying mouth and trying to gnaw on my head through the glass.

I moaned and grabbed the knife strapped to my ankle. As I brought it within sight of the zombie, the zombie let go and fell back as another pushed it out of the way.

I paused for a moment, glad I didn't have to cut off a zombie's hand, before jumping up and grabbing the keys from Matt. I shoved them in the ignition, and the bus roared to life.

"Why is she driving?" moaned Karl.

He was going to complain now of all times? I glanced at the giant rearview mirror hanging over my head to see if he were serious.

"Oh man, now I'm really scared." Sara rolled her eyes and glared at Karl. "Would you rather stay here?"

"I'd rather someone else drive."

Matt chuckled but looked at me. "You know how to drive a bus?"

"Can't be that hard, right?"

I shifted into gear, then bounced through the sand and scrub brush until the tires found solid pavement. The zombies fell away from the bus, a few still clinging to the open windows. They were quickly dislodged.

"Don't hit the zombies with the bus," Matt warned.

I looked at him suspiciously. "I don't think running over a few dead people is gonna hurt a bus."

He shrugged. "Still, I don't want to take that chance."

There had to be something to this whole not running over dead people thing. That, or Gavin and Matt collaborated just to drive me crazy.

Chapter 19 ☣

"Where did they all come from?"

Matt shook his head as if to clear it, then looked at me. "Sorry?"

"Where did they come from? I thought it was bright enough we would've seen them."

"Yeah, me too, but look at them. They're all coming from the same direction."

I watched the zombies stagger across the desert. "That doesn't make me want to go the way we're headed."

Matt shrugged. "Might mean we're headed in the right direction." Matt squinted while we watched the zombies. "Crikey. Look at what they're wearing."

My mouth dropped open. "That's why we didn't see them at first!"

We looked at each other and spoke at the same time.

"Camouflage!"

"The military base!"

"Karl, get up here and use that radio of yours! We're closer than you think, mate."

Deserting me, Matt joined Karl at his radio, trying to interpret the squeals and blurbs coming through the static.

Gavin dropped lightly into the seat closest to me. "It looks like you and Matt the man had quite the time of it up here."

I laughed. "Yeah, it was pretty rough. I'm glad he was able to help me."

Gavin didn't say anything.

"Don't tell me you're jealous," I joked, giddy from the adrenaline wearing off.

He didn't answer. I spun around, searching his face before turning back to the road. "Oh, come on. You're joking."

"Maybe I'm not the best judge when it comes to relationships, but all I know is you were busy telling me you aren't that kind of girl one minute, then running off with Matt the next."

My jaw dropped, and my gaze darted to the rearview mirror. The roar of the bus engine ensured this remained our own private conversation—thank heaven.

"Are you kidding me?" I spun around to look at him again, taking longer to look back at the road. "Matt and I had guard duty together!"

"Oh, so it's Matt now, is it?"

I glared at him. "Do *you* know his last name?"

Gavin squirmed. "I'd feel a whole lot more comfortable if you'd watch the road."

I spun back to the highway. "And I'd feel a whole lot more comfortable if you chose a different time to talk about this than when I'm driving!"

"Fine."

"Fine."

"That's just great."

"Yeah, it is."

Gavin got up and moved away, muttering something in a thick, Scottish accent. I strained to hear what he was saying, my fascination with all things Scottish overcoming my ire for just a second. But only a second.

I heard his heavy tread pause, then return. Seriously? Gavin had the audacity to come back for round two? What was he going to say this time? That I was putting my friendship with Sara before him too?

A little voice warned Gavin wasn't Peter as I lit into him.

"And if you think for one second I'm the kind of girl who just drops one guy for another, well then, oh boy, you are sadly mistaken, buster!"

"Wow. I think I'm relieved I missed the rest of that convo."

My head jerked around. Matt. My face flamed to life, and I spun away. *Somebody end me right now.* I stared out the windshield, wondering what to say.

"Oh. Uh, I thought you were someone else."

Not the brightest thing, but it was something.

"I gathered that."

"I see. So, what did you find out?"

"Besides the fact you don't consider yourself a two-timer?" Matt chuckled when I didn't say anything. "I can kiss you, if you want, and give him something to really be jealous over."

My flushed deepened. "Um, no." The words stuck in my throat. Most awkward moment ever. "But, thanks. I think."

He chuckled again. "There's not a town on the map for miles. In fact, this road isn't even on the map from what we can tell. Coffey's sure if we follow it, we'll find our false front."

"Awesome."

Matt stretched and leaned back. "Well, I was gonna talk to Sam, but I think I'll give Gavin a run for his money."

I spun around and stared at him, my mouth open.

"But I do agree with Bailey I'd feel safer if you watched the road, not me."

I turned back, more embarrassed than ever. "You heard that? Was that all you heard?"

"Would you believe me if I said yes?"

"Not really."

"Okay then."

Matt changed the subject, talking about his hometown in Australia. I laughed. He flirted. I tried *not* to feel guilty. But if Gavin wanted to join us, he was more than welcome. I wasn't hiding a blasted thing. I peppered Matt with questions, and by the time he grew quiet, I wanted to visit Australia as well as Scotland someday. If safe travel were ever an option again.

I glanced back at Gavin once but found him glaring at me through the giant rearview mirror.

Swallowing, I tried not to look back again, vowing to apologize when we stopped next. It wasn't worth holding on to grudges, especially since none of us knew how long we had left.

Everyone else dozed as light tinged the sky. I squinted into the sunrise, trying to keep my eyelids open.

Matt had his crossed feet propped up on the railing, wide hat pulled low over his eyes. His hands were clasped over his firm stomach.

Glancing back, I studied Gavin for the umpteenth time. He'd fallen asleep fairly soon after I'd started driving, able to forget our little spat. I, however, had been replaying it over and over.

A ginormous yawn split my mouth once again, and I blinked rapidly after it ended. The bus drifted to the edge of the road, and I overcorrected, bringing it dangerously close to the other side. Someone else needed to drive. I glanced around, hoping someone would stir. Yep, all of them, still fast asleep.

I scanned the horizon. The flux of staggering zombies made it impossible to pull over and pass out myself. There'd been spans with just a few, but I wasn't comfortable giving even a couple of them a chance to tear me to pieces.

Matt stirred and dropped one of his hands onto the seat next to him. "What? Hmm?"

My grin was cut off by another yawn.

"I don't want to take over driving," he mumbled, trying to get comfortable once again. He sighed and dropped his feet off the hand railing by the bus's door. "Ok, fine," he grumbled.

He tipped his hat back and froze when he saw me watching him.

I grinned at him, delirious. "Thank heaven you were dreaming about being my replacement. I was getting ready to take a snooze right about now."

He laughed nervously. "Yeah, sure, some dream."

I slammed on the brakes, knocking almost everyone off his or her seat.

Groans and "What the—?" accompanied by a few choice words exploded all over the bus.

Jumping up, I tripped over the raised middle console. "Whoopsie! Sorry, everyone, didn't mean to brake that hard." I cackled like a crazy person and dropped onto the seat Matt had just vacated. I was out as soon as my head hit the bench. I didn't even feel the bus lurch away.

I was falling, falling. Into soft, ethereal butterfly silk. Or was it butterfly milk? Dr. Seuss was confusing me. I grasped for branches on the apple tree where I'd been reading my book, but they slipped through my fingers, waving goodbye to me. I waved back. Dr. Seuss stood on a creaky wooden ladder propped against the tree, watching me fall, still reciting line after line from the extended edition of *The Lorax*. I'd kept trying to read, but the man wouldn't shut up. Was I still falling? The branches and Dr. Seuss all leaned forward as I fell away in slow motion. A thought scratched at me. I wasn't certain, but did Dr. Seuss really look like a giant purple teddy bear in real life? I opened my mouth to ask him, then slammed into the ground and woke with a start. What the—? I looked up into Matt's concerned face.

"Sorry, mate. I didn't stop that fast, but you must've been right on the edge."

"That's okay," I mumbled, pulling myself back onto the seat. Probably payback for doing that to everyone else. I covered my head with my sweater, wanting nothing more than to return to the peaceful apple orchard. Minus the weird stuff. Voices floated and mixed above me. I just wanted them all to shut up.

"This has got to be it."

"It's not on the map."

"The signal is coming from around here somewhere."

Sara huffed. "Glad you figured out exactly where, Coffey."

"Hey, this is pretty darn good for how messed up everything was. And don't call me Coffey. It's disrespectful."

"Sam does."

"Okay, children, once you've stopped arguing, you can join us in making a game plan. Sound good?"

Gavin joined in. "We should check the hospital first. We might find a sub-level of the secret base, and getting some bandages and medicine wouldn't hurt, either. Most of our medical supplies were lost with the doctor."

"I've got my first-aid kit."

I peeked up at Sara displaying her red medic bag to a completely uninterested audience. Which included me. Tugging the stretchy fabric over my eyes, I willed them to go away and leave me alone. But their voices just got louder.

"What about the bus? Are we really going to leave it here?"

"We can't exactly drive it into the hospital with us. Besides, the base should be close."

"But, what if the base isn't here? We're gonna have to use some kind of vehicle."

"Jeff and I could stay here and guard it," Trevor offered.

I peeked through the gaps in the loosely knit material before squeezing my eyes shut. *Go away!*

Sam shook her head. "No. Too dangerous. I want us all together. We're going to need all the firepower we can get."

"What about food? We've only got a couple days' supply each."

"We'll find what we can. I'm sure the military base will have supplies as well."

"Yum. MREs."

I threw the sweater off my head. "All right!" No wonder their voices were so loud. They were standing in a half-circle around my seat. "Could y'all take this discussion elsewhere? I'm nowhere near caught up on sleep." I flung myself back down on the seat, tossing the sweater over my head.

Mumblings of "Sure," "All right," and "She doesn't have to be so grouchy," reached my ears as the voices moved to the back of the bus.

"Y'all? I thought she was from California."

Sara's comment made me chuckle before I dozed off once again.

Chapter 20 ☣

Someone was shaking me awake. Again. I grumbled and swatted at the person, smacking him in the face. I sat up with wide eyes as Gavin groaned and held his nose.

"I guess I deserved that."

I didn't say anything, shocked he was waking me, let alone speaking to me.

"We really need to get going. We've waited too long as it is. We need to find that military base."

I nodded, and Gavin stood after watching me briefly. He reached out to touch my face, pausing right before he made contact. Dropping his hand, he moved past me.

Jumping up, I grabbed my backpack with my toiletries in it. I was going to apologize to Gavin—right after I brushed my teeth.

Sam and Sara covered me as we took turns using the nearby bank's facilities. Deposit slips littered the floor, and I felt a momentary urge to peek in the open vault. Not that cash would do me any good right now.

The guys met us outside with armloads of sodas and ice cream bars.

I looked at Karl askance as he handed me a few. "For breakfast?"

"Yes, for breakfast. Unless you want a couple crispy hot dogs and dried-out old buns."

I stared at the ice-cold packaging resting in my palm.

"I can eat that for you if you want."

Karl swiped for it, but I moved the ice cream bar out of reach.

"No, thanks."

I cautiously tore into the packaging, not sure I wanted to start off the morning puking.

Trevor offered apologetically, "The convenience store still had a generator on, but only the ice cream bin and the cold case of sodas were working."

"And the hot dog spit," threw in Coffey. "Burnt to a crisp, they were."

Trevor nodded. "Everything else was dumped on the floor and smashed. Sorry."

I nodded and took a couple of bites, the sugary ice cream roiling in my stomach. I did not do well with anything sweet for breakfast—cereal, orange juice, pancakes with syrup. Gavin must've noticed the nauseated hue to my face, for he disappeared and soon returned with a box of Cheez-its—my favorite sinful snack food. I attempted a grateful smile and ate a couple of the orange squares, but my appetite was pretty much ruined.

Matt tossed me a couple of apples and bananas that he, too, had disappeared to get me.

"Thanks!" My smile beamed at him, and I tore into a banana, glad for some real food to start my morning. I froze when I saw the look on Gavin's face. Acting as if it were no big deal, I slowed on chowing down the banana. Feigning nonchalance, I tossed a couple of the orange crackers in my mouth with the banana for good measure, chewing with my cheeks puffed out like a chipmunk's. It wasn't the best food combination, but I hadn't meant to gush over Matt's gift and not Gavin's.

And I hadn't meant to start World War III, which was exactly what I'd done by the look of things.

Gavin glared at Matt, and easygoing, non-confrontational Matt crossed his arms and gave Gavin a "make my day" look. My palms turned clammy while I watched two of the most gorgeous men I'd seen in my life stare each other down. Over me. Me. Did anyone else get how crazy ridiculous this was?

The rest of the team watched with interest, having nothing better to do. Well, except Jeff. Besides jumping in to help when we were attacked by zombies, he hadn't paid much attention to anything.

Gavin took a step forward, and Matt straightened from leaning against one of the bank's pillars, arms still crossed.

"Okay." Sam interrupted whatever was about to happen, thank heaven. "Let's move out. The hospital is about a block down the street, and..."

Bang. The hollow sound came from the other side of the bus. We froze, all staring at each other with wide eyes. At least, I was staring at everyone else with huge eyes; they were checking weapons and inching around the bus.

I hurried to catch up, rounding the corner the same time as Gavin. One solitary zombie was running into the side of the bus—over and over again.

Jeff lifted his weapon, quickly downing it. The thing got to its feet and walked straight back to the bus, running into it again. Jeff shot it again, but it got up and did the same thing.

I looked at Gavin in shock, and he met my gaze. Confusion marred his expression.

"What's going on?" I asked.

"I have no idea."

Jeff walked toward it, firing again and again. The zombie paid no attention but kept getting up and going right back to slamming itself into the bus.

Sam called after him. "All right. That's enough. Jeff, let's go. Jeff!"

Reaching the zombie, Jeff fired at close range. It jerked crazily, then—yes, you guessed it—went after the bus, not Jeff.

Jeff started yelling and cursing, smacking the zombie over and over again with the butt of his rifle. Sam and Trevor ran to Jeff and dragged him away from the unresponsive creature.

"Snap out of it, Jeff!" Sam got right in his face. "I understand you've lost someone you love. We all have. But if you're going to get us killed, so help me, I will leave you here to fend for yourself. Anyone not helping the team is no longer a part of it. Understand?"

Jeff's struggle to calm down was apparent. He finally nodded at Sam.

"Good. Now let's move out, before that thing notices us."

My gaze darted among the members of our team. Did no one else find the zombie's behavior strange? As we trailed Sam, more banging reached my ears.

Hurrying across the street, we moved down a side road. We'd parked the bus close to the edge of the town, hoping it would draw less destructive attention that way. Matt rounded the corner first, Trevor bringing up the rear. I froze when I reached my motionless team.

Zombies littered the street before us, all walking in the same direction. Those who met obstacles pushed right through them or ran into them until they gave way—or didn't. They were all headed in the same direction: the way we'd entered town.

My eyes locked on to a female zombie to my right. She ran into the glass window of a store with a repetitive *thud*. The window shattered, and she fell headfirst into the room. I followed her, that stupid, curious part of me wanting to see what she would do. Peeking through the wide-open window, I watched her.

Stumbling to her feet, she walked methodically to the back of the room and ran into the wall over and over again. It was going to take her a while to get through that.

I felt someone behind me and spun around. Gavin was looking at her, too. "Come on. I don't want you left behind."

I nodded, warmth flooding me at his kind words. Now was the time to apologize. I searched for the right words, but my mind went blank. He finally grabbed my arm and directed me toward the group, which had started to leave. I stayed close to him, wanting to say, "I'm sorry," more than anything, but the words stuck in my throat.

We avoided the zombies, ducking behind anything we could find. The big, white hospital loomed before us, still a couple of blocks down the street.

Sara tripped and tumbled out of her hiding spot, falling right in front of an advancing zombie. Matt, Gavin, and I ran for her. The zombie tripped over her, falling face-first onto the pavement, before staggering to its feet and continuing down the road. Matt, Gavin, and I stared at each other, then down at Sara.

Another zombie walked behind us, running into Gavin's shoulder. It didn't even look our way.

"What's wrong with them?" I asked.

Gavin answered. "I don't know, but it's really getting to me."

Matt helped Sara to her feet, and she snorted. "Really? More than when they chase us?"

"Yeah."

"Me too," I added. "And I have no idea why."

A few more passed us. Matt stepped out of one's way.

"I have an idea. Instead of standing here and chatting all day, how about we get to the hospital?" Sam hurried past us, keeping her gun trained on each zombie she passed.

We rushed to catch up with her and the rest of the team. Racing up the steps of the sprawling building, we headed for the automatic sliding doors, and they noiselessly slid open.

Sam and Matt rushed in and waved us in when they determined it was clear—for the moment, anyway. I glanced behind me as I slipped through the doors and abruptly halted. Gavin ran into me.

"Hey!"

"Sorry," I mumbled as I stared.

He paused. "You okay?"

I nodded toward the street we'd just left. I could see most of the town from the elevated steps. Zombies, all in a trance-like state, were streaming through the town in the same direction, heading straight for the desert. Civilian clothing and desert camo mixed in a confusing array of colors.

Gavin hesitated a moment longer before he placed a calloused hand on my shoulder. "Candace, we really need to keep moving."

I nodded and followed him into the building.

Chapter 21 ☣

Sam quickly located the security room, complete with personnel badges and security cameras. The hospital appeared to be deserted.

"If this is a cover for the base, there's gotta be some kind of elevator that will take us to a sub-level."

I glanced at Sam sharply. "Is that a good idea? Possibly trapped underground with a bunch of zombies? What if it's not the base, and we get stuck in the basement?"

Sam didn't reply. She just kept pilfering things from the first pristine desk I'd seen in ages.

"Please hold all questions till the end of the tour. Thank you!" Sara snapped her gum and grinned at me.

"Very funny," I muttered, a tad on the grumpy side, as I looked for a better map of the place. The map in the lobby only told visitors where to go. I wanted to know where employees could go—especially employees with privileges.

Matt scooped up a fistful of badges. "Let's see where this takes us, ladies and gents."

He distributed the badges. I guess I was Dr. Richards today. Why had he left his badge?

Sara held up hers. "Hospital educator. Hey, look! I really am a tour guide. That's what they do, right?"

No one bothered to answer her, so I shrugged. I had no idea. Didn't faze her a bit. She started introducing us to the furniture.

"And this, ladies and gentlemen, is a hospital chair, and this is a hospital desk, and this…"

I tuned her out. I was so done. With everything.

"You coming?"

I glanced up. Apparently I was the only one in the room still. I nodded and followed Matt into the hallway. I tried not to lag behind, but I was getting really tired of running around lost, without a plan. Oh, sure, find the military base—that was the "plan"—but I wanted a nice little list of steps A through D. I wanted to know *exactly* where I was going and how this whole mess would end.

We climbed a staircase, opting to stash away a few medical supplies in case we didn't find the base.

"Hey, you guys, this is a restricted area. Maybe we'll find something here?"

Sam backtracked at Sara's voice. The sign stating the floor level had been splintered to pieces and tossed down the staircase. "Does anyone remember what's on this floor? What is it? The 4th floor?"

We all shrugged and looked at each other.

"Well, then. Let's check it out." Sam scanned her badge, and the lock clicked open.

I risked asking Gavin a question as we slipped through the doors. "How much longer do you think electronic stuff is going to work? Why is there electricity in some places but not others?"

Gavin dropped back beside me from our single-file line. He kept his gun raised to the side, scanning hallways as he answered me. "I'm not sure. It makes sense things like badges will keep working until there's a glitch. Then, without someone to fix it, it'll eventually shut down. We had electricity in the bigger city, except for the places where the linemen had fried themselves in the transformer boxes, remember?"

"I remember you telling me about it," I mumbled, guilt from being jealous over the adventures he'd had with the now-zombie Peaches assaulting me. It's one thing to wish someone would die; it's quite terrible when you actually get your wish.

"Here it seems like the power is out completely, but everything has back-up generators, making it even more likely the base is nearby."

"Makes sense. Thanks."

He looked over at me and gave me a roguish grin, but his eyes held a hint of seriousness. "You're welcome."

A noisy sigh from Sam interrupted the shy smile I was giving him. "Head back, it's just the..."

Sam's voice faded from my mind as faint wailing reached my ears. The cries were pitiful and sounded unlike any of the guttural noises I'd heard a zombie make yet. They were higher-pitched, and the voices blended together.

My feet moved of their own accord as I followed the noise. As I rounded the corner of the wide hallway, a bright light shining out of a large window caught my attention. I moved toward it in slow motion, my breath shallow. The wailing increased. I stood in front of the glass.

My eyes roved from bassinet to bassinet. The little bundles inside of them squirmed and kicked. Each little one's skin was gray and lumpy. Tears filled my eyes and streamed down my cheeks as I stared at their faces. Every tiny little baby was a zombie.

Anger such as I'd never felt boiled inside of me. I screamed a rage-filled battle cry and swung a wooden chair against the glass with all of my might. Not even sure where it came from, but it was now in my hands. Footsteps rushed up behind me as I hoisted the chair once more. It weighed nothing to me. I slammed it into the glass again.

The bulletproof window shook but held, not even cracking. The pitiful little cries increased in volume. I had to get them out. I had to save them. Something so cruel could not happen to someone so innocent and small. It couldn't. I heaved the chair once more. It froze in the air. I tugged, but the chair wouldn't budge.

Matt wrested the chair from my fingers. Gavin wrapped his arms around my waist and pulled me back. "Candace, we have to go."

"No!" I fought him. I had to get back to that window. He picked me up and carried me down the hall. "No, Gavin, stop! We can't just leave them. I can't stand by and do nothing. Please, I am begging you, take me back!" He didn't let go of me. "We have to—oh, Gavin."

I crumpled in his arms and sobbed. He adjusted his grip and carried me down the staircase to the floor below. We went through several doors before Sam led us to a room overlooking the front of the building.

"Bailey! Bring her in here."

Gavin carried me into the room and set me on a cool, smooth surface. I leaned against his shoulder and sobbed harder. He wrapped warm arms around me and tried to comfort me. I didn't want to be comforted. Someone needed to do something! I didn't even know I *had* mothering instincts, but here they were, raging over the injustice done to those so tiny, so innocent.

My cries rose in pitch and volume. I was having trouble breathing.

Sam marched over and yanked a syringe from the haphazard mix of medical supplies our group had snagged. Smashing a glass case in the room, she lifted small vials of liquid, reading the labels. I half-wondered what she was doing while I keened on the table, beginning to hyperventilate. She filled the syringe and stomped over to me, shoving it in my face.

"Candace, do you see this? It's a sedative. Pull yourself together, or I swear to God I'm gonna shove it in your arm so fast you won't know what hit you. Got it?"

My eyes widened as the syringe came into focus. I gulped in air and held my breath, trying to get my crying under control. I nodded a few times and started hiccuping.

"Fine." Sam marched away and shoved the syringe at Trevor. "Put this somewhere. We might need it."

The last thing I saw was Trevor placing a cap over the needle before I squeezed my eyes shut. Gavin gently pushed me back on the stainless steel table and whispered, "I'm right here, baby. You're safe. Shh."

I clutched his arm and looked up at him. "Gav-Gavin please. W-we *have* to do some-something. Can't we d-do something?"

I tried to say it quietly. Basket case or not, I still didn't want a needle the size of a pencil shoved in my arm.

He looked, his eyes sad. "There isn't anything we *can* do. Not yet. We have to find that base. They might have the answers we're looking for."

I nodded and curled into a ball, clamping my eyes tight. Silent sobs wracked my body as images of tiny little bundles screaming in terror played over and over in my mind. I had to do something. But what? What could I do?

Gavin stayed with me while the rest of the team left to raid other rooms. He rubbed my back, saying nothing, allowing me to sort through my feelings…to mourn. After my tears were spent, I just lay there for a while, staring at the wall. No one came back to get us, so I assumed they hadn't found the elevator. Or they had, and hadn't bothered coming back for the crazy girl.

I sat up on the table, rubbing my swollen, gritty eyes.

"Are you okay?"

I shook my head no at the soft-spoken words.

"Do you—do you need anything?"

I shook my head again.

"K. I'm right outside the door if you need me."

Gavin kissed my forehead and slipped from the room, letting the door ease shut behind him.

I took a deep, shuddering breath, and sterile hospital smells assaulted my senses. I let my head fall back. How much more of this did I have to endure? Things were spiraling out of control. From the tension between Gavin and me, to wondering what had happened to those I loved, to the bone-wearying pace we'd been keeping to stay alive, I was at my limit. Sliding off the table, I made my way to the large windows far above the rest of the little town. I leaned against the casement and did the only thing I could do. I prayed.

"God, please help me. I don't know what to do. I want to make this right. Ha. I don't even know what to pray. Just…help me. Please."

I waited. No lightning-bolt answer came. I sighed, heaviness resting on me. I tilted my head and glanced at the ceiling.

"All righty, then. I trust you."

My gaze skittered out the window before I turned away. I froze.

The zombies were still eerily walking in the same direction, but I could see even farther from my higher vantage point. I followed their progress, then looked where they were coming from, my eyes riveting on their origin.

"Um, guys? Guys!"

Gavin pushed open the door. "Candace? You okay?"

"Get Sam. I don't think we're going to find anything else here."

Silence met my ears, so I turned to see if he'd heard me. Gavin stood immobile behind me, and Sara hesitated right behind him. Trevor popped his head in the room.

"Find something?"

"Get Sam."

Gavin walked to my side and whistled low when he saw what I was looking at. "I think you may be right."

Sam came huffing in aggravation around the corner, followed closely by everyone else. "This'd better be good, Marshall."

"See for yourself." I shrank from her anyway, looking for any pointy objects she might be carrying.

Sam grunted. "Good work, Candace. Everyone, down the stairs and back to the bus!"

"But, wait! What about all the stuff we came to get? Did we get enough? Aren't we gonna try that key to see if the elevators go past the basement?"

"The base isn't here, Coffey, and, if my guess is right, Marshall found it."

I glanced back at the small-town airport, heavily gated with barbed wire everywhere. Way more than I'd ever seen at a regular airport, especially a small-town one. Bunkers peeked out of dips in the landscape.

"Explain to me why we didn't just drive around and look for the airport to begin with?" grumbled Sara.

"Because we saw the hospital first. Any more stupid questions? All right, let's go."

We filed behind Sam, Matt bringing up the rear. The staircase was still clear, and the hospital, too quiet. I shuddered as I recalled the infants' piercing wails, and Gavin placed his hand on the small of my back. Our eyes met, and I gave him a smile I hoped conveyed my gratitude.

I shook off the melancholy that threatened to overtake me once more, determined to find the base and with it, a cure. Sunlight streamed in the staircase as Sam burst outside, swinging her weapon in all directions. Matt caught up to her, and the rest of us rounded the corner of the hospital and crouched behind bushes. Sam and Matt conferred quietly between themselves, eyeing the main steps we'd used to enter the building. The zombies were still oozing by, not acting any weirder than any other zombie walking around in daylight, ignoring perfectly tasty human beings, all walking in the same direction. Sam briefly made sure we were all accounted for.

Sam darted first down the steps, Matt and Karl close behind. Sara, Jeff, and Trevor dodged Gavin and me. I took a couple of steps, then stopped. Something was wrong.

"What is it?" Gavin asked, close to my ear.

I shook my head. "I don't know. Something's…different."

Sam halted abruptly. Matt matched her move, but Karl ran into her. "Oops! Sorry." He grinned. He didn't look all that sorry.

"They've stopped moving," I said in a hushed voice.

"Sam?" Sara questioned.

"Well, her, too, but no, I meant the zombies."

"Thank you for that insightful bit of information. I was getting ready to ask Sam what was going on."

"Oh, sorry. I didn't realize. I thought you were asking me—"

"Quiet!" Sam's voice echoed around us, then faded into nothing.

My breathing grew loud in my ears as our group remained frozen on the wide-open steps of the sprawling hospital. Gavin slipped his arm around my waist and squeezed. I reached across my weapon and squeezed his forearm in return, holding on for strength.

We all jumped as one of the zombies howled in what appeared to be pain and dropped to the ground. Scattered howls echoed throughout the city. More zombies fell to the ground, convulsing and writhing.

"Move!" Sam shrieked, and we bolted.

Opting for the fastest way back to the bus, we ran down the middle of the street, jumping over and running around zombies. They watched us as we sprinted past, howling in ungodly tones. Some scratched their way toward us.

Rounding the corner where our bus was parked, we skidded to a halt. One of the zombies, standing between the bus and us, was grabbing his head and writhing frantically, looking as if he wanted to tear his head off of himself.

"Are they in pain?" I asked in disbelief.

"I have no idea," Gavin answered.

"Well, that doesn't follow any zombie lore I know," cut in Sara.

"And what makes you the expert?" Karl just had to pick a fight every chance he got, didn't he?

"Shut up, all of you!" Sam inched forward.

Another zombie convulsing on the ground grew still, then slowly stood. Those in front raised their weapons; Gavin and I checked behind us. The one in pain ran straight for the other zombie, grabbing him and tearing at his limbs and clothes, as if the motions would somehow stop the sensation in his head. The other zombie did nothing at first, not reacting to the other's frantic motions.

Then it slowly turned, looking at the zombie pulling at it. With a quick, jerky motion, the zombie grabbed the frantic one around the neck and lifted it straight into the air. The zombie kicked and struggled, clawing at the hand latched on to its throat. Suddenly, the zombie stilled, hanging limp in the other's grasp. The first zombie marched to a nearby storefront, slamming the zombie in its grasp into the glass window. It shattered, sending both tumbling through.

We edged forward, wanting to get past them but extremely curious about what would happen next. Okay, I was. I was the curious one. I think everyone else only paused because I was gawking like a freaking rubbernecker.

Both stood, facing off. They regarded each other, expressionless, and stood rigid and hunched over, arms dangling. Simultaneously, they lunged for each other. They took turns picking each other up and slamming each other into the walls, counters, merchandise.

"Does anyone else notice they're moving faster?" I stage whispered.

"Or that they're actually attacking each other?" Sara added. "I haven't seen them do that before."

"Does anyone else think we should get on the bus and get moving?" Sam darted past the shattered window, making a beeline for our poor, dilapidated bus. We scurried after her. One of us, reluctantly. That would be me.

I glanced at the window before following, and my heart plunged to my toes. The first zombie was staring after Sam in vacant fascination. The other zombie attacked it. The first zombie swatted it aside, clambering out of the window toward our group's retreating backs. The other zombie stumbled up and after the first, also getting distracted by our group. Setting its sights on Jeff, it staggered after him.

"Sam, watch out!"

I pulled up my gun and fired. I missed the zombie, but everyone in the group hit their knees. True, I was shooting in their direction, but I was a better shot than that. At least, I thought I was. I checked my sights, baffled at how I'd missed.

Both zombies kept going, running as fast as their awkward gait allowed. Which was pretty darn fast for some reason.

Shoving the gun away, I bolted after the zombies. The others scrambled to their feet and fled, but the zombies were gaining. Matt and Gavin slowed and looked back for me at the same time. I dove at the one right before it reached Sam and wrapped my arms around its legs, making it fall headfirst onto the concrete. It instantly recovered and turned toward me with surprising speed and strength. I pulled my knife, but Gavin tripped, knocking it out of my hand. The butt of a rifle came into view, and the zombie's head snapped back.

Matt pulled me to my feet and threw me over his shoulder, turning and running to the bus. My stomach protesting the jarring ride, I watched as Gavin smashed the zombie's face with his rifle once more. He snatched up my knife.

Once again, I got tossed onto the front seat right before Matt dove into the driver's seat. So getting old.

Gavin was the last one on the bus after he pelted the other zombie with a few rounds to slow it down. Another zombie slammed into the doors as they closed. Matt peeled away from the curb, revved the engine, and raced for the airport.

"What in the world is going on?" I demanded.

"I'm not thrilled with the new development," quipped Sam.

"No kidding," added Trevor.

"Hey, guys, take a look at this," Matt called from the front.

We scurried to the shattered windows.

Zombies stood, looking lost and forlorn, staring in all directions. As the bus rumbled by, they blinked and stared at it. Breaking into a run, one by one, they loped after the bus. Their awkward, stiff gait would've been comical if it weren't so terrifying.

Matt floored the gas, driving as quickly as he dared. The bus's tires screeched around corners as the bus lurched from side to side, knocking us all off our feet. The engine revved as Matt accelerated.

Jeff fired out the window at a zombie.

"Save your bullets!"

Jeff gave Sam a dirty look before grudgingly acquiescing.

One of the zombies launched itself at the bus, grabbing hold of the open window and pulling itself up. Gavin lifted his rifle, but the zombie flew away with a blast before Gavin could pull the trigger.

Jeff stood across the bus, grinning.

Gavin marched over to him and grabbed his collar. "You try that little stunt again, and you'll have to worry about more than zombies."

Jeff shoved his nose into Gavin's face. "Is that a threat, actor man?"

"Knock it off, you two!" Sam wedged herself between the two men —an impressive feat, considering how fast the bus was barreling down the road. "Gavin, back off. Jeff, you'll get your chance. The zombies are the problem, not us, okay? Just calm down."

Jeff glared at Gavin, and Gavin matched his stare. Finally, Jeff relaxed his stance, nodding once at Sam while keeping his eyes on Gavin.

"Try not to shoot any of us, okay?" Sam turned and staggered to the front, not waiting for a response.

Gavin made his way toward me and dropped into the seat next to me. I clung to the seat in front of me, holding on for dear life on this crazy roller coaster masquerading as a bus ride.

I glanced out the window, then clutched Gavin's sleeve.

"Gav—" His name died on my lips. I stared in utter horror. A school bus lay on its side. A tattered little boy stood on the side of the bus, staring at us with a vacant expression. I could not tear my gaze away from him. His torn clothes revealed graying skin draped over scrawny arms and legs. Blood stained his ragged clothing. I saw no other schoolchildren, so I could only assume they were long gone or trapped inside the bus—neither option one I could think about long. His empty stare followed our progress until we rounded a corner.

Sara piped up from behind us. "There sure are a lot of families for a military base."

"There usually are," asserted Trevor, barely loud enough for me to hear.

Matt hit a curb, and we all bounced into the air with the bus, landing hard on the seats. Matt drove off the curb with a jolt, dodging more zombies. He pulled onto the main road. "Sam? You need to see this."

Sam got up from where she was also clinging to a seat and

stumbled down the roiling aisle. "Just drive through it."

"You sure?"

"Yeah."

"Everyone, hold on tight!"

Gavin grabbed my waist, shielding me with his body and bracing both of us against the seat. Matt sped up, and we slammed through the chain link fence I'd glimpsed before being shoved onto the seat. The jolt hit us hard, and the bus swerved before Matt regained control. Gavin sat up, pulling me with him. He kept his arm around me, though, and I leaned into him.

Gavin watched out the front window, but I glanced behind us. Zombies poured through the broken fence, falling over each other. Those that broke free ran after the bus but were quickly left behind. I looked around. There didn't seem to be any other zombies within the fence. Glancing back again, I stared at the figures falling far behind us, fear slinking like a snake down my spine.

Sam's voice fought to be heard over the roar of the bus engine. "Head toward that hangar."

"Um, guys, there's another fence," Sara pointed out dejectedly. One look at her face, and I could tell she was done with being thrown around like a rag doll. So was I.

"Look!" screeched Karl, making me jump. "Down there! The gate is open!"

Matt twisted the giant steering wheel, rocking the bus on two wheels, and barely missed plowing through the second fence. The bus settled on all four wheels, jarring my teeth, before squealing toward the opening.

Matt pulled through the gate, speeding ahead. The small-town airport look changed into military precision once we entered the second gate.

"Stop the bus! I'll close the gate so no zombies get in here," Sara yelled, peeking over her seat.

A chilling sound filled the bus. No way.

"Um, guys? The brakes aren't working!" Matt called over the roar of the engine as he pumped the unresponsive break pedal. "Brace yourselves!"

I dove for the ground, and Gavin dropped on top of me, protecting me with his body. He barely kept me from rocketing to the front of the bus under the seats as we crashed into the side of the hangar. The bus settled, sticking halfway in the hangar and half out. Gavin and I slowly untangled ourselves and staggered off the floor in time to see Matt and Sam race off the bus. The rest of us took longer to follow, but soon we were all standing inside the hangar.

Sam burst through the open door of the shelter, Matt close behind. I turned toward them in a daze.

"Gate's closed. It should hold them for a while. Trevor, Jeff, let's do a perimeter sweep. Make sure there aren't any more open gates."

Trevor and Jeff took off with Matt and Sam. They soon returned and were surprised to find us standing dejectedly around a solitary table in the middle of the echoing hangar.

"What is it?"

"There's nothing here."

Chapter 22 ☣

"What do you mean there's nothing here? How can there be nothing here?"

No one listened to me as Sam combed every inch of the building. She sighed. "There's nothing here, folks. Just a radio with a repeating message."

"That's what I said," muttered Sara.

Our group stared at each other, slumped shoulders following the pronouncement. We had come all this way. Gone through so much. Lost so many. Jeff roared in frustration and kicked the transistor radio against the wall, breaking it and silencing it forever. No one else moved, said anything, or even flinched. One by one, our motley group turned and trudged back to the bus crashed through the side of the military hangar.

"Wait! That's it? You're just giving up?"

"There's nothing here, kid." Karl looked at me in pity, anger sparking in his eyes.

"But, wait a second! This is a military base..."

"He *said*..." Sam softened her voice after a pause. "It's over. Let's go."

"No! Wait!" Everyone kept moving, not listening to me. Even

Gavin wasn't paying attention. "Listen to me! We can't just…we don't even…I said *wait*." I removed my revolver and shot it straight into the air.

They stared at me in shock, then Sam headed straight toward me. I tried not to flinch, but, well, I did.

"Put that thing away before you shoot somebody! I don't know what you're trying to prove, and frankly, I don't care. Get on the bus. Now."

"No! If you would just…"

She shoved me in the bus's direction. I whirled toward her, furious. I marched right up to her and got in her face.

"I will *not* get on that bus, and you *will* listen to me."

Sam folded her arms and opened her mouth. I cut her off. Surprise flickered across her face before she snapped her mouth closed.

"This is a *military* base. There are most likely hundreds of underground levels where they keep the super-duper secret stuff."

Sam's jaw dropped. "*Super-duper* secret stuff? Really? Did you really just say that? Out loud?"

"Never mind what I said! My point is there could be hundreds of perfectly normal people directly below our feet, with answers, and we might never even know about them because we gave up after a few seconds of staring at a radio!" My arms began flailing. "Why don't you use your brain and look for, oh, I don't know, underground tunnels!" I'd had it with this woman and her bossy, know-it-all ways. "Why don't you use your superhuman skills of bossing people around and make a smart decision for once? Why don't you—?"

"Okay, okay, blondie, we get the point. Matt, you and Trevor take Jeff and check out the area, inside this fence first, for anything out of the ordinary. Ventilation port, tunnel entrance, bunker—anything. First sign of trouble, get your butts back here, ya hear?"

"Sure thing, Sam."

"But I'm not even blonde…"

"Gavin, you and Sara help us dig out the bus and move it out of here pronto."

Gavin nodded, and he and Sara moved toward the bus.

"But why did you call me…?"

"Because you act blonde, genius. Let's move."

She breezed past me, and I only waited a second before I rushed to catch up with her. Being left alone in the hangar wasn't exactly appealing.

"Hey, Sam, check this out." Matt pointed.

I scrambled after Sam and Matt, covered head to toe in desert grit. The good news? The bus was out of the hangar's siding, and we could still drive it. Sans brakes. That would be the bad news.

"We didn't even see it until we rounded that hill there. We didn't find anything else. Not in this area, anyway. If anyone's still here, that's our best bet."

"Nice work, Matt."

"Thanks."

I craned my neck to see. A bunker, dug into the side of a hill, was nearly invisible until we stood before it. It sank into a depression and sat far back in a cave-like entrance.

I joined the guys at the face of the bunker. The pounding sunlight disappeared in the shade of the overhanging rock. They'd gotten the blast doors open and had already checked out the inside.

The bus slowly rolled up behind us, easing to a stop parallel to the sloping depression. Gavin and Sara climbed out and joined us. They looked as dusty as I felt.

"As far as we can tell," Trevor drawled, lazily shoving his thumb behind him. "You need some kind of code to get through that door right there."

We leaned our heads together to see through the doorway. A rectangular panel rested beside two stainless steel elevator doors.

"Let's check it out." Sam led the way into the bunker. "Coffey, watch the bus."

Karl sputtered and fumed as we filed past him. Sara ducked past with a shrug and a grin when he tried to grab her to take his place. He followed us and stood in the doorway, watching us instead of the bus.

Gavin handed me my knife. I tucked it away, avoiding eye contact in case he asked where I got it. He moved past me, and I breathed a sigh of relief.

The room was bare. We crowded together, staring at the panel—the only thing in the room. Sam inspected the door with Matt and Gavin. Not able to budge it, they starting punching random codes in the panel, causing it to flash red with every rejection.

"You need an eighteen-digit code!" yelled Coffey, trying to prove his usefulness. "Try the President's birthday and SSN plus one."

Pausing, everyone turned to stare at Karl.

"Or his phone number?"

No one blinked.

"Oh, for the love, I was just trying to be helpful!" Shoving his hat down on his head, Karl stormed out of the doorway, finally taking up his post of guarding the bus. And watching for zombies, I hoped.

We all turned back around, exchanging glances.

"Does anyone even know the President's soshe or bday?" grumbled Trevor.

Gavin shrugged. "I know his personal cell, but I'm not sure about his other phone numbers."

Our stunned gazes swung to Sara when she spoke up next. "And his birthday is August 4, 1961."

Sam interrupted the shocked silence. "Anyone want to surprise us with the soshe?"

We all looked at each other, waiting for the next person with totally random info to speak.

"All righty then, let's give this a shot."

Gavin rambled off a phone number, then Sara repeated the birthdate.

"You don't think it will actually work, do you?"

"Of course not. We're just trying to get attention."

Of course. I felt stupid for even asking.

Sam tried different combinations of the numbers, getting red flashes every time. A whirring noise startled us from behind the door. Sam motioned for us to get back. Sara and I competed for the "first one out of the bunker" gold medal.

Karl spun toward us as Sara and I burst outside. After seeing we were alone, a smirk touched his lips.

"Was the suspense too much for you? Maybe you should let the men handle this."

He strode toward the bunker, his stick-thin chest puffed out, but we stared past him with wide eyes. He froze when he realized we weren't looking at him.

The giant of a man standing behind Karl shoved his gun's barrel into Karl's back. "Drop the weapon, nice and easy now. Hands on your head."

The man's deep voice and camo uniform left no room for argument. Karl threw the gun from him and dove face-first on the ground, clamping his hands on his head.

"Don't shoot! Don't shoot!" wafted up from the sandy ground, slightly muffled.

Next, the man pointed his automatic rifle in our direction as two more military men emerged from nowhere to cover Coffey.

"That means you, too."

Sara reluctantly shoved her rifle to the side. Dust poofed as the weapon hit the ground. Pulling several handguns and a long knife from her belt, she tossed them aside and started to raise her hands. The man motioned to her leg. She sighed noisily and lifted her pant leg, revealing another gun and knife strapped to her ankle. I had no idea the girl was that loaded. She rolled her eyes as she huffed a few more times, like any good teenager, while removing her bounty. She sank to her knees with her hands on her head, eyeing the man defiantly.

I stood there completely frozen, staring at the massive weapon pointed right at me. I was incapable of movement. I'd never had a gun aimed at me before in my life—the trucker zombie did not count, mainly because he was not aiming, nor was he this close to me—and I had to admit, it was terrifying. I clutched my shotgun tighter, starting to shake.

"Easy. Easy now. Just lower the weapon to the ground."

My shotgun pointed harmlessly at the sky, but all I could think was my last few moments on earth would be spent experiencing searing pain as bullets ripped through my chest. I might not have watched many horror movies, but I most definitely had seen enough Rambo movies with my brother to be terrified of this bulky man holding an enormous military weapon to my chest.

"Just do what he says!" shrieked a hyperventilating Karl Coffey out of the desert sand and rocks.

The man opened his mouth to say more, then snapped it closed. He dropped the tip of his gun, swinging it wide, and raised his other hand. He stifled an objection from behind him with a sharp hand gesture and took slow, steady steps in my direction.

"I'm not going to hurt you, but I need you to put the gun down."

"Are you crazy? Do what the man says! Do you want to get killed?" squawked Karl.

Sara groaned and rolled her eyes. "You're just making it worse," she said in a sing-song voice.

The man continued to advance. He was no longer pointing the weapon at me, true, but now a man four times the size of Rambo, with enough face paint to be Rambo's cousin, was heading straight toward me. I backed up—right into the wall of the bunker.

The soldier reached me. He grasped my shotgun in a firm grip. Shaking, I clutched the gun for dear life.

"It's okay. I need you to give me the gun. Now."

I nodded but didn't release my hold. He tugged, prying it from my fingers. My hands hung suspended in the air between us, and I was certain I would faint at any moment. Maintaining eye contact, he nodded at the gun on my belt. I wrenched it from its holster and held it off to my side. He reached down and grabbed my wrist. My knees buckled, but the strong wall at my back kept me from falling into the man's chest. He slid his hand down and safely dislodged the weapon from my trembling fingers.

As soon as he'd secured my weapons, he nodded at his team. They clustered at the entrance of the bunker, watching their leader. He left me standing where I was but made sure I knew he was still watching me.

I sucked in a breath for the first time in what felt like an hour and sagged against the bunker. Oxygen snuffed out the dark spots invading my vision. Then I started to panic. Again. He hadn't asked to see under my pant leg. My knife was still strapped to my ankle. Beads of sweat dotted my forehead. I thought for sure he'd shoot me if he found out I was hiding a weapon.

My head jerked in the direction of the bunker. The soldiers were going in a few at a time, sneaking up on our unsuspecting team.

"Gavin!" I shrieked.

The leader snapped his head in my direction. I ducked, cowering against the wall of the bunker with my arms over my head, not waiting to see if the guy was going to strike me or shoot me. His boots stopped at the fringe of my vision while I stared at the ground. I squeezed my eyes shut.

"Way to go!" hissed Karl.

"Shut up, Karl!" snapped Sara.

Nothing happened. After what seemed an eternity, the boots crunched away. I slowly lifted my head, peeking out from under my arms.

A soldier rushed out of the bunker. "Bunker secure, sir."

Chapter 23 ☣

"What happened?" I whispered, my voice hoarse.

"I heard your shout and spun around to find soldiers rushing the bunker, yelling at us to drop our weapons. At the same time, the elevator door opened to more soldiers telling us to drop our weapons. We were surrounded."

I stole a look at the stoic faces surrounding us in the wide, stainless steel elevator. "They aren't going to hurt us, right?"

"I wouldn't think so. It doesn't make sense for them to."

"But, I mean, shouldn't they be glad to see us or something? We are, after all, the only other normal things around here."

Karl snorted.

"That's yet to be seen," mumbled one of the soldiers in the back.

I spun to look at him, surprised they were allowed to talk.

"Eyes forward." The soldier behind me shoved my shoulder, and I whirled back around.

The elevator slowed, and I readied myself to step out. We all swayed when it picked up speed—going sideways. I looked at Gavin with wide eyes. He grinned at me.

"Cool." Sara snapped her gum.

The elevator slowed once more before continuing its descent.

The doors slid noiselessly open, and we faced a long, white corridor. Two soldiers exited the elevator before us. I saw Sara pull out her wad and stick it on the spotless interior of the elevator. Disgust marred a soldier's face as he stared at it. Sara gave me an impish grin, and we exited before I could see what he did about it. If anything. They marched us at a brisk pace down the corridor, surrounded on all sides.

White lights flashed as we walked under them in the tube-like, spherical hallway. I started to get lightheaded as the lights pulsed and flickered. Gavin placed his hand on the small of my back. I tensed, then swung around to look at the guard behind me. He looked at Gavin's hand, scanned my face, then looked straight ahead. I checked a few more times to be sure, but it didn't look as if he cared Gavin was touching me. Shocker.

They led us into a gray room. Seriously, these people had no decorating skills. Gray ceiling, gray walls, gray floor—I wanted out. I started feeling claustrophobic in the small, bland room, thinking of how deep we'd traveled in the elevator. How far underground were we, anyway?

Two guards posted themselves outside the chamber before the doors slid shut on the other soldiers' retreating backs.

Jeff walked over to the door and tried it, just for kicks. It didn't slide open, and there was no way to open it from inside.

"What now?" I asked.

Everyone looked at Sam. "I guess, I mean, I don't…know. I wasn't expecting this."

"Maybe they need to test us first, make sure we aren't infected?" Sara questioned.

"Or, maybe they meant to infect everyone and are upset there are survivors."

"That's enough, Coffey."

"What? It's totally possible! They certainly weren't happy to see us."

The back wall slid open—a hidden door at the back of the room.

Several high-ranking officials entered, along with another squad of soldiers.

"So, these are the idiots who led the zombies back into our base."

We exchanged glances.

"Would you care to explain what's going on?" Sam asserted.

"We ask the questions here, not you. Sit."

There were enough chairs for us all, and I sank into one next to Gavin. The officers sat across the table from us, and the guards posted themselves behind us at intervals.

"I'm General Craig, and these are Lieutenants Blake and Jersey. How did you find us?"

"We deciphered a repeating message, asking survivors to come here," Sam answered.

Karl cleared his throat and shifted in his seat. I eyed him. Why was he nervous?

"Intriguing. Do any of you have a military background?"

"No, not that I'm aware of."

The general leaned forward, folding his hands on the gleaming table. "Really. How interesting. Would you mind explaining to me, then, why an encrypted military code, highly secret, brings an unsolicited—and unwanted, I might add—group of civilians to our door?"

Sam's jaw tightened. I, for once, felt sorry for Karl. He was most likely going to get shot as soon as Sam had her gun back. She leaned forward. "Am I to understand you're not looking for survivors?"

"Correct."

Sam looked down, anger flitting across her face. "Then what, may I ask, are you doing to fix this mess?"

The general's cool gaze met Sam's, a hint of humor lurking in its depths. "I assure you, it's under control."

"I bet it is," mumbled Trevor.

Thankfully, General Craig ignored him. He released Sam's glare long enough to shuffle through a few sheets of paper neatly stacked before him.

"I believe the Air Force is the branch you are looking for, Samantha Tidewater." His patronizing tone and amused gaze locked on to Sam once more. "They're in charge of finding surviving civilians."

I snapped to attention. "Uh…" Everyone glanced at me. Heat crawled up my neck. "I'm looking for my brother. And parents. His name is—"

"Not my department."

That little prick started in the back of my neck that said I was about to do something stupid. "But—"

"As I said, find the Air Force, then you can bother them with the unimportant questions."

My fists clenched. I considered strangling him, but never got the chance.

Sam took over. "How do you suggest we find them?"

"That's your problem." He smirked. "If you can get past our friends above ground, that is."

Sam shot to her feet. The soldiers pointed their weapons. Matt bounded in front of her. I tumbled onto the ground.

"Easy, Sam. We don't want any trouble. General, are you telling us there is nothing you can do to help us?"

"Once again, correct."

Matt blew out his breath and ran his fingers through his hair. Sam eased into her chair, keeping a frosty glare fixed on the general. Gavin helped me back to my seat as the soldiers lowered their weapons.

One of the lieutenants slipped General Craig a sheaf of paper. He raised an eyebrow and gave the man a questioning look. "Are you certain?"

The lieutenant nodded. "Acting Chief of Staff's orders."

Resignation soured the general's stern face. "We are relocating to a safer base of operations once transportation reaches us, one free of the —undesirables. I suppose, since you're here, we might as well take you with us." He held up his hand, stifling the hope springing to life on our faces. "It's a top-secret military base, not unlike this one, so we will take you to the closest Air Force rescue point. No farther, and not out of our way. Unless we can use you, of course. Am I clear?"

Grudging nods made their round in our group. My bobblehead tendencies may have taken over. It was better than getting left behind.

The doors behind him slid open once more, and a lower-ranking officer entered. At least, I assumed he was lower-ranking—he didn't have as many bar thingies on his sleeve or as many medals on his chest as the others. Whispering in the general's ear, he handed the general a message. General Craig briefly scanned it.

"If you will excuse me."

Leaving the lieutenants and all the other soldiers in the room with us, the general strode from the room. We sat quietly, waiting. The silence stretched on, but we started exchanging worried glances.

"What is that pounding?" Sara demanded.

The officers exchanged looks before answering. "It's coming from the areas that aren't secure. We only have control of a few of the levels down here."

"And you think it's a good idea to be this far underground?" I nearly shrieked.

"What was that about letting zombies into the base, then?" an indignant Karl sputtered.

"We had cleared the surface of zombies before you arrived. Breaking down our fence brought them right back in."

With how talkative these two were, I dared to ask another question. "How in the world did you clear them out?"

One of the officers shrugged. "The drug still affects them. They flock to extremely high-pitched frequencies, so we administered more of the drug and emitted the sound in the desert. All on the surface left. We were working on getting the ones down here out through the transport tunnels leading to the surface. We were drawing the zombies out when the drug wore off, and then you guys showed up, luring them back below."

The other officer cut in. "We were going to blow them up and trap the experiments down here, but the general wanted to secure the base for ourselves. We weren't sure how long it would last, but the drug wore off sooner than expected and changed their infrastructure once more. They came clamoring back."

The first officer continued. "They seem to be faster and a bit more crazed. It's fascinating."

"Fascinating?" Jeff choked out. "Don't cha think it's dangerous to keep experimenting instead of figuring out a way to get rid of them?"

Both officers clenched their jaws, and their expressions became guarded. I tried to get them talking. "Is there a way to stop all of this? To change things back to the way they were?"

Granite faces met my words. I tried once more. "How widespread is this? The general mentioned another military branch is looking for civilians. Are there many survivors? A way to look for friends, family? Please? Anything?"

The officers busied themselves with a couple of folders before them, effectively cutting off any further conversation. Tears burned at the back of my throat. Gavin reached out and clasped my hand, gently kissing the back of it.

The doors slid open once more, and the general entered. Chairs squealed on the concrete as we all stood, facing him.

"The helicopters are here. We can only take one of you."

"Take Sara, then," Jeff said with no hesitation.

Karl shoved Sara aside. "Take me. I'll go with you."

Sara's mouth dropped open.

Sam sputtered. "Are you serious, Coffey? She's just a kid!"

Karl ignored them and spoke directly to the general. "I have experience in communications and intel. I'm the reason we found this base."

Sara snorted. "In your dreams. We found the base in spite of you."

The general glanced at the other members of the team.

"No! I'm the one who deciphered the message, and I got us here. I can crack any code, anywhere, anytime, and decipher any message." His high-pitched voice rose even higher. "I will be your biggest asset. You won't regret it."

The arguing took on an otherworldly tone as I tried to grasp what the general was telling us.

Sam gritted her teeth. "Coffey, I'd hate to think you knew all along they didn't want civilians to come here, only military."

Karl ignored her, stepping forward. "I can be of service to you!" he screeched.

Gavin held up his hands in a placating manner, edging toward the general. "Hold on, now, we can work this out. Sir, if you are short on pilots, I can fly one of the helicopters if there is an operational one on base. That way, we all can go."

The general eyed him, interest lighting his eyes. "You're a pilot?"

Gavin nodded once, maintaining eye contact.

"Would you consider going?"

My heart plunged to my toes.

"Not without the rest of my team."

The general grunted in grudging admiration, and I breathed once more.

Karl shoved his way forward, standing between the general and us. "Give me a code, any code, and I'll break it for you. Need a new code? I'll make one for you in no time flat. I guarantee no one will be able to figure it out. I've worked with some of the biggest computer companies, writing unbreakable cryptic text for their software."

Matt spoke up. "General, please, take the kid."

Thoughtfully, the general regarded Karl. "No…no, I think we can use you. Move out!" he called to his men.

Gavin and Jeff stepped forward, and the soldiers immediately trained their weapons on us.

"I don't want to shoot any of you, but I will. Move out!"

Sara defiantly took a step forward as Karl turned to leave the room. "That's it, Coffey, turn your back on your team once again. Why don't you explain to Jeff before you go why Jenifer didn't make it on that bus?"

Karl twisted to face her. "Shut up! What do you know? You don't even know what you're talking about." He sneered.

"Yes, I do. I saw it from the bus's window."

My eyes widened, and Gavin and I stared at each other. I slowly turned to Jeff, praying he wouldn't do anything rash. Jeff marched forward, pressing himself into the barrel of a soldier's automatic rifle.

"What is she talking about?" Jeff ground out through clenched teeth.

Sara rushed on while she had the general's attention. "Way to go, General. You picked the one guy who'll do whatever it takes to save himself, even if it means sacrificing everyone else."

The general hesitated, looking Karl over once more. He shrugged. "Sounds like the kind of guy we need."

With a roar, Jeff elbowed the soldier nearest him, knocking him out cold. Gavin and Matt grappled with the guards closest to them, sending them crashing into oblivion as well. Gavin, Matt, and Trevor trained the weapons on the officers while the soldiers in the room slumped, unconscious, on the floor.

The general was the only military personnel still holding a weapon. After swinging his aim to several different people, his gun settled on Sara. Her face went white, and everyone in the room stilled. Swallowing hard, I stepped in front of her. Gavin made a noise like he was being strangled.

The general shrugged. "One woman is as good as another."

My rage fought with my fear over his words. The fear won. Having a weapon pointed at me twice in one day was enough to make my entire brain go to mush. Who knew I was such a scaredy-cat? Oh, that's right. Me. I did.

I glanced at Gavin. He was paler than I'd ever seen him, and he shook his head and mouthed the word "no." Returning my gaze to the general, I stood firm. Sara clutched the back of my shirt in her fists. She was shaking. I was about to join her any second.

"I am done bargaining. I will shoot her, and it will only be a matter of time before she tears each one of you to shreds. Now, put the weapons down and face the wall."

Our team exchanged glances as the soldiers on the floor began to groan and shakily stand.

Angrily, Jeff swiped tears from his eyes. "What does it matter? Either way, we all die. This way we make sure you die with us."

"Do not test me." The general's steely glare never wavered.

"Put the weapon down, Jeff," Gavin begged.

"Not until I know what happened." Jeff, closest to Karl, took three steps and shoved the gun's barrel into Karl's stomach. "Start talking. I know the general will leave you here if he has to."

Straightening his arm, the general aimed at my head. "One..."

"All right! All right!" Gavin heaved his gun away from him, placing his hands on his head. He desperately motioned for the rest of the team to follow suit. Sam slammed her weapon to the ground, furiously twisting to face the wall. Gavin did not take his eyes off me. The others dropped their weapons, and the soldiers quickly retrieved the guns. Jeff was the only one still holding his.

"Two."

Jeff threw the weapon down and grabbed Karl's throat. "Why didn't she make it on that bus?" he roared in Karl's face.

Karl began to sputter and gasp for air.

Sara spoke up from behind me. "He shoved her out of the way when he was trying to get ahead of the rest of us to get on the bus. She stumbled, and the zombies grabbed her. Karl's the reason your sister's not alive!"

I wanted to smack her. Why was she egging him on now, of all times?

"Three."

The report of a gunshot ricocheted throughout the room, and I felt all the air leave my body. My knees went soft, and I drifted toward the floor. But I didn't feel a thing. Was I in shock?

Gavin's strong arms came around me, holding me upright. He shielded me with his body.

My gaze riveted on Karl, who pulled Jeff's hands off his throat and stumbled backward. Jeff slowly sank to his knees, holding his stomach. Karl held a small handgun in his blood-speckled hand.

"Jeff!" Sara cried.

I struggled to breathe as it slowly sank into my brain I hadn't been shot. The soldier closest to Karl wrenched the weapon away from him and slipped it into his empty holster, looking disgruntled Karl had filched his weapon. The military personnel streamed out of the room, cramming into the elevator. The general gave us all a salute as the silver doors slid closed.

Karl reached the doors as they fastened, shouting, "No! *No*!"

I relaxed in Gavin's wonderful arms. I never wanted to leave. My lungs filled with oxygen as tears flooded my eyes. Clinging to him, I buried my face in his chest. Karl's cries filled the room, and I lifted my head to watch him. Even though he'd betrayed, abandoned, and practically tried to kill us all, a part of me still felt sorry for Karl.

Sam and Matt lifted Jeff, trying to look at his wound as Sara tried to embrace him. Jeff shoved their hands away, stumbling after Karl. Karl was still screaming, trying to get the elevator doors open. Sara slumped on the floor, crying. Sam and Matt stared at each other, then tried to subdue Jeff once more. He shoved them away, staggering after Karl with deadly determination. Growing horror spread throughout my body. Gavin held me tighter.

Jeff's gait grew slower and slower as he struggled to get to Karl. Jeff paused a few steps away, dropping his head. Karl turned. Taking one look at Jeff, he started to cry. "No, not like this. Please, not like this."

An eerie change came over Jeff's stance as he passed from a human being to another sort of being. He charged. Blood spattered the spotless walls as Karl's shrieks echoed down the corridor.

We moved as one toward the heavy door, prying it from the wall with our fingers. It closed inch by inch, filling me with terror. Karl finally slumped to the floor, a bloody, pulpy mess. The zombie lost interest as soon as the life left Karl Coffey's body, and it slowly turned toward us.

"I can't get it closed!" I shouted.

"Wait! I've got an idea. Help me." Trevor hollered.

He struggled with the heavy, stainless steel table in the room, and Gavin and Matt quickly joined him. Sam and I worked on closing the automatic sliding door. Sara still sat, limp, on the concrete floor. They slid the table out of the room into the corridor, blocking the door. They heaved chairs on top of and in front of it, hoping to slow the creature.

An air-release noise sounded as the zombie staggered toward us. The former Karl started to twitch. The door slid shut as the zombie reached our makeshift barricade.

"Now what?"

We faced the smooth back wall, the door the officers had come through earlier. Sam looked at Gavin. He nodded and hurried to the wall. Tapping until he found what he wanted, he kicked the wall until it gave way. He reached through the opening and grasped a tangle of wires.

Scraping chairs and clambering on the steel table reached our ears from the other side of the door behind us. Sara cried out and pointed.

Blood-covered and already graying hands pried the door open.

"Hurry, please," I whispered to Gavin.

Shooting sparks marked Gavin's success. The seamless door slid open, and Gavin stood in the doorway to make sure it didn't close. The door behind us began to creak and grind as it slowly slid apart. Two sets of hands clawed it open. I marveled at the irony of their working together now they were dead.

Matt ran back, grasped Sara under her arms, and hauled her to her feet. I made sure he got her out before I darted out of the room.

We faced a long corridor before us, much like the others we'd been through. It twisted out of sight. The faint banging we'd heard before was now much louder and unquestionably closer.

The zombies wedged themselves through the slit in the first door as Gavin allowed the second door to shut. It slid closed well before the zombies reached it.

Matt held on to Sara, supporting her drooping frame.

"Hurry," Matt urged.

Sam led the way, but Trevor held back. "You guys go ahead. I'll stay here and make sure something slows these things down."

"Trevor…"

"No, no, don't talk me out of it. We've lost too many already. I need to give you guys a chance to get out."

Sam walked back to him, her voice surprisingly gentle. "What will help us most is having you with us. Believe me, we need your firepower once we get weapons, and your strength in case we have to fight more of these things. What we *don't* need is three zombies chasing us instead of two." She placed her hand on his arm. "Please, come with us."

Trevor nodded, rubbing sweat from his face. Without another word, Sam took off down the corridor, disappearing from sight. Gavin and I exchanged amazed glances before we rushed after her.

Chapter 24 ☣

The pounding rose and faded in volume as we rushed down corridor after corridor. Some of the barricades keeping the zombies out of the "secured" area were ridiculous. A few were made of brick and mortar—I liked those—and others were comprised of stacked blue barrels full of something heavy. One was piled office furniture in front of a swinging door. That made me feel really safe.

I could only assume it was a matter of time before the Karl and Jeff zombies reached us. The tunnels twisted, leading us into the world's most confusing maze. They all looked the same: gray, round, and endless. We were hopelessly lost. Finding a small kitchen, we took turns guzzling water.

"The general spoke of a safe place, where those who hadn't been infected could go, right?"

Sam gulped more water before answering me. "That depends on whether you want to sit around with a bunch of other people who have no idea what's going on and trust the powers that be'll figure it out, or go to the military base ourselves and get answers."

Trevor snorted. "Like the answers we got here?"

Sam didn't say anything, but she got that familiar, obstinate look on her face.

"I take it you want to find the other secret military base, not the Air Force?" I continued.

"Yep."

"So, we just have to get out of here and find it."

"I wish it were that easy. He made it very clear it was for military personnel only, and it'd be extremely hard to find. We had enough trouble finding this place, and we don't have…" Grief swept her face as her words hung in the air.

Coffey. I cleared my throat. "When the general got the message about the helicopter escort, that lieutenant mentioned there were tunnels leading to the surface, right?"

Sam just looked at me.

"Well, does it feel like we're going up or down?"

Sam groaned, but Matt answered, "There's no way to tell down here, mate."

"Maybe there is." I looked up, searching the ceiling. "What if we go through an air vent and try to find the next level from there? Then, we can try to find the next level's air vent. That way we're always climbing up. Maybe we'll stumble on an elevator shaft or those bigger tunnels the lieutenant was talking about."

Gavin smiled wryly. "Not all air vents are big enough to climb through."

"And not all the levels down here are stacked on top of each other like a typical building," Trevor added. "There could be huge gaps of dirt or rock between each level. We have to find a map before we try anything like that."

"Well, we've got to do something other than wandering aimlessly. We should at least mark our path or something. We need to know if we're traveling up, not farther down."

"You do realize once we leave the secured area, we face a countless number of zombies here, underground?"

I swallowed. "Maybe we could double back, try to get back to the elevators?"

Matt shook his head. "Even I couldn't find those anymore, I'm so turned around."

A muffled crash from nearby made Sara and me jump. Matt scurried out of the room. He poked his head back in when no one followed. "I suggest we get going."

"But where?" Okay, I admit it, I was getting kinda whiny. No, forget that. I was downright surly. I was done. I'd had it with this awful place. "We need a plan, or an escape route, or a map of this stupid..."

The lights flickered and went out. I couldn't help it. I screamed. Gavin put his arm around my waist and pulled me close, kissing my hair. I think he thought all the kisses soothed me or something. He may have been right...

"Wait for the backup generators. They should kick on in a sec," Matt soothed.

"Uh, guys? I think those *were* the back-up generators," Sam added.

"No way. Even *I'm* not doing this in the dark with a bunch of zombies."

I couldn't agree with Sara more. More crashing boomed from the hallway.

Matt called out, "Everyone, stay where you are."

Since he'd been standing closest to the door when the pitch black hit us, he shut the door and locked it. He fumbled with nearby chairs, shoving them in front of the door. If I could see anything, I'd so be helping. A loud buzzing filled the air, and the lights flickered on and off again. Fighting for dominance, a few of the lights finally came back on. Only every fourth or fifth one lit, and they still pulsed and flickered dangerously.

A terrifying crash advertised the last of the office furniture barricade had been dislodged. Zombies soon pounded on the door. Matt made his barricade more secure while Gavin and Trevor moved to the other door in the room.

"Hey, Candace, come here."

I rushed to Gavin's side. He nodded at the door, and the first grin in ages lit my face. I reached into my hair for a bobby pin but came up empty. I'd forgotten I'd lost them. All of them. He handed me a thin strip of metal. I had the lock picked in no time. I stood back, then Gavin kicked the door open.

One light throbbed in the small office as they scattered to make sure the room was zombie-free. I scurried after Gavin, not wanting to get separated from him. The room held an oak desk with a computer and a phone resting on it. A door hung to our right—currently barricaded by fallen office furniture on the other side—and another door marked "General Joseph Craig" stood at the back of the room.

I had that door open in no time, too.

Gavin went first, again, and the noise faded as I followed him. I glanced at Matt and Trevor as they locked the office door leading to the kitchen and moved the oak desk in front of it. Turning my gaze back to General Craig's office, I stopped inside the doorway.

Warm colors instantly swallowed the never-ending gray and white of the rest of the base. An opulent mahogany desk sank into plush carpet at the back of the large room, and tall bookcases stuffed full of leather-bound books lined either wall. I paused to admire the richness of the room. One light burned in this room also, but it wasn't flickering like the others.

"Candace, check out that closet."

I tentatively moved to do Sam's bidding, certain I was about to get jumped—by Sam if I didn't move fast enough, or a zombie when I opened the door—either was equally as terrifying. The door swung open to complete darkness, and I stepped back.

"Here." Sara appeared at my elbow, a giant, odd-smelling candle in hand.

"Phew. Where did you get that?"

"The secretary's desk. She had a couple of them."

"Smells awful! Like rank perfume was poured all over it or something."

"You got that right. Gallons of it."

We both snickered as Sara struck a match, presumably also from the secretary's desk, and lit the candle. Light flared in the small room, revealing a space neatly stuffed full of flares, flashlights, and other supplies. We grabbed a couple of the flashlights.

I enclosed her shoulders with my arm as she fingered other supplies. "I'm sorry about Jeff."

She shrugged off my arm and looked at everything else in the room except me. "Yeah, well, it's okay. He was never interested in me, anyway."

I touched her arm. "That doesn't mean you can't miss him."

"Hey, guys! Check this out!" Sara called to the rest of the group, dousing any further personal conversation.

Our room was swiftly invaded, and the shelves were soon depleted of flashlights, blankets, and first-aid kits. Sam and Matt started rifling through everything else in the room, and I squeezed my way out. It was way too crowded in there.

Gavin walked up to me.

"Find anything?" I asked.

He put his arms around me and took a shuddering breath. "What in the world possessed you to step in front of General Craig's weapon like that? You don't even know Sara that well. You met her a couple of days ago."

I shrugged, running my hands up his perfectly sculpted back as magic wended its way through my entire being at his nearness. A delicious shiver coursed through me. "I couldn't let her die."

He pulled back and shook me gently, bending so we were eye-level. "I don't care who it is, don't ever do something like that again. Ever. It killed me to see a gun to your head."

I dropped my gaze, staring at the burgundy carpet. "I can't promise that, Gavin."

"But why? I can't lose you, Candace."

He wrapped me in a tight hug. As difficult as it was to breathe, I snuggled closer.

"When...when I was a little girl..." I started haltingly. "I saw something...terrible...and I swore, if it were ever in my power, I would help. No matter what."

He pulled back and looked at me. He hesitated for what seemed like an eternity. Finally, he ran a finger down my cheek. "What happened? You...you don't have to tell me if you don't want to, you know."

"I know. I want to."

He pulled me down to the carpet, and I sat next to him, cradled in his arms.

"My grandparents had this dog—the 'diggingest dog,' my grandma called him, after her favorite children's storybook. Well, my grandma decided after a while she liked her fiction dog much better. Especially after her entire yard had been destroyed."

Gavin chuckled, and I shared a smile with him.

"One day, after this dog had torn up half of my grandparents' beautifully sculpted backyard, I happened to look out the window. My grandpa had his belt off, beating the poor thing with all of his might."

Tears clogged the back of my throat. Gavin squeezed me, and I cleared my throat.

"I'm so sorry," he said huskily.

"Me too. I ran outside and screamed for him to stop. The dog—I don't even remember his name—was lying on his side, whimpering in pain. Nothing I said mattered, and Grandpa told me to go back inside. I obeyed, and he kept whipping. It never even crossed my mind to do anything more about it. I swore when I got older I would never let anything like that happen again."

"You've got to know it wasn't your fault."

"I didn't even do anything! I yelled at him, sure—something I never did before or after that, I might add—but I could have at least put myself between the dog and that belt."

Gavin frowned at me. "Candace, you can't blame yourself. He was in the wrong, not you."

"But I should have done something more! I was too little and too scared. I can't do that again. I won't. Besides, as much as I love animals, people are way more important. I couldn't let Sara die."

He gathered me close and kissed my cheek. "Oh, little girl."

I punched his thigh lightly. "Hey! I'm not so little anymore."

"So I've noticed."

He pulled back and looked at my lips with a devilish grin. He leaned forward. My heart stopped, then raced out of control. My eyes slid shut.

"Hey, Gavin!"

My eyes flew open.

He looked disappointed but grinned anyway. "The leader beckons."

"'Tyrant' is more like it."

He laughed and stood, moving to the closet's open doorway. I climbed to my feet and wandered over to the desk, running my hands over the smooth, cool wood. Immediately, I started fiddling with the drawers. Remembering the knife Matt had given me, I slipped it from its case and used it to pry open the locks, looking for secret places. I started pulling drawers from the desk, rifling through the contents and turning the drawers over. Finding nothing, I moved to the bookshelves. Fingering the volumes, I searched for something out of the ordinary.

Trevor relocated to the secretary's office, keeping an eye on the barricaded doors.

After thoroughly searching the bookcases, I noticed some family pictures on a matching stand behind the desk. A plant draped its spindly leaves over several of the pictures, and I brushed it aside so I could get a better view. Unfortunately, I smacked one of the pictures, sending it crashing to the ground. It hit the desk's leg, splintering the glass. Everyone came running at the sound.

I held up my hand. "It's okay. I'm all right. It's just me, being klutzy."

I turned to find the wall sliding partially open, just enough for a person to slip through.

"Well, that was convenient," I muttered.

"Way to go, klutz." Sara patted my shoulder as she slipped through the seamless door, her flashlight beaming before her. Matt and Sam quickly followed. I hesitated, unsure of how smart—or safe, really—it was to jump into all of the new places we discovered.

"After you." Gavin gestured with a flourish and a bow, reminding me of our coffee shop date. I reached out and squeezed his hand, wanting to be back in that café so badly. Without the awful zombie part following. He straightened and put his hand on the small of my back, ushering me through the slit in the wall. Gavin and Trevor had a harder time wedging their tall, muscular bodies through the small opening, but they managed to squeeze through.

Everyone had flashlights—Sara had two—and were inspecting the room, the bright rays slicing through the darkness. A large conference table stretched the length of the oblong room, and paper maps littered the walls. Computer screens lined one wall, and two large monitors hung over the opposite ends of the conference table. All were blank and dark.

I heard a click and swiveled my flashlight behind me. Solid wall met my gaze where the door had been. Bright light flooded overhead. The monitors came to life. Sara and I cheered, making the guys chuckle and Sam roll her eyes.

Sam strode to the giant map of the underground base splayed on the wall and began searching for an escape route.

Matt located guns and ammunition, instantly winning Gavin and Trevor's attention. They *oohed* and *aahed* in appreciation and selected more weapons than I thought they could carry. I admired the newer, shinier military weapons, certain they were the nicest guns I'd seen in my life. After grabbing a few for myself, I joined Sam and Sara, who were pouring over maps. Maps that showed the tunnels leading to the surface.

Yes! Finally. "Hey, guys, look at this," I called.

Our three remaining guys came over, loaded with weapons. Rambo would've been proud. He also would've felt underdressed. I turned my laugh into a cough when I saw how serious they were. My amusement evaporated when I realized they'd soon be using all of those weapons to defend themselves and us.

Sam turned back to the map. "This is where we need to go. If I have my bearings correct, it's not far from us." She hesitated.

"And the bad news?" asked Matt.

She took a deep breath. "The bad news is, not only will we be going through zombie-infested areas to get to the tunnels marked 'unsecured' on the map, but also the tunnels themselves will be teeming with zombies, since the officer said it was how they were getting in and out. Unless…" Sam's voice trailed off, and she shook her head.

"Unless what?" Gavin asked after the buzz from the lights and the monitors became the only noise in the room for too long.

I spoke up. "Unless we use these smaller tunnels here, here, and here. They're closed off by grates and don't run the entire span of the underground base like the large tunnels do. And several—here—lead straight up for quite a few meters until they join others. We'd be dodging fewer zombies that way, and the smaller tunnels should be relatively secure once we're inside of them."

"What are they used for?"

I shrugged. "Service tunnels, ventilation—I'm really not sure."

"The important thing is, we have a way out," Sam interrupted. She studied the clocks on the wall, which showed 24 different time zones. "It looks like it's around midnight here. This room seems secure. Matt, make sure it is, please. Sleep in two-hour shifts, two watching and four asleep at a time. I'll take the first shift."

Trevor volunteered to stay awake with her. Sara produced some pillows from a nearby storage room, and Matt dimmed the lights after making sure all entrances were secure. Sara curled into a ball in the corner, and Matt situated his bed close enough to her that anything attacking would go through him first.

I turned to Sam. "How long do you think it'll take to get through all the tunnels and to the surface?"

She yawned. "I don't know. Most of the day tomorrow, I'm sure. Oh, I forgot to mention, I'm fairly certain where the other military base is located." Sam pointed to a world map on the wall, a big grin splitting her normally stern face. I gazed at the map, and my smile matched hers.

"Thank you, General Craig."

She chuckled and moved near Matt and Sara, getting her own bed ready.

A bright red pin marked a spot in Colorado, with arrows from many other smaller red pins, including one in Arizona, where we were, pointing the way. A radio frequency was scribbled next to the marker, something that looked like it was done in great haste.

Now we just had to figure out how to get there.

Turning to find my own blankets, I saw Gavin had already made our beds. Close together. I smiled and plowed into the covers, snuggling into him. I saw Trevor making his bed before I drifted into sweet slumber.

Chapter 25 ☣

I woke with a start, sitting straight up in the makeshift bed. Soft snores and heavy breathing reached my ears, but nothing else. Glancing around the room frantically, I rubbed the sleep from my eyes, looking again. Everyone was asleep. Not one person was watching for zombies. I checked our time zone clock: 10:17am.

I shook Gavin, whispering hoarsely. "Gavin. Gavin!"

"Hmm…what?" He looked up at me and smiled, half-asleep, and reached for me. "Come back to bed."

He tried to pull me into the warm covers, but I yanked them off him. "Gavin, seriously, wake up!"

He groaned and sat up, rubbing his eyes and running his fingers through his hair. "What is it?" he mumbled, stretching and yawning.

"No one is watching. Zombies could attack at any moment, and no one is watching!"

My voice grew progressively louder, and Sara piped up from under her covers, "Oh, calm down. Matt himself said zombies couldn't get in here without some kind of security code."

"I don't remember…"

"Well, I do. Shut up and go back to sleep."

She buried her face under her pillow once more. The thought of payback, hovering over her and talking loudly while waving her red first-aid kit around crossed my mind, but I refrained.

Trevor yawned. "Oops."

Matt stretched and sat up. "This room's tight as a drum. No worries, mate. I'm glad everyone got a decent night's sleep."

"I'm glad no one got eaten," I muttered as I started picking up my bedding.

"Leave it." Gavin pulled me next to him, draping his arm across my shoulders. "Enjoy the peacefulness of the moment, before we have to go back out there."

I nodded and slowly relaxed, thankful we were all still alive somehow. I leaned against him as the others stirred and took turns using the one-room restroom off the conference chamber. Gavin nuzzled my neck, sending shivers skittering up and down my spine. I kissed the strong curve of his jawline, and he captured my lips with his. Sam interrupted us with a grunt and a roll of her eyes, handing us breakfast foods she'd pilfered from the kitchen the night before. She then disappeared into the restroom.

Gavin and I ate while the rest of the group went about their morning rituals, silent, preparing for another difficult day. After a while, I noticed Gavin had grown pensive.

"What is it?"

"You know, I always wondered how I would stand up in situations like this, without knowing my lines or what scene would come next." Gavin stared at his clasped hands, his jaw clenched.

I placed my hand on his knee and squeezed. "You're doing a great job."

He snorted. "Really? Then why do the people I try to protect keep dying and turning into more of those monsters?"

"Gavin, you can't blame yourself. You did everything you could to help them. All of them. And you've done a great job keeping me safe." I tried to lighten my tone, sending a teasing smile his way.

"Yeah, some great job." He touched my still-bandaged arm and lightly traced the fading bump on my forehead where I'd been hit by that stupid baseball. After a moment, he ran his fingers through my hair. "I like your hair without all that junk in it."

I cleared my throat. "Yes, but how will I ever be able to pick a lock without my trusty bobby pins?" I tried to joke, but it came out more like I was being strangled.

His hand moved to the back of my head. He pulled me close. "I guess we'll just have to figure out something else." I could feel his breath on my lips.

Sam entered the room and threw our newly acquired packs at us. "Come on, lovebirds. Let's go."

Groans met Sam's pronouncement, but we all grudgingly moved to obey.

Matt led the way out of the conference room, followed closely by Sam and Sara. Gavin nodded for me to go next, and Trevor took up the rear.

Sam clutched a rough map she'd sketched from the large map in the conference room, giving brief, one-word commands to Matt, telling him which way to go.

I held a flashlight with one hand and my Glock with the other, my new, military-grade shotgun slung across my back. I had two more handguns strapped to my hips. Sam insisted we use the sparse lighting in the base in order not to draw further attention. I was fine with that, but I wanted my flashlight handy in case those blasted lights blinked off again.

Matt paused at the end of the hallway. We lined up against the wall with Gavin and Trevor keeping watch behind us.

"This is the end of the secured area," Sam hissed. "We are about to enter a large warehouse filled with..." She squinted at her map in the dim lighting. "Generators. We need to make it across the room and up these stairs. The first of the tunnels is here."

She pointed, and Sara and I crowded to look, even though we'd memorized the thing last night.

"You guys ready for this?" She speared Sara and me with a stern glare, but her concern peeked through.

I snorted a laugh. "Would it matter if I said no?"

"Nope. Let's move."

Rounding the corner, we saw one light at the end of the hall, blue barrels piled in front of what was hopefully a door. I looked behind us. Complete darkness stretched in the other direction.

I clicked on my flashlight and shined it down the hallway, but the beam didn't penetrate the darkness. The back of my neck prickled, and I hoped nothing was hiding just out of sight.

We took turns standing two at a time with weapons drawn while the other four moved barrels and piled them against the wall.

"That should be enough," Sam declared as we hefted most of the stacked barrels out of the way. She studied the map and punched a code into the panel next to the door. We raised our weapons. The panel blinked green, and the doors slid open.

Peeking around the corner, Matt gave us time to observe the layout of the room before giving the signal to move out.

Giant generators filled the room, lined in neat rows, blocking our view of the staircase on the other side of the room. A wide-open space to our left revealed a circular, glass-paneled room where most of the light was coming from. A lowered walkway spanned its circumference, and Matt pointed to it. Only a few zombies staggered about the room, and none had noticed us yet.

Matt covered Sam as she darted past him, hiding behind a wide post before dropping into the circular walkway. Sara went next, following Sam's exact movements. Matt joined them, and Gavin covered me. I made it to the support pillar, then peeked around it before I dashed to the walkway.

One shallow-breathing zombie paused, staring in my direction. I held my breath until it resumed rambling about the room. Staying low,

I darted to Matt, Sam, and Sara. Gavin and Trevor soon joined us.

"Whew, that was close!" Sara whispered to me.

Sam raised her finger to her lips. We filed silently behind her as we made our way, crouched low, around the glass room to our left.

Matt held up his hand and pointed, and we all dove against the wall to our right. Shuffling footsteps passed nearby, and I could see the zombie's reflection in the glass as it walked by us. My brow furrowed. Why couldn't they smell us this time? Nothing about these zombies made sense. Matt checked to see if we were clear.

I craned my neck and peeked over the edge, wanting to see what he was looking at, yet not wanting to at all. Zombies in military uniforms staggered all over the room, disappearing and reappearing behind the giant generators.

Matt motioned, and we inched forward. Once again, Matt had us crouch next to the wall as he conferred in hushed tones with Sam. A raised walkway led out of the lowered track, and Matt pointed to it.

We filed out of the walkway, still staying low, and scrambled to the nearest generator. Keeping the generator between an advancing zombie and us, we rotated as one with its footsteps, staying out of its sight. It staggered by.

Glancing behind me, my eyes fastened on the glass room behind us. Zombies in white lab coats milled around, bumping into the glass walls and furniture before turning to do the same thing again. The room was in shambles. Glass tubing and beakers were splintered everywhere, and empty wire cages stood on their sides, ripped apart. Now the zombies were trapped with nothing else to do.

Sam motioned frantically, and we dashed between several generators, barely dodging a wandering fiend. Keeping a generator between us and another zombie, we all moved around it and came face to face with another zombie.

"Well, poop on a stick."

Gavin quirked an eyebrow at me as the female zombie hissed and lunged for Sam. I made a mental note to remember to kill my brother later for saying that stupid phrase all the time. After I found him alive and well.

Sam and Matt downed the zombie with their three-burst semi-automatics, the loud *pops* echoing throughout the room.

"Run!"

We bolted for the staircase that was still too far away, in my opinion. I emptied my handgun, threw it, and swung my shotgun to the front. Instead of simply jerking, now the zombies flailed and fell back with each shot. I pumped it and trained the shotgun on another zombie, hoping not to use too many more rounds.

Getting there first, Gavin and I tore up the staircase. When we reached the top, we fired down on the zombies holding part of our group at bay. Sam and Sara broke free and dashed up the stairs.

I turned to see zombies coming at us from both sides of the raised metal walkway.

"Sam! Where's the first pipe?" I shouted.

She took one hand off the railing long enough to point. I blasted away a zombie, then pivoted to see where she was pointing. A grated circle rested near the ceiling, at the top of a metal ladder fused into the wall.

Turning my attention below, I saw Matt sprint up the stairs, Trevor close behind. Gavin swung at an advancing zombie, sending it hurtling over the edge and crashing into a swarm of bodies below.

"Trevor!"

I shot another zombie coming at me before looking for the cause of Sara's shriek. Zombies clutched Trevor's ankles, pulling him down the stairs. I desperately fired on the zombies closest to him, but grasping hands replaced the ones falling away. Trevor clung to the banister, kicking frantically and crying out in pain. Gavin and I downed a couple of zombies near us before I turned my attention, and my bullets, back to Trevor.

I pulled the trigger, but nothing happened. I whacked a zombie with my shotgun. The creature plummeted to the ground below, giving me enough time to reload. Matt rattled off his three-burst semi, trying to free Trevor from the hoard pulling at him.

Trevor twisted around, holding on to the banister with one hand and shooting wildly with the other. He disappeared below the mass as they pulled him free.

"No! Trevor!" Matt ran down a few steps, firing into the hoard.

Sam cried out. "Matt! No! Leave him!"

No other zombies climbed the stairs; they instead focused on our fallen companion. Matt took another step forward. The swarming stopped, and they turned their attention back to Matt. A bloody and completely changed Trevor rose in their midst, staggering toward the staircase along with them.

"Matt! Come on!"

Matt bolted up the remaining steps. He and Gavin quickly cleared the walkway of zombies and threw their bodies below. Sam heaved one down the staircase, momentarily halting those scrambling up it.

I was nearest the ladder. I swung my shotgun across my back and clambered up, tears stinging my eyes. We weren't going to lose anyone else. Not if I had anything to do with it.

The grate wouldn't budge. Slipping my knife from my ankle, I wedged it into the crack and pried it open. The grate gave way so easily, I nearly fell. Lifting it free, I almost dropped it, it was so heavy.

"Lower it! I've got it."

I handed it to Matt. My knife tumbled from my fingers and clattered all the way to the floor below us. *Great. Just great.*

Matt spun and rushed the zombies with the shield of metal. They tumbled from the vertical staircase to the ground below, buying us just a little more time.

Gavin nudged me. "Keep going, Candace."

I looked into the tunnel. It was big enough for two to crawl side by side, and it was clear. As far as I could see, anyway. I toppled in, Gavin and Sara close behind. Sam and Matt scrambled in, and I looked back just in time to see Matt secure the grate. It clicked into place just as smelly fingers invaded the small openings. I made sure the zombies couldn't move it before scrambling away. Sara crawled next to me as we took off down the tube. She sniffled and wiped sweat from her face.

"How do we know there aren't any zombies in these tunnels?" Sara called back to Sam.

"We don't, but I hope to God there aren't."

"The grate should keep them out," I encouraged. "It was tricky to open. I don't think a zombie could get it undone by sheer force."

Sara swiped at her face again.

I glanced at her, and my heart skipped a beat. Blood oozed down her arm from her shoulder. I didn't know how the zombie bug worked —I, after all, hadn't been turned into a zombie from my wound—but it seemed like several others were merely wounded, not killed, when they'd turned. I desperately hoped she wouldn't be one of them.

She scrubbed at her face again, her voice catching. "How much longer do we have to be in these stupid tunnels?"

I prayed not much longer, especially with that vicious wound. I crawled faster, keeping my eye on her, pleading with God she wouldn't turn into a zombie as well.

The other grated end came into view as we rounded a bend in the pipe.

"Thank God," I breathed.

I paused and speared Gavin with a look, indicating Sara with my head. He looked puzzled but watched her as I tried to open the grate. At least, I hoped he kept watching her. It wouldn't budge.

"Here." Matt passed his knife up to me.

I checked on Sara once more before releasing the latch with the knife and slipping open the grate. I poked my head through the opening.

The pipe emptied into a narrow concrete chamber stretching far above my head. The walls curved out of sight in both directions. Grates lined the outer walls above in a spiral reaching upward. I cautiously stepped out of the tunnel onto the concrete floor, and the rest of the team tumbled out after me. I stepped back and pulled one of my handguns free, ready to train it on Sara if necessary. Maybe I could shove her back into the tunnel and pop the grate back on? *Please, dear God. No, no, no. Please, no.* She plopped onto the rim of the tunnel and took a shuddering breath.

Sam and Matt took off in opposite directions, soon disappearing from sight. Gavin stayed with Sara and me, guarding us. I eyed her with concern. She sniffed and wiped her eyes, gingerly touching her shoulder until Sam and Matt returned.

"Dead end," Sam offered.

"Same here," Matt agreed.

They sat on the ground next to each other, looking dejected.

"No zombies, either."

Yeah, unless we'd brought one with us.

Gavin looked around the vault before his eyes settled on my face. I glanced at him, then nodded at Sara again, my weapon ready. He followed my gaze, and his eyes widened. *Finally.*

As Matt and Sam looked above our heads and consulted the map, trying to figure out which tunnel to take, I slipped my gun away and sat next to Sara.

"Sara?" I kept my voice low.

She looked at me, panicked, trying to hide her wound with her hand.

"Are you all right?"

She nodded at me, frantic. Then tears filled her eyes, and she slowly shook her head no. I swallowed back a sob and squeezed her shoulders, well away from the wound.

"Would you—would you mind if I prayed for you?"

She shook her head and buried her face on my shoulder.

Everyone stilled as my quiet voice filled the small space. "Dear Jesus, please heal Sara. Don't let her turn into one of those things. Please, dear Lord, protect us and get us out of here safely. Amen. Oh, yes, and may there be a cure!"

"Thank you," Sara whispered into the fabric of my shirt.

Gavin, Matt, and Sam stared at each other, clearly unsure of what to do next. They weren't the only ones. I was normally embarrassed to pray out loud, but I pushed aside caring what they thought. My friend was worth a little discomfort.

Suddenly, Gavin tugged off and ripped open his backpack. And I jumped. Of course. He pulled out his first-aid kit and grabbed the alcohol and a wad of bandages. He turned Sara away and blocked my view before pouring the alcohol over her shoulder and down her sleeve. She cried out. I tried to see what was going on. He poured it a few more times before placing gauze over the open wound and wrapping it in bandages.

Sam nudged me. I looked at her, and she shoved the map in my face. "We need to find this tunnel. But, which one is it?"

I lifted the map from her fingers and studied it. It was a hastily made, and therefore badly done, copy.

"We're in a big three-quarter circled area," Sam advised. "And it's not on the map."

"What?" Gavin and Matt crowded around the map.

Sam took it from me and spread the crinkled paper on the ground. "If I had to guess, we're in the center of the base, and this area wraps around the elevator shaft." She pointed above our heads. "Each grate opens to another service tunnel, presumably above each hallway in the base."

Gavin looked puzzled. "Shouldn't that be on the map? This service tunnel was."

Sam sighed. "I hate to admit this, guys, but I don't think I read the map very well. I vaguely remember this room being on there, but I thought it was insulation or something. It was really confusing, but I *know* most of these tunnels weren't on there."

I groaned.

"Now I wish we'd lugged it with us," grumbled Matt.

"What? You mean the giant map that was part of the wall?" I hadn't seen her direct a glare at Matt yet. Guess she had to glare at somebody since Coffey wasn't around. "Anyway, now I know what it is," Sam asserted in her best grumpy voice, in charge once more, "I say we climb to the highest one." She pointed to the map. "The tunnel we need ends here. Then we can either double back in the hallways and try to get on the elevator, or go through one more tunnel to get to this vertical ventilation shaft"—she circled it with her finger—"To the surface. Only problem is we might need a welding tool to get the raised cover off above ground, and it's a mile climb straight up."

We all groaned.

"Hey, at least we've got a way out," Sara spoke up.

"The only question is—besides where we'll find a welding torch—which tunnel do we want to take?"

We looked above our heads at Gavin's question.

"If I remember correctly, only one of those will take us to the ventilation shaft, and we've got—what—five, six to choose from?"

Sure enough, six grated ends poked out of the top of the wall, the farthest two curving out of sight. Hundreds more stretched between those six pipes and us. The design made me think of a giant sprinkler going off from the elevator shaft, stabbing the walls with service tunnels instead of water. How big was this place? And why on earth did they take us to the deepest level?

Sam tapped the map and stared at the tunnels. "Which one is it?"

I glanced at Sara. Besides looking weary and full of pain, she looked just like, well, Sara. I glanced at the grate resting next to her feet. A small, muted blue tag tied to the grate was barely visible. My gaze darted to the grates nearby. Smidgens of dusky red, green, and a few other colors—none of them bright—met my gaze wherever I looked. But there was no other blue.

Grabbing the map from Sam, I looked at her sketch of the pipe we wanted. Dotted lines connected the tunnel we'd just come through to the one high above our heads. I glanced up.

"What are these dotted lines?" I asked.

Sam squinted at the map and shrugged.

"It was on there, so I copied it. See something, Marshall?"

"Not sure yet," I muttered.

I studied the grated rims above my head before choosing one. Grasping the grooves in the concrete that served as ladder rungs, I mumbled, "Here goes," before starting to climb.

"You want us to join you up there?" Matt called.

"Not yet. I want to make sure I'm right."

Reaching the top of a row of pipes, after *way* too long, I found a green tag instead of the blue I was hoping to find. "No, that can't be right."

I took a moment to suck in some air, hoping my burning legs and shaking hands wouldn't make me fall.

"What are you mumbling to yourself about now?" called an exasperated Sam. Her voice bounced up the chamber, reminding me how far away I was from the ground below.

"Just a minute."

"'Just a minute,' she says. Of course."

"Be careful up there, please," Gavin called.

"Sure thing."

Taking a deep breath, I gripped the rung tighter and looked side to side, not daring to look down. Heights were most definitely on my never-to-do list.

Dark red and dingy yellow tags clung to the grates on either side of me. A gray-blue tag snagged my attention as the wall curved out of sight. I pointed.

"There! That's the one we need!"

"How can you tell?" asked Gavin.

"Look at the grates. There are colored tags on all of them. The pipe I'm at has a green tag, and that pipe right over there has a blue tag, just like the one we crawled through. It must be the one we want!"

Gavin and Matt looked at each other and shrugged. "Makes sense to me," Matt said.

Sam called up again. "Are you coming back down now?"

"No, if I can just…"

I stretched to the right, leaning over nothing but concrete floor a ridiculous distance below. My hand grasped the grate next to me, and I stepped from the ladder to the rim. My heart flip-flopped as I released the concrete rungs entirely and gripped the cool metal.

Gavin cleared his throat nervously. Glancing down, I saw him standing below me with his arms outstretched, ready to catch me.

Man, I hoped that wouldn't be necessary.

Swallowing my heart back down into my chest, I balanced on the rim of the pipe and reached for the next ladder over. I repeated the same agonizing process past the grates with grungy yellow and orange tags before perching on the ladder next to the blue. I was breathing heavily—not from exertion but from fear. Forcing myself to take calm, even breaths, I realized it probably would have been just as fast to climb down, then scale the ladder I wanted. *Great.* I had risked my life for nothing.

Gripping the bottom edge of the blue-tagged pipe, I used Matt's knife to pry open the latch, then pulled the grate free. It teetered in my grasp.

"Watch out!"

The heavy grate slipped from my fingers. I lunged after it, keeping a firm grip on the ladder, but the grate plunged below me. I closed my eyes and prayed it wouldn't hit Gavin. I peeked below me once the loud echoes faded. Gavin stood plastered against the wall, the grate sprawled on the ground next to him. I breathed a sigh of relief as he moved away from the wall and stood below me once more. I slipped the knife into my ankle strap. It was now or never.

Stretching over empty space, I pulled my shaking self slowly into the pipe, after peeking to make sure it was clear, of course. I slipped and plunged toward the ground below me.

Sara gasped, and Gavin called out. "Candace!"

Clutching for something—anything—my fingers grasped solid metal. I clung to it, my legs swinging and my arms burning from the sudden stop.

I looked around. I'd dropped past several pipes. That's okay. I had about ten more chances or so before I hit the ground. Time to think about something else before I hurled. I stretched across to grip the ladder before beginning my ascent once more.

The others waited in silence—holding their breath, I'm sure—until I made it safely back to the open tunnel. I pulled myself in and turned around, sticking my head out of the opening. "Who's next?"

Gavin wordlessly began the climb and soon dropped into the tunnel next to me. He grabbed the back of my head and pulled me toward him. "Don't ever scare me like that again." He stifled my apology with a passionate kiss.

"Are you guys about done already?"

My eyes widened, and I pulled back. Gavin's grin could only be described as smug. Sara peeked into the tunnel, her grossed-out tone not matching her sparkling eyes. She climbed into the pipe with Gavin's help, lightly punching me in the arm as she moved past. Sam's head popped in not long after Sara's.

I followed Sara, getting out of the way so Gavin could help Sam, too. "How did you get up here so quickly?"

Sara rolled her eyes. "It took me forever to get up here with this arm, even with Sam's help. I think you were a bit distracted."

My face heated as she grinned at me.

Matt joined us not long after Sam. They crawled past us all to lead the way down the tunnel. Gavin tugged at my heel, and I dropped back to crawl beside him. There'd been so much more room next to Sara, especially since he took every opportunity to rub against my arm or kiss my cheek.

"I'm really glad you're okay," he whispered.

"Okay, knock it off, you two," Sam called.

I flushed, but Gavin took the opportunity to give me another kiss. This time on the lips.

I laughed self-consciously. "Shouldn't we focus on getting out?"

"Absolutely." He kissed my nose.

I must've really scared the poor guy.

"How do you think I managed not to turn into a zombie?" Sara asked.

"Don't know," Sam quipped.

"Well, we prayed," I suggested.

No one said anything.

"You both got wounded and didn't turn. Maybe you *are* the cure," Matt proposed.

"Ha! Take *that,* General Joseph Craig!" Sara laughed.

Sam grunted and paused, grabbing her water bottle—her only remaining item from her pack—and guzzled. We stopped to do the same. My knees were thankful for a respite.

"Okay, I'm not sure what we'll find in the next couple of rooms, but I want to get through fast without losing anybody else." She gave us all a stern look.

I couldn't help it. I laughed. My laugh ended in a choked sob. I ducked my head and cleared my throat. If only that's how it worked. Then she could've given the group that little pep talk at the beginning. None of them would've dared turn into zombies. Gavin squeezed my hand.

Sam leveled a suspicious glare my way and continued. "This tunnel empties into a small room. We'll have to go down two separate hallways before we get into the room with the next tunnel." She studied the map. "It's also near the ceiling, but I can't tell by my scribbling how we're supposed to get to it. I'm sure we'll figure it out. Any questions?"

No one said anything.

"Good. Let's do this."

After a few more bends—I wondered if the tunnel would ever end—the grilled enclosure came into view. Matt held up his hand, and we all checked and reloaded our weapons. I passed Matt's knife back to him. He and Sam clicked off their flashlights, edging toward the grate. Peering through, they motioned us forward. We huddled near.

"Ready?"

"Ready."

Sam unlatched the grate, sliding it free without a sound. She held it in place as Matt counted under his breath. "One. Two. Three. Go."

The grate clattered to the floor as Sam pulled her weapons. Matt and Sam jumped out, firing at the zombies in the room. I clutched my shotgun tighter and jumped out, Gavin right behind me. We stayed close, darting past the zombies falling backward. The first hallway held only a few zombies, who got blasted as we raced past them. The hallway T'd, and Matt turned to the left.

"No, Matt! This way!"

Matt backtracked toward Sam's voice as the rest of us turned to the right. A light illuminated the end of the tunnel, showing an open doorway. I heard scuffling and swung my flashlight to the pitch-dark behind us.

Matt had apparently stumbled upon a swarm of the creatures. They teemed after us, filling the hallway to the brim. We burst into the next room, and I looked frantically around.

Low-hanging, much smaller pipes ran the length of the room, suspended by wires from the ceiling. A grated shelf spanned the length of the pipes to our right. The room was an extension of the hallway, taller than the passage we'd just exited. Another hallway opened at the end of the room, not far from us.

"There! There's the pipe!" Sara screamed and pointed.

We had seconds to get to it. Metal ladder rungs melded with the wall, and we clambered to them at once. Sara and Sam climbed first. Matt used the rods holding the shelf to the ceiling to swing himself up. Gavin picked me up and shoved me in Matt's direction. Matt yanked me up beside him. My shotgun slipped from my fingers and clattered to the ground below. Gavin bolted up the ladder as the creatures burst into the room. He lunged past the last few steps, lifting himself to safety.

The zombies swarmed the room, filling every available inch of ground below us. They couldn't reach the grid, so they tugged on the rods holding the shelf as they tried to get to us.

Matt, Sam, and Sara scrambled down the length of the room, pulling the grate free of the next pipe. They had to stand and boost each other up to climb inside the pipe. Matt grabbed a metal rod lying on the shelf.

The bucking, swaying ledge was difficult to climb across, but Gavin and I were almost to the end when a sickening crunch rent the air, and the grate dipped crazily. I jumped to the next one, but the zombies had already torn it free from the wall.

Chapter 26 ☣

I was falling. With a mighty cry, Gavin grabbed for me, heaving me up toward the metal grate. My fingers closed on solid metal, and I hoisted myself up. I turned around for Gavin, but he was gone.

The teeming mass of the undead swarmed him, far below me.

"Candace, go on! Forget about me. This is your chance—use it!"

He shouted a resounding victory cry, pulled his gun from his holster, and fired into those grasping him, clawing at him.

"No!" was wrenched from my soul. I couldn't lose him. I wouldn't.

"Come on! Hurry!"

Matt, Sam, and Sara waited for me. We were almost to freedom and safety, whatever that meant.

"No!"

I pulled both guns from my belt and fired at the zombies holding him, as close as I could without hitting him. My bullets were soon spent, ineffective against the undead. But his plan had worked. They were all focused on the tasty meal before them, momentarily forgetting about the rest of us. That wouldn't last long.

"Candace! Now! Get your butt up here!" Sam commanded in her best no-nonsense voice.

A sob stuck in my throat as I looked up at them. They didn't understand. I wouldn't leave him here, not after all he'd done for me. Matt lowered the metal rod from his higher vantage point, waiting for me to grab it so he could pull me up. I quickly crawled in their direction. Relief washed across their faces. No one would have to come bodily carry me out, crying or wailing or whatever. I grasped the rod and yanked it as hard as I could. Matt let go in surprise, not expecting the sudden jerk.

"Candace?" Sara's timid voice floated out of the pipe.

"You're going to have to go on without me."

I held Sam's gaze for a second before turning and launching myself into the last place I'd seen Gavin. The moment I landed on the backs of the undead, I began swinging for all I was worth, clobbering as many as I could. They immediately turned their attention toward me, advancing methodically. I located Gavin and swatted moving dead bodies aside so I could stand next to him. He was on the ground, bloodied, but he still seemed to be moving and fighting, *alive* alive. I hunched over him, not letting the creatures get close. I screamed and swung, screamed and swung, tears streaming down my face. This was it. My last few moments on earth.

They backed away, probably regrouping before swarming us again. I caught sight of another pipe with a grate covering it tucked almost out of sight, just big enough for us to squeeze into.

"Stay with me, Gavin. Stay with me!"

"Candace?" He sounded dazed. "I thought I told you to leave…?"

"Not without you, I'm not. I'm not going anywhere."

Gavin groaned. "Candace."

I grasped the back of his shirt and pulled, still swinging my metal bat. The parting of the sea of bodies miraculously stayed.

"Come on. Over this way. Can you help me out?"

He shook his head as if to clear it, not able to move much. I cried out a sob, close to hysterical, and wrapped my arms around his broad chest and pulled. I paused only to swing my club at advancing zombies, but they stayed just out of reach, milling about uncertainly.

I could barely get the words out, but I wasn't going to let him slip away. Not if I could help it.

"Don't you dare leave me, Gavin. I'm not done kissing you yet. You know how you asked what I wanted to be? Well I want to be a photographer. Not paparazzi. A pro. And I haven't done it yet. I haven't done anything with my life." I sucked a breath into my air-starved lungs. "You have to make it. You have to make another movie for me. You have to see me become a world-class photographer. And guess what? Neither of us are dying till that happens."

I planted a swift kiss on his unresponsive lips, then peeked up at my destination. The grate.

I peeled the grate off the wall and scrambled inside. Using every ounce of strength I could muster, I tugged Gavin after me. The pipe was just big enough for me to crawl on top of him and click the grate into place behind us. A few of the undead were looking at each other as if they were unsure of what to do next. I clenched the metal rod under my arm and pulled Gavin's dead weight along the length of the large metal pipe.

I cried out and gulped air as sobs wracked my body. I wasn't sure how much longer I could pull the hulking man. I was still crying when I reached the end of the tube. I looked out of the grid the best I could. It seemed safe, as safe as a building overrun with zombies, ready to jump out at no provocation whatsoever, could be. I couldn't breathe from how hard I was crying. I tried to unlatch the grate. There was no unlatching mechanism as there were on the other grates. I turned around and kicked until it gave way.

I pushed Gavin out of the pipe, sobbing, past exhaustion. He lay in a crumpled heap on the floor. I dropped out behind him and cried out in dismay to find a few zombies scattered about the room. They were all staring at us in surprise, a few with their mouths open, and a few holding Styrofoam coffee cups.

I grasped the metal rod that had clattered to the floor and positioned myself over Gavin's body, certain our luck had run out. This would be our last stand. I could not get my crying under control. I was gasping out sobs, beyond hysterical, beyond everything. The room began to darken and spin. I couldn't breathe. The zombies looked at each other, but none moved toward us. I dropped to my knees, unable to stand any longer.

"What...are...you...waiting...for?"

I feebly lifted the rod, ready to defend us. It was too heavy, and it dipped to the ground. I cried "No!" and desperately tried to lift it.

A loud sound reverberated through the room, and I jumped. No one else seemed fazed by it. It sounded like a bell at recess, only a thousand times louder.

Strong arms wrapped around me. I wrenched myself from them with my last ounce of strength, spinning to look behind me. Gavin stood there, clothes mussed and blood crusted on the side of his face, an infinitely sad look on his face.

"Gavin!" I managed to strangle out. I dropped to my knees once again, barely able to hold on to consciousness. "I'm...so sorry I... wasn't able to...save us."

Now I cried from relief as well as despair. More zombies entered the room, all staring, none advancing. The pregnant pause before the kill. I looked back to Gavin, half-expecting him to be a zombie and attack me first—half-expecting him to be able to save us yet again. He bent and tenderly gathered me in his arms. Those wonderful, strong arms. If I were going to die, at least it would be like this. I sighed and rested my head on his shoulder, hoping it would be quick.

"Candace, look at me. It's over. It's all over. You're safe now. Do you hear me? You aren't in danger anymore."

I looked up at him, still crying, but quieter now that he was holding me. He obviously hadn't seen all the zombies in the room with us.

"You have such nice eyes," I whispered. "Thank you for being my friend."

I kissed his cheek, smearing snot and tears all over him, and buried my head on his shoulder, waiting for the screaming and killing to start.

He held me, looking up after a little while. He'd finally seen them. I tensed, tightening my grip.

"Is she all right?" I heard a vaguely familiar voice ask. Where had I heard that voice before?

I felt Gavin shake his head, then lower me to the ground, sitting with me. "Candace, sweetheart, look around you," Gavin said softly, soothingly close to my ear.

I reluctantly pulled back and regarded him. The last thing I wanted to see was a freaking zombie's face before I died, and I was still expecting him to turn into one. I cowered against him and stared up at him, wanting to ask a question. I just wasn't sure what it was. I was just so darn *tired*.

"Miss Marshall?"

My head snapped around. The distinguished gentleman from the zombie movie pre-screening! The guy who'd started my entire nightmare.

"You!" I flew at him.

Two zombies darted toward me. I scrambled back, then noticed a gun lying on a table off to the side. I yanked it from its holster, aimed, and fired at the first zombie.

My hand was thrust into the air at the last second, and I fired harmlessly at the ceiling. Shrieks erupted from all over the room, but they sounded…human. Scared. Eyes wide, I stared up at Gavin, who handed the gun to a man dressed as a security guard. I did a double take. The guard's face was normal, not decaying in the least. He looked embarrassed and flustered.

I turned back to Gavin, my eyes huge. What was going on?

"Candace, sit down. It's over. It's fake. All of it. Make-believe." He crossed the room to the nearest zombie and pulled bits of mask and makeup off his face. "See?" He walked to a water cooler and poured a cup of water. He dipped a cloth into it and rubbed his own face. "It's fake blood. I'm not hurt. Do you understand?"

I grabbed for something, anything, as I sank to the floor. A zombie reached for me, but I shrieked and shrank away. Gavin was instantly by my side. He threw the rag at the man.

"Go take off your makeup," he ground out through clenched teeth.

He sat on the floor next to me.

Movement caught my eye. Our team—those who'd made it and those who'd been killed or turned into zombies—stood nearby, regarding me. All eyes somber. Unsure. A cry caught in my throat when I saw Jenifer. My gaze slammed back into Gavin's.

"You mean, everyone—everyone I love, everyone I knew—they aren't dead?"

Gavin shook his head no, his eyes full of sorrow.

"You mean, the babies, the children, they haven't really been killed, turned into zombies?"

Regret and shame flared on Gavin's face. He once again shook his head.

"Why?" I whispered.

Gavin didn't answer me. I looked around the room. Looks of shame, embarrassment, discomfort, and interest surrounded me. My eyes rested on the older gentleman who'd started my nightmare.

"Why?" I whispered once again. He returned my gaze, not answering, yet not looking regretful in the least.

My mind shut down. I began to sob. Deep, soulrending sobs. I curled up in the middle of the floor and cried like a baby. It was too much. I didn't understand. Gavin's heavy hand rested on my back, and someone later told me he cried with me.

Chapter 27 ☣

I rolled my eyes as the props guy showed me yet another "fancy movie trick." Blood sprayed, and I jumped. Eying him warily, I barely restrained myself from slapping the guy as he shoved another popped blood pack under my nose in an attempt to show me how the actors had been shot or mutilated on set without my knowledge. How I'd been tricked into thinking it was real. I think it was the studio's attempt to mollify me so I wouldn't sue the crap out of them. As if.

I was still fuming over Matt's—er, Kyle, was it?—reaction. As Gavin was leading me from the set—at least *his* name was the same—Matt had sported a wide grin and clapped me on the shoulder.

"What a sport! You rocked it, dude! Give me some."

His lifted hand remained high-five-less as Gavin shouldered past, trying to shield me. I stared at Matt—er, Kyle—tears drying on my face, numbness the only thing I could feel. Matt—Ky…oh, heck! I'm just calling him Matt!—had shrugged.

"Whatev."

Australian accent? Gone. Surfer accent? Sadly horrible.

It was the first in a series of even better events. "Better" as in: Worst. Day. Ever.

Gavin had been whisked away, and strangers had crowded me,

asking me what I needed. Over and over.

What I needed was their grimy hands off me and a moment to think. Then I'd been shoved into a room and left alone for a few hours, and I'd realized how much I *didn't* want to think. Then I'd been shown everything on set. The set I was on, anyway. As if my brain could handle it.

Now props-dude held me captive. Any other time, I would've found this stuff interesting. Not today. Today I wanted to strangle him. Along with a few other people who shall remain nameless.

No need to give the cops further investigative leads when I finally snapped.

Excited voices in a room not far from where we stood kept grabbing my attention. I nodded and grunted in the guy's direction as he moved closer to the voices, displaying a table full of instant gore makeup.

"Each gash or flesh wound had to be carefully set up and tested far in advance so it could be slapped on the actor in seconds. See?"

He oozed glue all over a deep, grotesque piece of gnawed-up flesh and slapped it on his arm. Beaming with pride, he shoved it, too, under my nose.

Time to take control of the situation.

"Uh-huh. Right. Anyway, what I'd like to know is how you shut down an entire city for filming. Several cities, actually."

I think it was the first question I'd managed to ask. I guess the props guy wasn't as intimidating as some.

He grinned as if he held the world's best-kept secret. "It was a logistics nightmare. Had to shut down large sections of Phoenix and the highways, then move you in and out as quickly as possible and still get all the shots we needed."

My eyes started to glaze over. Come to think of it, he knew quite a lot for a props guy. Maybe they chose him to turn my brain to mush because he talked so much.

"Acción wasn't a real town before we built it, you know."

I hadn't.

"Whole thing was a set. A thriving town now, by the way. Everyone wants to live there."

I just bet they did.

"It was part of the agreement Walmart and IMAX made with us to build there."

"But, Phoenix?"

"You don't want to know."

Actually, I did. He moved on anyway. I didn't push, although I really wanted to.

"You've got to see this. Right over here…"

My next question stuck in my throat, but I managed to get it out before he showed me whatever was so freaking important.

"Did I, you know, hurt anyone?"

He pushed his glasses up his nose. "Huh?"

I fiddled with something rubbery on the table, my eyes flitting from prop to prop.

"I hit someone with a two-by-four. Among other things."

His scrunched face relaxed. "Oh. That. Yeah, you broke the guy's nose, but no biggie. He signed a waiver. Like I was saying, these over here—"

"I broke his *nose*?"

"Yeah. Anyway—"

"And how exactly am I not going to get sued for that? Is he even okay?"

"He signed a waiver. No legal action. Nadda. You're good. He's fine. End of story." He drew the words out like I was the dumbest person on earth.

I may have looked that way with my mouth hanging open.

"But…you guys gave me a *knife*. I could have killed somebody!"

"Naw." He waved away my concern with a flick of his wrist. "You needed it for the grates. We made sure you didn't have a chance to use it on anyone."

My mind was practically exploding with what could've gone wrong. What if I'd cut off someone's *arm*?

"And these over here are little explosive packs, or squibs."

I looked at him blankly, my mind still swirling with words like *Phoenix* and *broke his nose*. What the freak?

"You know, so it would look like you shot what you were aiming at. Oh! Look at this!"

He jumped toward a container and peeled back the lid. I sighed. I guess I couldn't fault the guy for loving his job, even if that job included making me look like an idiot. He spun around to face me, and I stumbled back a few steps, my eyes going round.

"Graying powder for the face. Perfect for someone to turn into a zombie in an instant without needing a makeup crew. Normally, the makeup crew takes care of this part, but we needed to be versed in every aspect of costuming, makeup, and props to make sure it came off without a hitch. You just take a handful and..."

I think he finally noticed my pale face, huge eyes, and scared self.

"Oh. Uh, I'll just, um, I guess I could...if you'll excuse me." He fumbled for a rag and scrubbed at his face. He checked in a mirror. His appearance hadn't changed. "Sorry, it sticks really well. I'll be right back."

He darted out of the room, probably looking for makeup remover or one of the makeup crew to scour the nasty powder off his face.

I took a deep breath, and a corner of my mouth quirked up at the panicked look on his face. When I glanced at my hands, though, they were shaking. Making my way across the room, I sank into a chair I had seen earlier, half-hidden by a rack of smelly, torn clothing. The voices from the next room were clear now. I shamelessly eavesdropped and hoped it would be a while before anyone found me. It took me a minute to recognize the voices, but I was able to place the producer and director I'd been introduced to earlier.

"These scenes are gold, pure gold!" the producer enthused. "You got shots from several different angles, right? And the sound quality wasn't affected, was it?"

I leaned forward, edging closer until I could see around the corner.

The producer hovered over the director and one of the editors, who were viewing various shots on large iMacs before them. My stomach clenched at the different shots of my panic-stricken face, and I averted my eyes from a particularly awful closeup of a freaky-looking zombie.

"What about that truck exploding? I thought you were going to scrub that scene."

"We decided to give it a try. She walked right into it. I'm just glad it came off without a hitch," the director explained.

"And the helicopter?"

"Worked like a charm. Hydraulics on the ride didn't freeze up or anything."

"Good, good. That's excellent!"

Ride? *Ride?* I'd been on an amusement park-worthy ride and hadn't even known it?

Oh, these guys were good. I pretty much hated them.

"You can't do this. You can't release this movie."

The three men swiveled to face the intruder. I jumped and darted back around the corner, holding on to the wall for support. My heart pounded in my ears, and I took several steadying breaths.

"Well, well, Mr. Bailey. How good of you to join us. Have you seen some of these shots yet? Excellent work, my boy, excellent!"

"You cannot release this film." Gavin's voice was firm.

My curiosity got the better of me when there was no reply, and I peeked around the doorframe once more. The door behind Gavin stood wide open, and he glared at the producer with his arms crossed.

The producer's steely blue eyes studied Gavin. I held my breath.

"Need I remind you of the intricate details of the contract you have with us? I'm sure we could sit down with Mr. Jones and have a chat about it."

I clenched my teeth at the thinly veiled threat of legal action. Mr. Jones' name had come up in my own conversation with the man.

Gavin smirked and shook his head, his disgust apparent. "That won't be necessary. Yet. Can't we discuss this like gentlemen?"

"What's there to discuss? The film will release as scheduled, and we'll all be the wiser, and the wealthier, for it."

He winked at Gavin and turned back to the monitors. My hands clenched, and I considered marching in there and telling that producer what I thought of him. Someone needed to wipe that smug grin off his face.

"What about Miss Marshall? Shouldn't her feelings be considered?"

The producer didn't bother to turn around. "Our business with Miss Marshall is none of yours. If it makes you feel any better, she has a contract with us as well, although she doesn't know it yet. And that is something I am only willing to discuss with her or her lawyer."

Contract? What contract? I never…oh.

Oh, yes I had. At work. I couldn't have stopped the images if I'd wanted to. Peter rushing me, checking his watch, tapping his foot, as I initialed page after page after page. I'd signed the final sheet, and he'd snatched it from me, bolting from the stuffy newspaper office. I signed stuff all the time at work, so I hadn't given it another thought. Peter was being, well, Peter. Weird.

Since I was pretty certain Peter had in fact *not* been killed by zombies, it was clearly up to me to hire an assassin. ASAP.

Gavin stalked away from the producer. He paused at the threshold. His hand hovered over a monitor by the door. I wondered if he were going to launch it against the wall. Or at the producer. That was my vote. His hand dropped, and he moved past it.

Rage clouded my vision, and I bolted from my seat. Storming out of the giant, hangar-like prop room, I passed the props guy, his face scrubbed pink. It still had a grayish hue, however.

"Sorry, it's really hard to get off, but I can—hey! Where are you going? Wait a sec!"

I marched past him and flung open the door leading to outside. I wanted off this awful set. Now.

Chapter 28 ☣

"How was it supposed to end?"

I couldn't help but eavesdrop on the couple discussing my movie, which had debuted two weeks ago.

"They were going to kill off or turn all of her companions into zombies, leaving her alone in a safe room at the military base. She would've still been able to hear the zombies outside the room. They were going to have one 'loaded' gun in the room and see how long it took her to use it on herself."

Well, that's stupid.

"How tragic! And to think she had no idea it was just a movie set. I would have just died! So what happened? It certainly didn't end that way."

"No, she surprised the director and set crew by trying to rescue her love interest and take him out a way they weren't expecting or prepared for." The person cackled as if it'd been her idea. "It was brilliant! So they ended the movie with her dragging Gavin Bailey away, to what everyone assumed was safety. Didn't you see the tag scene?"

"No, my husband hates watching credits, so we left right away."

Good for you.

"That's a shame. It was *so* good! She ended up in some kind of break room, where the director and Gavin Bailey tried to break the news gently that she was on a set."

"Oh my gosh, how did she react?"

"I think she was in shock, really. She even tried to kill what she thought was a zombie with a real gun."

"No!"

"Yes!"

Yep.

"How did she get the gun?"

"Not really sure—some security guard left it lying around, I think. I believe I heard he was busy with one of the young ladies on the crew, if you know what I mean."

"Ooh…drama, drama. So has she seen the movie? Have you heard anything else about it?"

That it should die a painful death? That it should never be seen by another living human being?

"Not really. Oh! Except she had some pretty steamy scenes with Gavin Bailey. *Entertainment News* did a feature on it. Said they're a couple now. But we both know how long that'll last, considering she's probably only after his money and fame."

I may have snorted.

"His good looks don't hurt, either."

Both women, well into their forties by the looks of things, giggled like schoolgirls sharing a crush. I was never so relieved in my life when their ride pulled up to the curb, forcing a hasty departure.

The street vendor handed me the not-healthy-but-tasty hot dog I'd been waiting oh so patiently for. He gave me a strange look when I snatched it from his grasp and marched away, muttering to myself. I clutched it in my hand, smashing the poor thing to bits, and fumed.

I didn't care what the gossip rags said. Gavin and I were not—nor would we ever be—a couple.

The driver finished loading my luggage, and I sank into the glaring yellow cab, groaning to myself.

I'd come to New York to escape my movie, but here it was, just like every other blasted place I'd been.

My brother felt only slightly guilty—thrilled would be a better word—that he had set Peter and me up to be screened for the film. Peter was furious when he found out the little zombie tour they'd taken him on was nothing compared to the experience I got. He had the decency to call me up and chew me out about that one. Yeah, that was the last phone call I'd be taking from that jerk.

When I asked my brother why he would do that to me, he just grinned and said it was because I was such a scaredy-cat. He knew I'd be perfect for the role. Might be the last time I talked to him, too...

I sighed and stared out the cab's window. I was leaving it all behind me. All of it. It was time for me to take charge of my life and do what *I* wanted—not what Peter wanted, or my parents, or even my crazy-awful-but-I-love-him-anyway brother.

I dropped my head against the sticky vinyl seat.

Oh, well. I'd just give it a few weeks for the newness to wear off, and I would never, ever have to hear or think about the movie—or Gavin Bailey—ever again.

Chapter 29 ☣

I smiled and hung up my cell. It was sweet, Jack's attempt to brighten my day. What I really needed, though, was a latté from my favorite coffee shop in Manhattan. Since taking an internship at a prestigious fashion company in downtown New York, I had worked my butt off to forget everything that had happened. I wanted a future with this company, and I wanted it badly. They'd hired me as an intern, looking past my stint in the horror movie industry.

The film company had offered to pay for therapy, but the therapist and I had only stared at each other. I wasn't much for talking, anyway. Then I'd discovered work was my greatest therapy. I'd poured myself into the job and was so close to being hired after my internship was over. It was a prominent position, and rumor had it that it was between me and one other girl. And they were leaning toward me.

But today might have changed all of that. I attracted the strangest sort of weirdoes. All of them loved my movie and wanted my autograph. Today, one had gotten past security and had made a huge scene in front of a successful client. My boss was ready to dismiss me on the spot, but the client had intervened. The fan was dragged out of the building by security, screaming endearments and crying at getting to meet me the entire way. I wanted to die. Er, I mean, sink through the floor. Um, disappear, maybe? Still haven't gotten around to creating new phrases...

I'd tried to stop the movie's release, but the studio had great lawyers and even better contracts, which I'd signed. For real. I kept hoping it'd been a dream. It hadn't. Apparently it also didn't matter I didn't know what I was signing, since I had initialed every single stinking page. Stupid contract. Stupid pre-screening experience. Stupid Peter! I took a deep breath and let it out slowly.

The movie had been the largest-funded and most ambitious project in the history of filmmaking, and they weren't about to scrub it.

Didn't mean I had to like it.

My parents wanted me to move back in with them, but the last thing I wanted to do was move to a small town and take a dead-end job. I was somehow comforted by the teeming masses of normal, real people in New York. I loved being surrounded by crowds. Weird, but true.

And after God and I had a little "discussion" about why in the world He hadn't warned me just a little about being set up as the biggest fool on earth, I finally appreciated He'd used the experience to stretch and grow me in ways I was still realizing. Now if He could just make the nightmares stop...

As I neared my coffee shop, I dropped my iPhone into my Gucci bag and glanced up. Gavin Bailey stared at me from the entrance of the café, a paper bag in one hand and a tray of four coffees in the other. A rakish gangster-style hat tilted on his perfect head.

I stopped.

"Watch it, lady!" called an irate New Yorker. Had he just run into me? I hadn't noticed. Guess seeing the last person on earth I wanted to would do that to a person.

Now I needed a double espresso. Or a vodka. Not that I ever drank, but the occasion might call for it.

A gorgeous blonde stepped around Gavin—Mr. Bailey—and paused at his side. Tall, leggy—did I mention gorgeous? She followed his gaze and looked me up and down. Her gaze wasn't necessarily hostile, but it wasn't friendly, either. It was enough to get me moving again.

"Mr. Bailey." I tilted my head in his general direction and moved past him. He was not going to keep me from my coffee.

My traitorous self glanced back as I yanked open the door.

His head was bent as he whispered in the blonde's ear. Great. I could just hear it now.

That's the idiot who thought I was in love with her! Priceless!

I paused, glowering.

He shoved the bag and coffee tray at her. The coffee sloshed, she grimaced, and I whipped around and headed through the double doors. It put a smile on my face, I am mostly ashamed to say.

She could have him.

I got in the long line, waiting my turn to order. Refusing to peek through the glass doors at my back. Had he left? Taken his perfect blonde with him? The thought stung far more than I wanted it to.

A touch on my arm. Gavin's voice, too close for comfort. "Candace."

I jumped but caught myself before shrieking or spinning to face him. I could do this. Pulling every ounce of professionalism from my core, I turned slightly. "Mr. Bailey." I nodded to him, then swiveled back to peruse the menu board. *Maybe I should get one of each.*

"Candace, please, we need to talk."

I had ignored his calls, refused to see him, avoided him completely. I wanted nothing more to do with anyone or anything concerning that movie. Nor did I enjoy the unpleasant memory of falling in love with him while I thought he was falling in love with me, only to discover it was just another role.

I ignored him and casually studied the board, every inch of me tingling in awareness of whom was standing near me.

"Candy, please." He grasped my elbow, leaning close and sending a soft puff of air into my ear. A shiver wracked me without my permission. I spun toward him, dislodging his hand.

"You, sir, have not earned the right to call me that. And I'm completely convinced neither one of us has anything to say the other wants to hear. If you wish to whisper in someone's ear, there's a perfectly adequate blonde waiting for you outside."

My voice had gotten progressively louder, every eye was on me, and I was totally losing my cool. I had to get it together. Not throw my arms around him and burst into tears like I wanted to. I turned back to my board and inched a step closer to ordering.

"Candace!"

"Miss Marshall," I snapped.

He took a deep breath and waited. "That's my cousin and my new assistant."

I rolled my eyes. *Right. Can't believe he used two excuses.* Not that it mattered. I inched forward yet again.

"Candace."

"Miss Marshall!"

"Candace, I love you."

I sucked in a loud breath. *How dare he?* "You certainly have a funny way of showing it," I growled, thankful my voice didn't whimper like it wanted to.

"What, by doing everything possible to make it up to you, to make it right? I'm sorry, Candace. I'm so sorry. I never meant for it to go as far as it did. I never wanted you to get hurt. It kills me, knowing what I did to you. I tried to make it up to you. To apologize. You never let me. I did everything in my power to keep that film from being released!"

I spun and glared at him. Was he serious?

"Lady, you gonna move, or are we just gonna stand around and chat all day?"

I turned and took a half-step forward. My nose was practically touching the guy's back in front of me.

Gavin rested his cheek against my ear and spoke low, sending chills up and down my spine. His fingers trailed my arm.

"I have never felt so horrible in my life for what the studio did to you, and my part in it. The worst was falling in love with you, knowing you'd never believe me when you found out about the movie. I hated watching you be so scared while I knew it was all fake."

I inched forward, desperate for distance from this man who still held my heart.

"Candace, I can't stop thinking about you. Wondering if you're okay, if there's anything more I can do. I miss you. I want—"

I jerked back around and held up my hands. My traitorous, trembling hands. "It's okay. I'm fine. I forgive you. I just want to move on with my life, and I think you should as well."

I could not admit how much his words, his touch, had shaken me. I turned back to the board. I gasped as Gavin wrapped his strong, muscular arms around me.

"Candy, I love you. Please, say you'll give me a chance. I can't bear to live another moment without you in my life."

I blinked back tears, refusing to let them fall—telling myself I was ridiculous for believing him.

"You don't love me." I sniffled. "You don't even know me. All you know is how I act under pressure in a controlled movie environment. You don't even know—"

He yanked me around, gripping my shoulders. "You don't think I learned everything about you I could during filming? What began as a job became all I wanted to do. I want to spend my life getting to know you. Please, say yes."

I shook my head and opened my mouth, but he pressed close, covering my mouth with his own. My gasp caught in my throat. Then his kiss overcame all common sense, and my arms snaked around his neck. I returned his kiss, never wanting to be separated from this man.

I still loved him, dang it.

"Come on, people! Some of us have lives we want to get back to."

I started to pull away, but Gavin tugged me closer. He didn't even pause but kept going until he was good and finished. He pulled away, breathless. Or maybe I was the one who was breathless. Can't say *I* was finished, though...

The man grunted. "Some people."

Gavin started to turn toward the guy. I laid my hand on his arm. "It isn't worth it."

Gavin bent his head to say something to me.

"Okay, then. Whoopdy-do. Can we get back to the ordering coffee now?"

I was going to get dizzy with all the swiveling. I took two steps forward. There were still roughly twenty people ahead of us.

Gavin faced the man. "I'm sorry, but I need to make sure my fiancée is good and kissed."

"Your *what*?"

Yep. Dizzy.

"Too soon?"

"Um, yeah."

He took me into his arms with a rakish grin. His lips covered mine once more, and I melted. A couple of the patrons cheered.

"She's kissed, she's kissed. Now, order coffee!"

"Aw, lay off of them, Herbie!" said a lady from a nearby table.

"What? I just want my coffee. Nothin' wrong with that!"

I pulled back, everything else fading into the background. I looked into his eyes, wanting to believe I could trust him. "You really hurt me, Gavin."

Gavin slammed his eyes closed and rested his forehead against mine. "I'm so sorry," he whispered.

"I know, and, well, I forgive you. Truly. It wasn't easy for me, but…I have. Already. I—"

His lips, once again, cut off the rest of what I was going to say. I pulled away—far before I wanted to—and held up my hand.

"I'm not saying yes." I covered his lips with my finger, stifling his protests. "But I'm willing to give us a chance."

He grinned and threw his hat in the air with a loud *whoop*. "That's all I'm askin', Doll," he said in his best gangster voice.

I smiled and kissed him.

THE END

Epilogue ☣

Gavin and I exited the lavish Broadway theater, me gushing the entire way over the play we'd just seen. Even though I'd lived in New York for several months now, it was the first time I'd ventured to this side of town, and oh my word, was it worth it.

Gavin just smiled, chuckling as I kept claiming each part of the play as my favorite. He seemed to enjoy my ranting. I have no idea why. I would've told me to shut up a long time ago.

Crossing street after street to Gavin's car, I vaguely noticed the glances. We drew attention just about everywhere we went, and I was getting used to it. I even signed a few autographs on occasion without cringing or running away.

But tonight, we were drawing attention for another reason. Dressed in a tux and an evening gown, we looked good—I mean, ready for a photo shoot kind of good. The man could clean up. I, apparently, could too.

If only I didn't have to walk twenty blocks in heels. Guess that's what I got for forgetting to reserve a parking space, every parking garage full because of the newest show on Broadway. The one thing Gavin had asked me to do...oh well. My poor little toes would never let me forget this one.

At least Gavin had been gracious about it. He was pretty much the best guy ever.

Arriving at his black car, we both reached for my door's handle. I beat him to it—still chattering endlessly—and grasped the cool metal.

I yanked my hand back as if I'd been stung. "Oh man!"

"What is it?"

"My glove is all wet. Darn it," I complained.

Gavin chuckled, walking to his side of the car. "It's not like you can't get new ones or anything."

I laughed with him. "True. 'Cause these are the last gloves on... Gavin?" I tried not to panic as I looked at my hand. "Gavin."

"What is it? You okay?" He hurried to my side.

I stared at the glove in the dim yellow light coming from the streetlight. "Gavin, look. It's—it's—blood."

Grabbing my hand, he tugged it closer to the light. "Are you sure? It's hard to tell..."

"Look!"

Dark liquid pooled by the car at my feet, trailing into the alley nearby.

I started to freak out.

Why on earth had we chosen to drive instead of using a service? Limo? Cab? Anything. Why had Gavin insisted we park ourselves? Why were we next to a deserted alley anyway?

Suspicion grew inside of me, like a creeping, eerie vine. He wouldn't.

Gavin bolted to the trunk, pulling out a flashlight and a few other things from the emergency kit I kept back there at all times. The white light revealed what I already knew. Blood covered my white gloves and dripped from the door handle onto the cracked pavement.

I peeled off my gloves and threw them into the road. "We need to get out of here. Call the police," I said, doing my best to keep my voice steady. I would stay calm. I would.

"Tell me about it."

Opening the door for me with a wad of paper towels, Gavin froze.

We both heard it at the same time: a low moan emanating from the alleyway.

My temper exploded. "Gavin, I swear, if this is another movie trick —"

"Get in the car, lock the doors, and call the police. I'll be right back."

"I don't think so! I'm coming with you."

"No!" Gavin grasped my arms and turned me toward the car. "I don't want anything to happen to you. First sign of trouble, you get out of here, you hear me?" He handed me the keys. "Candace?"

I nodded, not convinced.

"Promise me."

"Gavin…"

"Promise."

I sighed. "I promise."

After seeing me safely into the driver's seat, he leaned across me and pulled a gun from the glove box.

"No way! Is it a real gun this time?"

He dropped the magazine and showed me a bullet. Yep, not a blank. I'm glad I now know the difference. He slid the magazine back into place. Tucking the gun into his pocket, he closed my door and eased toward the alley, the bright beam of his flashlight glaring before him.

Glancing at the middle console as I placed a call to the police, I spied his cell phone. I grabbed it and bolted after him, not wanting him to be without it.

He spun as he heard my footsteps. "Candace! I specifically told you…"

His voice trailed off as I stared past him, eyes wide. He reeled around, lifting his gun and his flashlight.

Blood was spattered all over the alleyway, and a lone figure bent over a body, sucking greedily from its neck. Looking up at us, his eyes flashed red as blood dribbled down his chin. He grinned, revealing pointed fangs, then disappeared into the night.

My call connected.

"911. State your emergency. Hello?"

A vampire. No freaking way.

Do not miss

Vampire Feud

Book Two of the Candace Marshall Chronicles.

Coming Soon from L2L2 Publishing.

Thank You! ☣

Oh my goodness, there are so many people to thank!

This book would not have happened without a plethora of people who have read, refined, and edited this pile of words into the book you hold in your hands.

First, my Lord and Savior, Jesus Christ. You put this dream in me, this burning desire to write, and all I want to do with it is please You. If I can show just one person how much You love them, my life is complete. What a fun story! Thank you for letting me tell it!

My husband. Dude. You were the first to be bombarded with my insane, insatiable desire to write. Through it all—the all-nighters, the frizzy hair, the makeup-free face, the pajama-clad body, the altogether scariness—you've encouraged me and stuck with me on this wild roller coaster, five-year publishing journey. Look! It's a real book you can hold in your hands and everything! Thank you, sweet love!

Blaze, Maverick, and Gwen. Blaze, you were only a few months old when I wrote this book. The whole thing poured out of me in a month, then I spent the next five years refining it. When I think of this book, I think of you. I held you, cuddled you, and snuggled you through so many drafts of this thing. I will always remember you in my arms when I read these pages. Maverick and Gwen. I am so glad it took this long to get this book published, if only so I can tell you how much I love you in these pages. You guys are my favorite, and I love each one of you with my whole heart.

My beta readers! My characters—and my writing—has grown and strengthened so much because of you. I tried to list everyone; *please* forgive me if I left anyone out!

Joyce. I'm so honored to be your first zombie book. It wasn't too gruesome, was it? Your insights and encouragement was invaluable!

Hannah. I'm so happy I made you cry! Thank you for loving my characters as much as I do!

Sarah. Thank you for your honest, real, totally-what-I-needed advice. Have I finally gotten the "show, don't tell" thing down? "Showing" is the bane of my existence! I. Will. Master. It. Thank you for the long chats about both of our books. I needed it more than I can ever say!

Nicole. I love your detailed, science-filled mind. You brought up things that never even occurred to me, and I hope I answered all of your questions with this completed tale. You rock!

Mary. I can't even tell you the wave of emotions that hit me when you handed me my manuscript, printed. On real paper. It was the first time I'd seen it not on my computer screen, and I cried. (When I got home. Cause I don't cry in front of people. I just don't.) Your comments made my day, and each one filled me with joy. You liked my book! I mean, you actually liked my book!

Crystal. Oh my goodness, your comments rocked my world! I treasured each of your suggestions and tried to implement each one to the best of my ability. You had such a fresh take on everything! And thank you Valerie for introducing me to her. Your introduction couldn't have been more timely or appreciated.

Sara Helwe. You did it again. I love your covers so much, I can't even stand it! I just want to show my book to everyone and say, "Do you see the amazing cover Sara created? She's the best cover artist in the entire world!" Art speaks so strongly to me, and your craftsmanship is priceless. Thank you!

Thank you, Dr. Dennis Hensley, for professionally editing my manuscript. I am so embarrassed over all the silly mistakes I made—thank you for your patience and kind explanations. I will never confuse "hangar" with "hanger," Ever. Again. You are a treasure.

Nadine. My favorite person ever. Thank you for your final polish on this manuscript! I giggled and squealed over your wonderful notes (you liked my book! Ahhh!) and anything that made this story better is because of you. Thank you for taking time for this author.

Have I thanked everyone on the entire planet yet? I certainly feel like it. But I mean it. *Thank you.*

And last, but most certainly never least, thank you, dear reader, for sticking with me to the end. What did you think? Did you enjoy my story? Tell me! I'd love to hear from you.

Happy Reading!

In Him,

Michele Israel Harper

The Author ☣

Michele Israel Harper is an addict. To books, to writing—if it includes ink and paper, she's all over it. When she found out she could write books instead of simply read them…well, let's just say she's rarely been seen outside of her office since. She adores her writer's group, the Heartland Christian Writers, and has no idea what she would do without the American Christian Fiction Writers. Being voted treasurer for her local Indiana Chapter of ACFW just about sent her into a happy coma. Which, you know, she's very much familiar with since that happens at the end of every good book she reads.

Visit **www.MicheleIsraelHarper.com** if you want to know more about her!

Reviews ☣

Did you like this book? Authors treasure reviews! (And read them over and over and over…) If you enjoyed this book, would you consider leaving a review on Amazon, Barnes & Noble, Goodreads, or perhaps even your personal blog? Thank you so much!

More from L2L2 Publishing

If you enjoyed this book, you may also enjoy:

Wisdom. She is furious. Her sister has destroyed countless of the Maker's creatures and shows no sign of remorse. Or of stopping. She knows Folly's end is near and cannot wait to staunch her sister's wrath. Forever. Now if only her heart believed her. Folly. Her hatred wanes with each passing day. What's the point? Her defeat has been promised, and its surety strengthens with each step of time's cruel march. Can nothing change her path? Why did she leave heaven's bliss for such a cruel taskmaster? But Wisdom has orders to thwart her sister. Folly's orders are the same. And both are determined to win.

More from L2L2 Publishing

If you enjoyed this book, you may also enjoy:

Jocelyn washes up on the shore of eighteenth century Ireland, alone, naked, and missing all of her memories. Taken in by a lonely old woman full of plots and schemes for the lovely yet enigmatic creature, Jocelyn knows only one thing. She longs for the sea with every ounce of her being. Yet it tried to kill her. Aidan Boyd loves two things. His ship and the sea. When Jocelyn is thrust upon his vessel in the midst of his superstitious crew, he finds himself intoxicated by her—willing to give up everything for her. He soon finds he cannot live without her. But something holds Jocelyn back. The whisper of another's love. The embrace of water. Does she belong to this world? Or could Jocelyn possibly be from the sea?

More from L2L2 Publishing

If you enjoyed this book, you may also enjoy:

Bound by Heaven. Hunted by Hell.
Liz Brantley has a gift she wants to return.
Able to see and fight demonic forces, she has spent her life alone, battling the minions of hell bent on her destruction, running from the God who gave her this curse. Drawn to her abilities, the demon Markus unleashes havoc on her hometown and pulls Liz further into the throes of battle. She's desperate for a normal life.
When she meets a mysterious man who seems unaware of the mystical realm that haunts her, the life she's always wanted moves within reach. But her slice of normal slips from her grasp when an old flame, Ryland Vaughn, reappears with secrets of his own. Secrets that will alter her destiny. Torn between two worlds, Liz is caught in an ancient war between good and evil.
And she isn't sure which side to choose.

CPSIA information can be obtained
at www.ICGtesting.com
Printed in the USA
FFOW02n2115120616
24861FF

9 781943 788088